A CHANCE TO CHOOSE

Second Chances Book 3

A CHANCE TO CHOOSE

Second Chances Book 3

JEANNIE SHARPE

Guntersville

A Chance to Choose
Second Chances Book 3

Fresh Ink Group
An Imprint of:
The Fresh Ink Group, LLC
1021 Blount Avenue, #931
Guntersville, AL 35976
Email: info@FreshInkGroup.com
FreshInkGroup.com

Edition 1.0 2020

Book design by Amit Dey / FIG
Cover design by Stephen Geez / FIG
Associate publisher Lauren A. Smith / FIG

Cataloging-in-Publication Recommendations:
FIC042120 FICTION / Christian / Romance / Suspense
FIC042060 FICTION / Christian / Suspense
FIC042040 FICTION / Christian / Romance / General

Library of Congress Control Number: 2019920518

ISBN-13: 978-1-947867-73-4 Papercover
ISBN-13: 978-1-947867-74-1 Hardcover
ISBN-13: 978-1-947867-76-5 Ebooks

Acknowledgments

To Mary Schmidt - Words can't express my gratitude to you for what you have done for me. You have been a godsend in my life. From helping me through every editing aspect of this book, to more than once teaching me how to edit a book and giving me tools to make me a better author, a huge thank you. Without you, my book would not be the quality that it is today. Thank you from the bottom of my heart. Not only did we edit this book together, we became close through the process and I cherish our friendship. I will never be able to repay you for your wonderful graciousness. Thank you, Mary.

To Vernette Williams – You are one of my most favorite people in the world. Thank you for continuing to believe in me. From the first thought of this book, you were there and stood by me and gave me support. I love you.

To My Husband, Vance – Thanks for always putting up with me while I disappear to write. It has become a passion to me, but I will always put you first in my life. Love you.

To Brent and Lauren – Thanks for believing in me and giving me your support. Love you both to the moon and back

To Bailey – You are so full of life and have the world in front of you. Thank you for your understanding and your support in my writing. Love you.

To Grammy – Love you. Thank you for always being so giving and showing your support in my efforts, even when I fail.

Jesus Christ, My Savior – Without you, Lord, none of this would be possible. I love you.

And lastly, to my readers – I want to personally thank you for taking the time to read my books and believing in me. My dreams as an author have been made possible because of you. Thanks!

Camden, Maine

1

"What in the world are you doing?" Chloe Terrison, owner of Camden Bakery inquired when she walked up to Ben Matney, her bakery assistant, who was sitting on the tile floor at the back of the shop.

He swallowed hard. "Eating my leftover dessert from lunch."

"But why on the floor?" Chloe stood transfixed at his feet. "Are you worried about flying to London?"

Ben sighed, shoved the rest of his brownie into his mouth and slowly savored the last of the rich fudgy flavor.

"Well?" Chloe stood waiting for a reply as she rested her hands on her huge pregnant tummy.

Ben wiggled his shoulders, slumped against the brick wall and closed his eyes. "I was trying to hide from you."

"You can't hide in here. This shop is way too small for that," she laughed as she slightly kicked the bottom of his shoe.

The bell above the front door chimed. "Someone's here," Ben snapped and jumped to his feet. "I'll go wait on them."

Chloe moved to her left to let him pass. "I'll finish ordering our supplies."

Like a madman, Ben dashed to the front of the bakery. White flowing sheers pulled back at the four oversized picture windows highlighted the sea-foam green walls. He glanced at the dark grey and white checkered floors that sparkled from the shop's overhead fixtures. They seemed cleaner than usual on his way to the cash drawer. *Regardless, they will still get mopped.*

Streetlamps up and down East Main flickered and brightened the darkening skies over Camden, which meant the end of his workday was near.

His smile broadened when a nice-looking woman drew near the main display case. "Welcome to Camden Bakery."

Like most of their customers, the young lady selected her favorites, paid him and drifted out of the bakery with two boxes tied with sea-foam green ribbons in hand. He stood by the front window and followed a stream of light on the floor, now prominent from the streetlamps that had brightened the night. He cupped his mouth and yelled, "I'm locking up."

"Thank you," Chloe echoed in reply.

Kandice Myers, the shop's other full-time employee appeared with her purse over her shoulder. "I'm heading out. Have fun in London."

"Yeah, okay," he moaned in a low voice. As Ben looked at her, he noticed a flour smear on the hip pocket of her blue jeans. "You have flour on your pants, Miss Myers."

Her brown eyes sparkled. With a wipe of her palm, she dusted off her slacks. "Did I get it?" She peered at him.

Her perfect olive complexion glowed as she moved closer. "Yeah, you got it." To this day, she'd grown to become his closest friend since moving to Camden, Maine four years ago. Chloe, he thought, was a close second, but Kandice... she had a way of cheering him up when he felt down. Over the years, she had listened to his complaints and let him share his dreams. In return, he paid attention to her funny stories that had him doubled over in sidesplitting laughter almost every day.

Ben sprinted to her. "You also have a little flour on your nose, silly girl." He wiped at the dust. "There, that's better."

Kandice rubbed at the spot. "Thanks. Why aren't you thrilled about your trip? It will be great."

"I'm just not." Ben cut his words as his brow tensed.

She studied him. "I don't get it. Ben, it will be fun."

"I'll spill it, okay, Miss Got-To-Know." With an odd twinge of disappointment, he uttered, "I'm scared... Why? I can't pinpoint it. But I keep getting these weird vibes." He put his arm around her shoulder. "Do you think I should go?"

"Whoa! Don't put that on me. What you've told me about that old girlfriend of yours, I wouldn't go, but I'm not you." She laughed and pushed him out of her way. "See you when you get back."

He pulled on the belt loop of her washed out denims as she opened the door. "Aren't you going to give me a hug goodbye?" He opened his arms.

She pivoted, threw her arms around him and fell against his embrace. "You are something, Mr. Matney." She patted his back and let go. "Have a good time," she iterated in a serious voice as she exited. With a knock on the front window, she stopped, put her thumbs in her ears and frantically waved her fingers back and forth making a funny face. "Have a good time," she mouthed and stomped her foot.

Bubbly laughter escaped his chest as he struggled to not listen to her quirky laugh, but it was impossible. *Got to love her.* While he appreciated the sentiment, could a second chance at love be awaiting him in London? *Listen to her, go and let the merriment begin.*

Upon finding a clean cloth and a bottle of spray cleaner, he hastily polished every surface near him, then veered to the 15 tables out front and wiped them. He continued cleaning along the back-wall bar then looked around the shop and smiled he'd finished the task. *It never gets old seeing a clean shop.*

Ben thanked God for his job. Was his luck changing? He snickered remembering his mother telling him there was no such thing as luck, just blessings. He pondered. It was a blessing he worked at Camden Bakery. As for the women that had been a part of his life... he pursed his lips, nothing but bad luck had enveloped him. *No blessing in that department came his way.* He rocked his head as he contemplated his unfortunate relationships with every girl he'd chosen. Even at 12, his sweetheart Anna kissed Evan, his middle school best friend. That kiss happened at a school football game and it broke his heart. Then in high school, every girlfriend he'd had cheated on him. *What is wrong with me?* Girls in college weren't worth dating until he met Tori Bailey and she too shattered his heart.

With the tables clean, he cruised to the back and grabbed the squeegee to scrub the floors. As he pulled and pushed back and forth, he realized that life had dealt him no luck at all or like his mother would call it, missed blessings. His head pitched upward as if he were gazing at God. *Why aren't blessings forth coming?* Was God choosing to bypass showering him with blessings? Did He care? "God, it doesn't have to be a thunderstorm, I'll take a sprinkle." A slight grin etched his face as he propped the squeegee against his hand. *Maybe.* Would going to London and seeing Tori bring back love he lacked?

With the bakery sparkling, he hurried behind the counter and scanned for any pickup orders that remained. *One box left.* He guessed they'd come tomorrow. As he was closing the sheers at the windows, the doorbell dinged. *I forgot to lock up.*

"Are you still open?" A high-pitched voice wailed from a small child who ran to him.

"Yes! What can I help you with?" Ben smiled and bent to the three-foot tall boy's level.

"My mommy needs her brownies," the kid hollered as he caught his breath.

Ben slid across the slick floor and pulled the single box from the rack. Under the sea-foam ribbon, holding the order slip, he glanced at the name."Is your mommy's name, Caroline Montgomery?"

"Yes, that's her." A bright smile appeared on the little one's face.

Before Ben could get his next question answered, the door flew open a second time. A small girl with striking red hair slammed the door shut with both hands and halted. "Is my brother in here?"

Ben pushed his silky blond hair behind his ears and crouched to her level. "Well, hello there, little miss. Is this your brother?" Ben pointed at the other red head who stood two feet to his left.

He shook her tiny hand. She's precious. *Where's their mother?*

"Uh-huh. He's my twin," she responded. With a quickness, she ran to stand beside her carrottop brother who looked just like her.

The bell above the entrance sang sweet notes. With a hard thrash, his pulse thumped against his chest when the most beautiful woman he'd ever seen quietly shut the door.

"You're closed, aren't you?" She shifted her shoulders.

"Hello! Welcome to Camden Bakery." Ben scrutinized her frown. He breathed in the *heavenly* scent of her perfume when she neared the counter. "I was about to lock up when this young man appeared. Then this little beauty came in." Ben lifted his eyebrows.

"That's Harry, and this is Penny," announced the woman as she pointed towards her smiling, bursting with energy, red headed freckled faced children. "They're my doppelgangers."

"They're adorable," Ben asserted stealing another glance her way.

Penny held her hand high above her head to high five Ben's hand. "Hey, Mister."

Ben fell to his knees and popped her hand. "High five," he shouted.

Penny laughed. "It's nice to see you." Her bright blue eyes twinkled. "May I have a cupcake?" She begged as she pointed at the display window. From cookies, cupcakes, muffins, donuts to blueberry scones, all the pastries were tantalizing.

Ben guffawed. "Mom?" He flashed his eyes towards her for approval and shrugged. "Please show me which one you'd like." He led the precious Penny behind the counter. "Pick one and get your brother one, too."

He guessed the woman was Caroline Montgomery.

She eased up to the display glass with Harry at her heels. "You don't have to do that. It's okay. Really! They don't need it."

With approving eyes, Ben admired her beautiful flowing reddish blond hair and blueish green eyes. "If you don't mind, I'd be glad to oblige."

She looked from one to the other, "It will spoil your dinner." Her lips flat lined.

"Please, Mommy, please," Penny screeched.

"Oh... all right." Her eyes lit up as she glanced in Ben's direction. She put her hand on Harry's shoulder and stopped him from proceeding to where Ben and Penny stood.

Ben's eyes froze on hers. "Are you Caroline Montgomery?"

"Yes." A perplexed gaze crossed her face.

"Before you came in, your Mr. Harry confirmed your name from your order slip. You ordered brownies, right?"

"Yes, I did." She opened her pocketbook.

"Let me get them for you." *She is drop dead gorgeous and not wearing a ring!* Not only did she have perfect hair, her jaw line was stunning. Lingering for a second, Ben backed away and skedaddled to the shelf. "Here you are." He placed her large box on the counter. "That will be $32.79."

Ben watched her dig inside her purse.

"Oh goodness, I should have had my card ready." From inside her oversized bag, she pulled out three cosmetic bags, two sets of keys, a small notebook and a tissue packet before she located her wallet. "Here it is."

Ben took her credit card, swiped it and returned it. "You want your receipt emailed, printed, or sent by text?"

"You can text it," Caroline uttered. She gave him her phone number as he entered it into the bakery computer system. "Okay, we're all done."

Caroline's mouth spread into a grin. "You're a lifesaver."

"Thanks for choosing Camden Bakery." *Where did that come from?* Ben followed the three to the exit. Chills spiked his spine when he glanced at her gorgeous figure, curving and regal. She, with her striking leggings and blue top, created a grand fashion statement standing there.

Caroline rotated, "Thanks again." Her gorgeous smile beamed.

"You bet. Please come back and visit us soon."

He beheld the trio as they made their way to their car right outside the bakery door and waved to them. All three-gestured in return. Upon their departure, he turned the deadbolt.

The last time? He questioned that thought. He ambled to the display case and emptied the shelves of the unpurchased pastries. Various sized white and sea-foam green boxes were under the counter to his left. He snatched a piece of tissue paper, selected the largest size from the bunch and hoped the leftover cookies, donuts, muffins and blueberry scones would all fit. Satisfied he arranged every pastry with none of them being smashed, he closed the lid and tied a ribbon around it for the children's home.

As he turned to put the box beside the cash register, he glimpsed his pink envelope, that must have slipped from his pocket, lying halfway under the ice machine. *It's the airline ticket Tori sent me. Why did that girl send me this ticket? What are her intentions?* The fluorescent lighting sent a brilliant glimmer to the iridescent packet. *Is it a sign of a happy ending?* He yanked it off the floor, pulled the flap and located the flight departure for the third time that day. His heart pounded against his ribs. Trepidations? He would board the plane en route to England regardless of how he felt.

Shattered memories rushed to the forefront of his thoughts. *Why can't I picture her?* Was it because he'd met the most spectacular woman ever just seconds earlier? As he tussled to remember Tori's beautiful face, Chloe walked up. "Are you ready to go?"

"Nearly. I need to empty the trash cans."

"Did you decide?" She pulled on his arm.

"Yes, I've decided I'm going." *Did that convince her?*

"Why the sad face?"

Was she scrutinizing him? It pained him to look in her direction. He nodded perfunctorily and turned in dismay. "I confess, I'm nervous."

Chloe's face turned white, and she lost her balance.

"You don't look so good." Ben grabbed ahold of her arms to help balance her footing.

"I don't feel so good." She grabbed her stomach.

The floor under her feet puddled with liquid. "Oh, my gosh! My water just broke! Help me, God!"

"You need to go to the emergency room." Ben followed the trickle of fluid to Chloe's office.

"We need to call Mitchell!" Chloe shouted.

What's a guy expected to do? This situation was almost unbearable. "I know nothing about delivering babies!" A sudden woozy feeling rushed to his head. "The room is spinning." His footing wobbled.

Chloe gripped his arm, "Don't you pass out on me!"

The dizziness in his head, passed to queasiness in his gut. "I'll be fine," he blurted.

Inside Chloe's office Ben gathered his wits. "Sit here." He reached for the phone receiver and dialed Mitchell's office. "Hello, may I speak to Mitchell Terrison."

"I'm sorry, he's away on a business trip." He put the phone back on its holder.

He frowned and grabbed her hand. "He's not there, Chloe, where is he?"

"That's right, I forgot. He went to Southwest Harbor today."

Chloe screamed sounds he'd never heard from a person. "This is making me uneasy."

"This pain is killing me!" Chloe seized his arm.

She's scaring me. He squatted beside her and picked up her free hand. "We need to get you to a hospital."

"We don't have time for that. The baby is coming out!" She screamed in his ear.

"What do you need me to do? I can google it." He got his phone from his back pocket and started a search.

She slapped his hand. "Stop that! Go get towels, and hurry. Get a pair of gloves and some hot water!"

He dropped his phone on the chair and ran through the shop. "I'm hurrying," he shouted and gathered clean towels from the dryer. The largest pot in the shop sat under the first bin by the stove. He snatched it and collected several pairs of gloves from beneath the sink. He flung the hot water knob. "Should I boil the water?"

"Shut up, Ben!" She hollered.

When he returned, Chloe was lying on the floor. "Now you're scaring me!"

Tears streamed down her face. "I need to get this baby out! Put the towels under me."

Lord, God, help me. "Can you lift your back?" Goose bumps the size of watermelons tingled his arms as he stuffed and laid four of them as neatly as possible under her. "Whatever you do, don't push." He glanced at her face. "I heard that in a movie once," he smirked as his eyes grew wider.

A wailing sound erupted. "Stop the staring. I will slap you." Her face twisted with strained sneers. "I've got to push!"

In a stupor, his mouth fell open. "I'm at a loss here. What am I supposed to do?" Sweat beads popped on his forehead.

"You've got to deliver this baby."

He inched towards her door. "I'll do whatever you say." Her body quivered. "We need an ambulance!"

"Help me get my pants off. I can't do it by myself. She's coming, you hear me!" She wrestled with the waistband of her leggings.

"Did you have labor pains all day or something? I didn't think babies came this quick."

"My back has been hurting for two days. Help me, please."

He crushed his eyes shut. Together they removed her pants and underwear. *You can do this!* "Okay, what's next?" He voiced in the calmest tone possible.

"Can you see her head?" Wailed Chloe.

Did he dare look? "I'm too scared to look."

"Do it NOW!" Her roar was so loud it could have been heard all the way to Seattle, Washington.

"Okay, okay." *Help me, Jesus.* In slow motion, with one eye open, he lifted her long t-shirt and squinted and stuck his head further under her shirt to get a better view. Before him was the crown of the baby's head. "I see her!"

"Ben, I remember from my birthing class... I'm supposed to push when I have a strong contraction."

"Are you having one now?" He leaned forward and gawked.

"Ouch..." A big splash of tears fell upon her face and intense sweat formed at the top of her brow. Perspiration rolled down her face.

Ben picked up a nearby towel, leaned over her and sponged her face. "Are you all right?"

Nothing but a frown etched her face. "Shut your mouth."

He remained beside her and stayed put. "I'm sorry. What do you want me to do?"

"Call 9-1-1!"

He stretched and grabbed his phone off the chair and dialed.

"9-1-1 Emergency, how can we help you?"

"I need an ambulance at Camden Bakery. The owner, Chloe Terrison, is having her baby. Please hurry!" He slammed the phone to the floor.

"Here comes a contraction!" She screamed.

"Chloe, push!"

Her mouth opened as earsplitting sounds bellowed from her. "This is awful."

"Push!" Ben yelled.

Deep breaths expelled from her. "I can't anymore, I'm too tired."

Knowing that response wasn't good, he leaned over her and inched towards her face, "You've got to push, her head is halfway out. I'll catch her, I promise. Try one more time."

"Push down against my knees," she sobbed through her wailing.

With as much force as he could muster, he balanced her legs as she grunted, hollered, and cried, "Ooh, she's coming now."

He collapsed to the tile. "I got her! I got her!" Soft cries from the little soul filled the bakery. "She's perfect."

I delivered a baby. His own tears fell. "She's beautiful, Chloe." With tender cuddling, he kissed the baby's head, wet a towel with warm water, wiped her face and wrapped her in a clean towel. He picked up a new, smaller cloth, wet it and stuck it in Chloe's hand. "Here you go."

She squinted. "You've got to cut the umbilical cord."

"What?" He wobbled as his head started to spin. Are you sure?"

"Yes, I'm sure. Go get the scissors and some string."

He placed the baby against her chest and flew out of her room. He opened the drawer under his workstation and on top of all the junk was a pair of scissors, exactly what he was looking for. Rushing to her side, he collapsed to his knees. "Is this going to hurt either of you?"

"No. Tie the cord off first, then snip it."

"Where do I cut it?"

"I don't know, just cut it."

"All right, here goes." He sucked in a deep breath, tied the string around the cord, placed the scissors on either side of it, squeezed his eyes shut and cut. "Chloe, are you okay?" He peeked out of one eye.

"Yes, I'm fine. You're doing great, Ben."

He dropped the scissors onto a chair. "Now, I'll finish wrapping the baby in the towel."

"Good idea." She handed the baby girl back to him.

With a gentle touch, he cuddled his arms around her tiny body, wiped her down then draped her in a clean towel.

Tears flooded Chloe's eyes. "I love her so much."

"She is so beautiful." He kissed her forehead and gently placed her on Chloe's chest.

Like a fountain, tears streamed down all three of their faces. Joy exploded within him. He raised his head to see Chloe kissing her sweet baby's face.

"Ben, I'm so proud of you." Chloe touched his hand.

"It scared me to death."

"It terrified me!" She twisted and stared at her baby.

He touched the baby's cheek. "Look at her, she's gorgeous."

He saw Chloe's face wince. "Stay still until EMS workers get here. I want nothing else to happen to you."

"I feel I need to push again. Hurry! It's worse than before. Oh, Jesus!"

With firm hands, Ben took the baby from Chloe and placed her in the middle of some unused wadded towels close by. Cries from the baby and the mother rang out. He slid in front of her to get a better look. "There's another baby coming."

"What?" Wet tears surfaced upon Chloe's face.

Ben put pressure against her knees. "When you feel another contraction, push."

They took deep breaths.

"That's easy for you to say. Here comes one. Ooooh!" She pushed, screamed, and pushed more.

"It's a boy, Chloe, it's a boy!" Ben, with quickness, reached for a clean rag, dampened it with water and wiped the baby's face. The squealing boy with jet-black hair and deep blue eyes sent chills up his arms. "I didn't realize you were having twins."

"I didn't either." Her sobs were uncontrollable.

"Take a deep breath." Ben inhaled a deep breath along with her.

"I'm happy." Chloe closed her eyes.

Loud sirens sounded in the distance and grew louder by the second. "It sounds like the paramedics are almost here." Ben grabbed another clean towel and laid the baby boy against Chloe's chest "Stay still. I need to go unlock the building."

Hard pounding noises and loud voices rang out. Ben raced to the to appropriate door and led the med guys to Chloe's office. "She's in here."

"Hello, ma'am. We're here to help." The med guy assessed the area. "I see you delivered your baby. Wait, there's two. Wow! Congratulations."

A female paramedic drew close to Chloe. "How are you feeling?"

"I think okay." She allowed the medic to take the baby from her chest.

"I see it's a boy."

"Yes." Chloe smiled not taking her eyes off the newborn.

"We will cut his umbilical cord and clean him up," the EMT announced.

"Ben cut the cord for my baby girl." Chloe watched with loving eyes. She touched Ben's arm.

A different paramedic took charge of the girl. He wiped her with a clean cloth, laid her in Chloe's arms while he unwrapped a sterilized blanket. "I'll take her from you again. Ma'am, she is one beautiful infant." Carefully, he bundled the baby tightly inside the heavy surgical cloth. "I bet you're exhausted."

"I am."

"Are you in any pain?"

"Uh... a little, I guess."

"We can administer some medication to ease it a bit."

"That's not necessary. I can wait until we get to the hospital."

The EMT cuddled the baby. "I'm going to take her to the ambulance. This sounds crazy, but we need a little paperwork completed with your names, etc. on the way to the hospital."

Chloe gripped a wet cloth and smoothed it against her brow, "That's fine."

A muscular paramedic stepped up to Chloe, "We will put you on this stretcher and then go to the ambulance. Your babies are already secured and waiting. You ready, ma'am?"

"Yes, Sir." Dreamy eyed Chloe, so in love, did as the EMTs told her.

The taller guy gave Ben a thumb's up. "You did a good job, man."

"Ben, please call Mitchell," Chloe yelled as she was being rolled outside.

Ben dialed Mitchell's number. "Hey, it's Ben."

"What's up?"

He released a pent-up breath. "Chloe had the babies."

The phone went silent. "The babies?"

"Yes. You have twins. A girl and a boy."

"Are you joking? Wait..."

"Yeah, Mitchell, you heard correctly."

"This is unbelievable."

"It happened so fast. One-minute Chloe and I were talking and the next thing, we were delivering your babies."

"You, Ben Matney, delivered my babies at the bakery by yourself?" Mitchell questioned.

"Yes, I know it's hard to fathom, but I did. They are in the ambulance as we speak heading to the hospital."

"Tell Chloe I'm on the way. This is surreal. She wasn't due for three weeks."

"I can hardly believe it myself. But, Mitchell, Chloe was the brave one. She told me what to do, and I did exactly what she said."

Mitchell laughed. "Was the bakery open?"

"No, thank God. I had locked up only a minute or two when it all started."

"Thanks for everything."

"You bet." Ben pressed the end call button. The proud father would soon be with Chloe and the newborns.

After snatching a large garbage bag from under the counter beside his workstation, Ben grabbed a mop bucket, some cleaner and hightailed it to Chloe's office. *Gloves.* He scampered and found a pair. Without a second thought, he rushed to the scene, slid on the gloves and cleaned. Why did scrubbing come natural to him? In the wonder of it all, did he inherit that trait? Was it because his mother was a super clean freak, or did he get his tidiness from his dad? He scrubbed the birthing place until it sparkled like new. After a quick tie of the trash bag, he opened the back exit and hauled it to the shop's dumpster. Satisfied Chloe's office was better than new, he turned off the lights. On his way out, he remembered the cookies for the kids. *I almost forgot.* He hustled to the front, stuffed the box under his arm and skedaddled to the car park.

A slight detour, a mile to the east, he zoomed inside the children's home and dropped off the desserts.

As Ben neared the hospital, a red light stopped him. He let his head fall against the headrest as he reflected the invigorating births of new life. *Thank you, Lord, for allowing me to help Chloe's babies come into this world.* God bestowed blessings upon his life after all.

2

Never in a million lifetimes would he have imagined, he could or would have delivered a baby, but *two of them*? A sudden grin crossed his lips as he slowed his Jeep Wrangler to a crawl in the parking garage of Camden Hospital. He wheeled into the first available space and thrust the gearshift into park mode. He pulled the sun visor down in front of him and gazed into the mirror. His bright blue eyes looked tired and murky, and a stubble had found its way onto his jaw. He slid his hand across the prickly beard, brushed his eyebrows backward, then tried to get his fly-away hairs a little tamer. *That will work.* He unfastened his seatbelt, opened his door, hit the lock on his key fob and headed toward the automatic sliding glass double-door entrance to the hospital. With brisk strides, he hastened through the corridor to the information desk. An aged woman greeted him. "Can I have Chloe Terrison's room number and can you direct me to the nursery?" She smiled and proffered directions, pointing her finger towards the elevators at the end of the massive lobby.

The deeper into the building he ventured, the more he smelled iodoform disinfectants in each hallway. The elevator doors opened as soon as he reached them. Several people exited before he stepped inside, after a man and an aging couple, along with a heavyset woman. "Can you push floor two, please?" Ben squeezed against the wall to make more room in the tight area. The guy responded and pressed the second-floor button. *Perfect.* When the elevator opened, a huge arrow with words in the middle 'Nursery This Way,' greeted him. He drifted behind the elderly couple to the thick-glassed window and gazed at all the cool pink and blue caps sported by the infants. Snuggly wrapped in matching blankets, some babies were sleeping and others crying their lungs out. Behind all the basinets, several attendants were dressing two babies, one in a pink gown and one in blue. *There they are.* He would recognize them no matter how far they were away. Delight pierced his heart. *I may be their God father.* He chuckled as he continued to view all the excitement going on through the glass.

Ben remained in the exact spot for several minutes. When the vicinity grew overcrowded, he backed away and proceeded to Room 207. He knocked on the door, waited a few seconds, then shoved it open. "Hey, Chloe." His straight blond hair tumbled against his cheek as he drew close to her bed.

"Ben!" She cheered in a jolly tone. "The hero has arrived."

He greeted her with a hug. "How are you doing?"

"I'm doing great, but physically just so, so."

He peered intently. "I'm sorry."

"Listen to this."

Ben shifted his footing. "I'm all ears."

"We get to leave first thing in the morning."

He caught a glimpse of a roll around chair across the room and pushed it next to her. "I dropped by the nursery and saw the babies. They're incredible."

"Thank you." Her cheeks tightened as she grinned. "The doctor instructed that we must get a bilirubin light for the twins to sleep under for a week or so. Plus, have them at his office every morning at 8:30 a.m. so they can check their bilirubin levels."

Ben tilted his head in a nod. "That means they have jaundice or something like that?"

"Yep, that's what the nurses indicated. One doctor informed me that a baby's liver doesn't fully develop until they are 40 weeks old."

"Wow, how old are they?"

"37 weeks today."

"I wasn't aware of that." He touched the bottom of his palm to his head, "Oh, before I forget, I chatted with Mitchell and he'll be here soon."

"Before you go, I want you to hear me out about something." She pulled the bedcovers closer around her.

Ben's eyes narrowed, "I think I know what you're about to say."

"Yeah, well, I've thought about it long and hard." Her grin faded. "I'm closing the bakery while you're in London."

"I knew it. Chloe, you don't have to do that." *Her statement startled him.*

"I've decided." She glared at him. "You deserve a vacation. I will be away from the bakery for at least a month or more and you may not have another opportunity to take a day off."

"I've agonized over going to London ever since I received that plane ticket."

"But still..."

"It doesn't seem reasonable to leave since the babies are here." He scooched closer and drove his fist into his palm.

"How long has it been since you've seen Tori, ten years?" She propped against her elbow.

"Eight years, almost nine." He counted his fingers as he contemplated when they first met. Tori was the cutest thing walking across the grassy area of the campus of NYU. It was the first time he'd set eyes on her. Those tanned legs. *Ooh!*

"Ben... Ben?"

"Sorry. I was lost in a memory," he sighed with exasperation.

"When does your flight leave?"

His voice went shaky as the words spilled from his mouth. "A little before five in the morning." He cleared his throat.

"The bakery will survive a week not being open. We can make a sign for the front window that says I had the babies and the shop will re-open in seven days."

He coiled his right index finger through one of his belt loops. "I don't believe businesses do that anymore."

"Well, this one's going to. You've been nowhere since you worked for me and... I've noticed you haven't dated either." She took a quick breath. "All you've done is stick close to the bakery. I'm starting to worry about you."

He stood and meandered over to the window. "You're embarrassing me." Blood pounded through his temples.

"Why haven't you dated?" She asked in a demanding timbre. "Once upon a time I thought you and Kandice had a thing going."

He eased to the foot of her bed. His hands started to shake as his embarrassment turned to annoyance. He gripped the bed railing in front of him. "Kandice is like a sister, nothing more. Can we please change the subject?"

"You need to think about looking for a wife. You aren't getting any younger. How old are you anyway?"

His back stiffened as his mouth clamped tight. Determined not to yell, he spoke in a low voice. "I'm 28, but you already knew that." A muscle quivered at his jaw. "I'll bring Tori back and we'll get married, is that what you want to hear?"

"Absolutely not. Why are you getting so upset? Look at me, I want happiness for you. You need to fall in love and start a family. And... with someone who won't hurt you."

He scratched his now steaming forehead. "How did you know Tori hurt me?"

"You told me a long time ago, you don't remember?" Chloe hit the bedcovers with her hands.

"Vaguely." He rolled his eyes. "You can't say I won't get hurt. Everyone suffers when it comes to relationships." He braced himself for her next words.

"You've got it all wrong." Her eyes were boring a hole through him.

The door to Chloe's hospital room flew open and two nurses ushered in the babies. Ben leaped towards the glassed bassinets, "Awe, Chloe, they're fantastic." He leaned over them and kissed their foreheads.

"Mrs. Terrison, we need to go over a few things with you. Do you want..." One nurse eyeballed him as if to say... get out, but she was nice enough not to state it out loud.

"I'll excuse myself so you can have your privacy." He teetered toward Chloe and gave her a slight squeeze. "Congratulations."

With his lanky self, Ben slipped from the room as Chloe's powerful words struck him like nails pounding into a wooden barricade. He had no time for romance. *Make time.* Something deep inside him yelled it so intense that he shuddered and stopped his trajectory. *What just happened?* "There aren't any girls my age around." Wait. There's Caroline and Tori. He'd fly to London and see what pans out. A smile found its way on his lips as he reached the elevator.

He took his phone, typed as fast as his fingers would move and sent a text. *Chloe. I'm going to London. See you in a week. Thanks for the pep-talk.*

* * *

Ben turned his Wrangler in the graveled driveway of his super small, one-story residence along Penobscot Bay. His headlights shone on the Tiffany blue siding he'd painted himself. It helped the dwelling capture a stately look amongst the similar houses on Water Edge Way. Upon inching up the icy porch steps, he noticed blown snow had accumulated against the front wall. He shivered as he jingled his keys to find the correct one. With the key shoved inside the lock, he opened the door and hurried to his bedroom to change his soiled clothes. He chose a pair of joggers and a jersey, then grabbed a soda from the fridge. After brief rummage through the hall closet, he turned up a suitcase. His cell phone buzzed in the distance. *It's in my pants pocket.* Without hesitation, he busted it to his bedroom, found his phone and pressed talk. "Hello."

"How are you, Ben? This is Tori Bailey."

At a loss for words, Ben stepped to his picture window and gazed at the snow hitting the water across the bay. He became agitated hearing her voice. *Why?* "Hi, Tori."

"Are you still coming to London?"

"Yes. My plane leaves at 4:55 in the morning. I should arrive sometime tomorrow night." He moseyed out the door and steadied himself against the iron railing on his porch. Huge wet snowflakes hit his face.

"Can I pick you up?" Tori volunteered.

"No. I'll call you once I get checked into the hotel." His neck tightened. *Why does she get on my nerves?*

Laughing sounds came from the other end of the phone. "I can't wait to see you. We'll have so much fun. Hey, listen, I won't be able to pick you up until 11:00 p.m. or so, is that all right?"

"Yes. That'll be fine." The whys still choked at his throat. Should he be blunt and ask her why she sent him the ticket or just let it go? Deep down he speculated she had alternative motives behind his visit. He squeezed his fists tight as he stopped himself from asking. "I'll see you tomorrow."

Click. *Was I rude? Why did she hang up?*

A fierce burst of wind sent a chill through his body. He pulled at his shirt and glanced at his bare feet. The mail. The snow-covered yard would chill him to the bone if he fetched it barefooted. *What the heck.* He danced across the yard, pried open his mailbox and pulled out an unusual pink envelope that laid on top of his bills, junk mail and other advertisements. The return address was hard to see in the dark. Is it from London? Why would Tori send a letter? As he stood in the snow gazing at the envelope, his feet went numb. "Get back inside the house, dummy." He made a mad dash. Halfway through the yard, he slipped and fell. A burst of laugher exploded from him. What else could happen today? Not giving up the opportunity to make a snow angel, he stretched out his arms and legs and started flapping back and forth. "It's freezing." He quickly jumped up and got out of the bad weather, raced to the thermostat, and flipped it up to 75. The now wrinkled, damp envelope, went on the nightstand and the junk mail tossed into the trashcan beside his bed. Soaked to the bone he stripped, hustled into the bathroom and turned the shower to hot. He tiptoed inside, let the hot water soak away the day's excitements and anxieties, then poured body-wash onto his hand and scrubbed. The steaming water soused his back. He wiggled his toes until the numbness went away.

The pink envelope on his bedside table came rushing to the forefront of his thoughts. He twisted the knob to the off position and snagged a towel from the rack. *What would be inside?* At his dresser, he dug through the middle drawer and drew out another pair of joggers. This time, he searched for a heavy pair of socks and put his hands on the first long sleeve t-shirt he came across, a Jack Daniels shirt given to him by a friend who lived in Lynchburg, Tennessee. He plopped onto his bed and grabbed the envelope. He tore away the nice smelling flap and unfolded the soft pink paper and read Tori's handwritten words:

Ben, will you please forgive me? I need to tell you so many things. My love for you is still at the center of my heart. All I can think about is your arrival. Tori.

That's strange. *It makes no sense.* He didn't believe the girl could care for anyone. "Why go to London?" His deep-rooted voice boomed inside his body. "I'll hope for the best."

Ben stopped in front of the cedar chest at the foot of his bed, took a deep breath and lifted the lid to old memories. *Her picture's in here somewhere.* He rummaged through the items inside. *Here it is.* He slid his fingers along the front of the large photograph album as flashbacks flooded his mind. To touch her again would be a dream come true. *Is that the reason you want to visit?* He pushed the notion away. Remnants of Tori and him gravitated upon his soul when his eyes glued to her picture on the first page. *There you are.* "You were so beautiful." He smoothed his hand over a closeup picture of her. "Why did you hurt me?" A tear fell onto the plastic-covered page as his emotions overtook him as he swung the old pages. A photo at the top right brought a second smile to his lips. The memory of them together at his brother's graduation reemerged. "We had a great time on that trip."

The past came alive as he strolled through the photos of them together. He was startled when he flipped to the last page. "What?" On the back flap, stuck with tape, was a yellowing white cloth. With a tug he ripped it off. As he unwrapped it, a ring dropped to the floor. "I gave you that ring." *How did it get in here?* The emerald embedded with diamonds sparkled in the light.

Upon re-folding the thin linen around the magnificent piece of jewelry, he slipped it inside the last plastic page among the photos of him and her. Did Tori put the ring in there? Another question that needed an answer.

The whys of how she'd hurt him was still a blur, but in a matter of hours, he prayed the whys wouldn't count anymore.

3

Packed and ready for his early departure, Ben felt growls trickle through his stomach as he sat on his couch watching TV. It'd been hours since he'd had anything to eat. A spaghetti special from his favorite eatery had his mouth watering. He dialed the restaurant's number and hit the talk button.

"Olli's Italian Gardens, how may we serve you?"

"I'd like to order a spaghetti special."

"With a dinner salad and bread sticks?"

"Yes." Ben twisted his wristwatch. 8:05 p.m.

"Sure thing. What is your preference on salad dressing?"

"Ranch, please."

"Got it. It will be ready in 10 to 15 minutes."

"Thank you." Ben blew out an exasperated breath. "See you then."

The short trip to the eatery turned out to be a fiasco. A three minute drive ended up taking 20 minutes. Cars at every turn were in ditches and wrecks at every intersection. From this snow? *What in the world?* He didn't detect icy conditions. Now his dinner would be cold. *Darn.*

To his surprise, a parking space at the front of Olli's was vacant. He slowed his vehicle to a stop, cut the engine, then slipped and slid to the door. *It is a little messy out.* There behind the hostess stand, of all people, was Caroline Montgomery. *Why is she here?* Low and behold, how could it be that he would see her twice in the same day. His mouth etched into a huge grin as he took in her wonderful beauty. He stopped in his tracks, smoothed his hair and ran his tongue over his teeth.

"Well, hello there. I met you earlier at the bakery." She smiled. "A table for one?"

"Uh… I had a call-in order." Without reluctance and gazing her way, he blurted, "It's nice to see you again."

She returned to the hostess stand and glanced at the book that laid on top. "Let me get your order." She flung her eyes away. "I'm sorry, what was your name again?"

"Ben." *I didn't make a good impression, did I?* He raked his hand down his face.

"Oh, yeah, Ben." A slight grin etched her face. "I'll be right back."

He chose a seat at the bar. The gorgeous woman with the most perfect figure, complexion and hair disappeared into the kitchen. Her green eyes against her reddish blond hair was breath taking.

Caroline returned with a silver bag in tow. "Here you are." She handed Ben his dinner.

"It smells superb." He took out a $20.00 bill from his pocket and placed it in her hand. "Keep the change."

"Awe, thanks," She slipped the bill into the cash register. "I hope you enjoy your supper."

Should he ask? He dipped his head. "Can we go out sometime?" *Rejection* started beating him down like a ton of bricks falling off a speeding truck. Here it comes.

"I'd like that."

What? It's a yes? His palms went clammy. "I'm going out-of-town, but when I get back, I'll come see you."

"That will be nice."

Ben strode to the entrance. "Catch you later." He took one last look before he left. *You are so beautiful.* "Bye."

Even though the streets were icing over worse than before, he avoided any serious traffic issues on his path home. *Thank God.* He carefully gathered the bag holding his dinner, and with caution, eased up the walkway. Once inside the house, he got a soda from the fridge and unwrapped his spaghetti. The room filled with rich flavors of garlic and baked cheese. After a quick blessing, he dug in and savored each bite. He nibbled at the salad and bread sticks to boot. In between bites, he flipped on the TV to check the weather forecast. The fellow on the tube rattled off several inches of fresh snow were expected to fall by dawn. He glanced at his luggage. Doubts of flying to London crept back into his mind. In a few hours he'd have to be ready to leave for Portland, Maine.

You will enjoy London. He kept reminding himself and set the alarm on his watch for 1:30 a.m. He needed to drive at a much slower pace than normal, at least until he reached the interstate.

* * *

Late that evening, 12 a.m. to be exact, Caroline Montgomery, along with three of her employees cleaned the large commercial kitchen of Olli's Italian Gardens, they mopped the floors, washed the dishes and wrapped the cleaned utensils in cloth napkins. Caroline locked up and scurried to her brand-new Mercedes GLA SUV. She wanted to dislike this vehicle, but the shiny, deep burgundy GLA, was the only substantial possession she gained from her nasty divorce. *How?* Eli Montgomery's father owned the Mercedes dealership in Camden, that's how. *Thanks Eli's dad.* She tossed her hateful regrets out the window when she passed her and Eli's old stomping grounds of Camden High School. Hate is a strong word; she contemplated and *knew* God said in His word not to hate. But all she had for her ex-husband was that and much more. *Remove Eli from my memory, please, Lord Jesus! And forgive me for hating him.* She rolled her eyes as she wheeled by their favorite hangout on Friday nights after their in-town football games. Large weeds and overgrowth had now consumed every inch of the closed, rundown, drive-in movie place where she'd received her first kiss. *I loved him then...*

The 27 year old carefully drove through Camden to her mother and father's place on Bay Avenue, collected her things and made her way up the walk to the front door. After digging through her oversized handbag for the house key, she entered the grand three-story hollow entryway. The heels of her boots echoed on the black swirling marbled tile. The foyer with crisp white walls held magnificent paintings. Lewis, the house butler, rambled down the way in his house shoes and asked if she needed him. "No thanks, Lewis, I'm on my way to my room."

With a quick tap on her parent's bedroom door, she turned the knob and cracked it. "Mom, Dad, I'm home."

"Hey honey. How was your night?" She could hear her mother's voice from the dark room.

"Superb. We took in a little over $7,000.00," she announced.

"Penny and Harry watched their favorite movie twice. They fell asleep on the couch. Your dad later carried them to bed." The silhouette of her mother, Elizabeth, eased forward from her parent's bed. "I think Harry is coming down with something. He felt a little feverish, so I gave him some Ibuprofen."

"Thanks, Mom. I'll check on him. I love you."

"Love you too. Night."

Caroline hastened to the basement of the three-story mansion. The luxurious estate covered three blocks on the east side of Camden. Thankfully, her father, David Gladden, provided her and her twins a roof over their heads, at least for the time being. She opened the door to Harry's bedroom; found him all twisted inside his comforter and chuckled as she got closer to the little bed. *How could he get so messed up in those covers?* As her smile erased, with gentleness, she touched her handsome three-year-old's forehead. *No fever. Thank God.* She untwisted the comforter away from his little body, straightened it and found the flat sheet. Making sure the comforter was secure, together with the sheet, she tucked him in under the covers. Upon kissing his sweet face, Caroline stood at the door and breathed a prayer. *Thank you, Lord, for my loveable Harry.*

A few short steps away, Caroline found Harry's twin sister, Penny, fast asleep. Her twins were her life and the only stable thing in her world.

"Mommy?" Penny's adorable voice called.

"I'm here." Her cell phone vibrated in her apron pocket. "Hello. Hold on, please." She brushed her lips on her daughter's cheek. "Night, Penny. I'll check on you in a minute."

"Okay, Mommy."

Caroline closed the wooden door and hastened to her makeshift bedroom. "Why are you calling me?" She plopped onto the wooden chair beside the bed and put the phone down to untie her tennis shoes. "Hello."

"I'm drunk baby," Eli indulged himself.

Caroline blew out a distressed breath. "Eli, they ordered you not to call me."

"I don't care about them." The conversation subsided.

"Are you there?" Caroline waited for a response.

"Yes, I'm here. I had to call... I want to know will you forgive me?"

Caroline pulled the phone away and stared at it. *I can't believe him.* Her chest tightened. "We are no longer married, Eli."

"I want us to be. You are all I think about."

With her free hand, she untied her Olli's apron. "I can't deal with you. Do you understand?"

"Caroline, I miss your beautiful face."

Her voice hardened. "I bet you do. Why don't you call one of your girlfriends and look at her face? Don't call me again." She ended the call, pulled her apron over her head and laid it on the bed. *Block his number.*

A quick trip into the bathroom, and Caroline washed the grunge from her face. She stared at herself in the mirror. *How did I get here?* She always made wrong choices. Thinking back, why did she give Eli an ultimatum of marriage? As she relived the last seven years of pure misery, her phone rang a second time. This time when she read the number, she saw London. "Hello, Tori?"

"Hey, Caroline. It's me."

Caroline's tone changed. "How are you? It's good to hear from you."

"How are you doing?" Tori inquired.

"I'm doing pretty good. Are you still in London?" She queried her old college friend.

"Yes, I'm still here. I don't think I'll ever come back to the states. I love it here."

"So, what's up with you?"

"You remember Ben, my old boyfriend from school, don't you?"

"No, I can't say that I do. I remember you speaking of him, but you two had split up by the time I started at NYU."

"Oh, that's right. Anyway, he's flying to London to see me."

Why is she telling me this? "You sound excited."

"I am. He'll be here for a week. I'm gonna try to get him to stay and work at my uncle's restaurant."

"Is that so?" Caroline snatched the clock, turned it around and checked the time. 12:45 a.m.

"Yes. He's in need of a chef and I thought Ben would be a perfect fit."

"Tori, I don't mean to cut you short, but, it's late and I've got to get my kids up early for school. It was great hearing from you."

"Yeah, you too. We'll talk soon."

Upon hanging up the phone, Caroline rushed back to Penny's room and found her asleep. She kissed her cheek, turned out the light, moseyed to her room and fell onto the bed. There was an urgency in her spirit to pray. She yielded her wants and desires to the Lord and prayed for her family. A quick scan of her daily devotion read *Blessed Are Those Who Hunger and Thirst for Righteousness.* She dug right in and made notes along the margin of the small devotional magazine. The study drew her into deep thought about her ever-changing circumstances. If she sought after His righteousness would life get any easier? *Lord, Jesus, please help me trust you more and help me seek your righteousness. I want to love you more.* As she prayed the words, her burdened heart lifted. Her eyes began to grow heavy and she fell asleep. She dreamed of the man who wandered into her restaurant for the spaghetti special. She woke and his name crossed her lips, "Ben." *His name was Ben.* What a coincidence that Tori's boyfriend has the same name.

4

The warm sun seeping through the jet's small porthole woke Ben. How long had he slept? He twisted his arm and pulled at his watch. One hour and five minutes. *Huh.* A stiffness traumatized his neck. Without a thought, he stood, stretched and looked around at the other passengers. *Yep, everyone's still here.* The lengthy flight was taxing, and restlessness trounced upon him. As hours continued to tick by, he tried to doze, but now wide awake, he forgot about sleep and attempted to remember the good in Tori Bailey. Finally, the plane descended toward land.

Reflections of Tori from long ago at a college party resurfaced. They were dancing when she stopped, dug into her pocket and placed a gold ring in the center of his palm. 'This is for you.' He remembered her saying, 'I love you.'

He twirled the band he still wore on his finger. *I loved you so much, Tori.* Now, nine years later, what would he possibly say to her? His insides flip-flopped at the thought.

To rid his boredom, he read article after article from different magazines and finally came across one on a children's home he found interesting. Right in the middle, an interruption of a crackling noise sounded throughout the cabin. "Good evening ladies and gentlemen, this is your captain speaking. We will arrive at Heathrow Airport in approximately 15 minutes. The weather forecast is calling for rain showers and is projected into the morning hours. The temperature is a cool 40 degrees. We thank you for flying with us and we hope your stay will be an enjoyable one."

How could it be raining just minutes away when the sky is such a deep blue and stars everywhere? Even if the rain fell, Ben promised himself he'd check into the hotel, take a shower, get acclimated to the area, and grab a bite to eat.

Without hesitation, and when the okay to unfasten seatbelts sign came on, he snatched his bag from the overhead bin and pressed the talk button on his phone to call Chloe.

Waiting for her to answer, doubt snubbed him again. "Chloe? Hey, it's Ben. I made it."

"I appreciate you calling. Have a good time and... I hope it works out."

"Yeah, me too." Could she sense how he felt? Scared, nervous, and unsure of what was in his immediate future rumbled through his head.

"Listen, if you need to talk later, call me."

"I will. Thanks. See ya." He pressed the end button and waited patiently for the passengers ahead of him to dis-embark the packed plane. The pilot was correct with the prediction, rain and fog greeted him when he passed through the sliding glass doors to exit onto the streets of London. *It's a beautiful place.* He caught the first taxi he flagged down. "Hello," he greeted as he ducked into the cab.

"Where to?"

"The Egerton House Hotel." Ben scooted inside and fastened his seatbelt. This man's cab was super clean, and no funky smells greeted him. Thank God.

"I'd be glad to drive you. It's a 10 minute ride. Welcome to London, England. Are you from the United States?" The driver turned on the taxi's meter then proceeded through the busy airport traffic.

"My accent gave it away?" Ben gazed at this watch. "What time is it?" He smiled at the driver gazing at him in the rearview mirror.

"A little before 7:00 p.m."

He quickly set his watch at the new time and sat back to enjoy the ride into town. "I'm kind of hungry. Do you know where I can get a bite close to the Egerton?"

"There are several places to be exact. My favorite, Twice Baked Restaurant, it's two doors up from your hotel."

"Thanks. I'll try it."

The taxi ride was fast and furious. He paid his cab fare, retrieved his luggage, and stepped toward the grand entrance of the hotel. While checking in, he exchanged some currency, then hurried to the eatery the driver suggested. The glass front building was quaint and boldly rustic. He entered and approached an attractive young woman standing behind the hostess stand.

"Greetings. A table for one?"

"Yes, thank you."

"You can follow me." She escorted him through a narrow hallway that opened to a huge red carpeted room with windows extending from one end to the other. It delighted him that he'd be overlooking the busy street while eating. Rain pelted the window-panes as he contemplated what to order from the oversized menu board to his right.

A short waiter stepped up. "What can we get you?" He asked in a grumpy voice.

Ben cleared his throat. "I think I'd like to try the twice baked potato with beef and cheese sauce."

"And to drink?" He asked as he steadily wrote on his order pad.

"Do you have bottled water?"

"It will cost you."

Ben wrinkled his face. "I'll be glad to pay." *What's with the attitude?* "Can I get a couple serviettes?"

"Uh, I'll be right back with that and your bottled water."

A deep growl permeated his stomach as rich aromas of grilled meat overflowed the top of a potato that was placed on a table across from him. *Man, that looks good*. He glanced at his phone. Should he call or wait? He was over-taken with extreme fatigue. He yawned several times as his eyes watered. To take a nap before he saw her was a must. A good night's sleep sounded even better.

He pulled up Tori's number and pressed talk. "Hey."

"Did you land?"

"I finally did." Ben pulled at his watch.

"I'm in a meeting until about 10:00 p.m. tonight. Can I come to your hotel afterwards?"

"I need to get some rest. Why don't I meet you for breakfast in the morning?"

"Okay, I'll pick you up at 10:00 o'clock."

"That will be fine. See you then." Ben ended the call when a different woman than before brought out his entrée and set it on the table. "May I please have a serviette and the bottled water I ordered? Also, Miss, I need a fork."

The girl looked around his table. "Sorry about that. I'll fetch them now," then turned and rushed off.

He trailed her with his eyes as she scurried up the narrow hall. At the end was a cabinet. She pulled it open and grabbed salt and pepper shakers, wrapped utensils and a bottle of water, raced back and flung them on the table. "We are busy this evening, sorry you had to wait."

A quick scan of the empty room, Ben wondered why she shared false information. Maybe the eatery was packed with folks before he arrived. He bowed his head and blessed his meal. The pleasant smell of cheese and beef filled his nostrils as he picked up his fork. With a tad of salt and pepper sprinkled on his large potato, the luscious tasting meal depleted his hunger. As he ate, he watched people going back and forth along the busy street.

Ben about choked on a piece of beef when he spotted a woman who highly favored Tori, holding hands with a tall man outside the window where he was seated. They were scrunched under a small purple and white umbrella that didn't quite cover their heads. His eyes grew twice their size when they stopped and kissed. *Was that Tori?* He frowned in disbelief as they crossed the road and dashed inside a storefront café.

What is going on? He scarfed down the last two bites of his potato, wiped his mouth, threw three euros down on the table and hurried to the entrance where an elderly gentleman was sitting behind a counter near the front door. "I was sitting in the back. Is it possible for me to pay my bill here? I'm kind of in a hurry."

"Sure thing. What did you have?"

"A beef and cheese potato and a bottle of water." Ben took out his visa check card and handed it to the guy. "Thank you." He pushed opened the front door and barreled onto the street. Now to find that woman.

* * *

"Dad?" Caroline jerked at her father entering her room early the next morning.

"We need to talk." He moved closer and parked himself at the edge of her bed.

"Yes, Sir." She drew the bedsheet to her neck. "Are you mad?" She was suddenly wide awake.

"I want to talk about your plans to move. Have you found a place?"

She knew this discussion was coming but didn't realize it would be so soon. "No, Sir. I thought we could stay here a while." Caroline felt the blood drain from her face. She imagined how pale faced she must have been.

What was he thinking? "Dad, you look upset?" She struggled to sit against her pillows without shifting the covers from her chest.

"No, not at the moment, but you and the kids living here is no longer an option."

Caroline diverted her eyes. "I'm not certain I follow you."

"It's simple. You have two weeks to be out on your own."

"But, Dad." If she could, she would have leaped from the bed and run to her mom for support.

He inched up to her and placed his hand over hers. "I will provide you an allowance until you are more financially stable. We, physically cannot keep up with Harry and Penny any longer."

A frown passed over her brow. "I thought Maxi was helping." Maxi, her dad and mom's main housekeeper had been with them since she was 10 years old.

"She's worn out, too."

"I'm sorry, Dad." She leaned into him and encircled his shoulders with her arms and put her head against his chest. A tear formed at the base of her eye.

"We love Harry and Penny, but we, along with Maxi, can't keep up with them."

"I understand. My priority will be to locate a house. I'll start looking today."

"I'll help with the closing costs and your allowance should aid with the mortgage payment."

"Is Mom mad?"

"Heavens no, she hasn't complained at all and she never would."

To hear that was a relief. "I'm glad. You still seem a bit mad though."

"I've had my moments, but I'm not upset with you." He shifted his weight and ruffled the comforter. "The situation with the kids has me concerned. You've been through plenty enough with Eli and more than anything we want you to be safe. That's why it's so hard to ask you to move. To be truthful, I don't think your mother can handle the stress, well... I can't either." He grabbed her face and turned it from side to side. "You've healed nicely. You can't tell you were hurt."

"My scars have completely disappeared." She grinned.

"It's time, Caroline." After they hugged, he stood and inched to the doorway. "We want you to come and visit any time. Mom and I will babysit whenever you need alone time. We will be a phone call away."

"Thanks, Dad."

He walked back to her and they hugged a second time, then he kissed her forehead. "You're doing a great job at Olli's, by the way."

"I love it."

"I can tell. Love ya, kid." He waved his hand and exited.

"Love you too."

Eight months had worn out their welcome. She understood Harry and Penny's demands and couldn't deny the fretful looks received from both her parents. It was a must they move out quickly to ease further tension.

* * *

Showered and dressed, the heels of her sandals clicked the wooden floors to Harry's room. Inside, she found Penny in bed with him. "What are you two doing?" A grin burst from her.

Harry made her melt. "We hun-gee, Mommy."

"We're hungry, Harry," Caroline repeated the phrase several times so he and Penny would learn the correct pronunciation of the word. "C'mon, let's go upstairs and get breakfast."

Bacon, eggs, hash browns and juice were waiting on them when they entered the huge dining room. "Good morning, Mom." Caroline reached and squeezed her mom's neck.

"Good morning."

Both twins jumped at their grandmother's lap. "Gummi, we love you," Penny slid her hand down her grandmother's arm. "Your skin is so soft."

"Me hun-gee," Harry announced.

"Me hun-gee too," Penny repeated.

"Okay! Get in your chairs." Caroline's voice grew stern.

Lewis, the butler, filled their plates with food and poured orange juice for everyone.

"Thank you, Lewis."

"You're most welcome, Miss Caroline."

Silence filled the room as the two precious twins ate their breakfast. "Mom, Dad and I spoke about us moving."

"What did he say?" She scooted her chair closer to her daughter.

"He told me I had two weeks to find a house and that he would give me an allowance, plus pay the closing costs for the new home."

"Are you okay with that?" She felt her mother staring.

"Yes, Ma'am."

"I'm sad it came to this, Caroline."

"Don't be sad, Mom, I completely understand." She peeked at her beautiful children finishing their meal.

"We'll manage."

"I pray so, Caroline."

5

Ben's feet pounded along the busy sidewalk as he nudged his way past a mingling crowd who'd paused at the front of the café where the Tori lookalike had entered. With little to no regard of the surrounding patrons, he casually eased across the charming restaurant and parked at the only vacant stool at the bar. Through scrutinizing eyes, he checked out everyone seated. Full of diners, but none of them were her. The woman who wore a brilliant green satin coat, would, at once, be visible when discovered. The man with the classic blue suit and brown penny loafers would mesh with the rest. A fanatic himself over shoes, he could seek them out but snickered under his breath knowing that wasn't possible. He rubbed his unshaven face as he continued his survey the space. Seeing neither, he crisscrossed through the mass spotting an adjoining room. It also was crammed to the max with people.

Bingo! *The green coat.* He drew close and strained to see the woman in the dim light. His brow squeezed as he studied the woman oblivious to anybody except the fellow with the perfect shoes. *What is that guy doing?* The slim built man with striking black curly hair, leaned across his dinner menu and kissed her. Ben's mouth tightened when her familiar face came into view. Her beauty was the same as he recalled, but maybe she was a little slimmer. He caught a glimpse of her majestic eyes, her best feature. With a strained breath, he ran his hand down the front of his sports coat, loomed upon their table, pulled out a vacant chair and sat in front of her. "Good evening, Tori."

"Hello." She smiled at the man glaring back at her.

"Do you remember me?" Her brown resplendent eyes clawed at him like talons.

"No, I'm sorry. Am I supposed to know you?"

Ben clinched his teeth to kill the outcry ready to burst forth and leaned close. "I'm Ben Matney."

Tori jumped, reached for him and squeezed his neck. "Ben, why didn't you call me?" Tori quickly returned to her chair and put her hand on blue suit's arm.

Ben humiliatingly felt the scrutiny he was under and grew helpless by the second as he shifted his attention to the man sitting across from her. "Who is this?"

"I'm her fiancé, George Stanley." He stood and palmed Ben's hand. "It's nice to meet you."

At a loss of words, Ben remained silent as the blood drained from his face. His misery, so acute, a sick feeling crushed at his stomach. He held it at bay as his body temperature started to rise.

"I'll explain." Tori hurried around George and seized Ben's shoulders. "I wanted you to come to London to find out if you'd work in my uncle's bar and grille. He needs a chef and as I understand it, you've been down on your luck."

"Down on my what? We haven't spoken in nine years." He stood, gripped an empty chair behind him and awkwardly stepped backward. "You have no clue what kind of life I've had or my employment status." He bit at his lip until it throbbed, then excused himself past a waitress.

"Ben, please come back and talk with us. We have a proposal to offer." She bumped her way through the tightly fitted table and chairs and grabbed ahold of his jacket.

"Who is we?" He gazed at her boyfriend five feet away.

"George and me. We're the managers of my uncle's place. We haven't had a suitable cook in three months. You'd be fantastic."

His mouth flew open. "You want me to be your Chef?"

"You'd make a crazy salary, I mean huge."

A chill spiked his spine. "So, me coming to London had nothing to do with our relationship? I'm appalled and..." he crept closer, "I am not interested." He turned to go. "I have an excellent job in the states."

"You work at a bakery for God's sake. There's no real money in that." She stepped between him and the exit. "I realize I brought you here under false pretenses, but will you hear us out?"

Stunned and more sickened, he spun around, repeated the words 'not interested' and stared a hole through her. "I love my job in Camden and will not move here." He covered his face with trembling hands and gave vent to the agony he was struggling to hide. Exhaling and demanding to rid his anger, with slow intention, he let out his instantaneous views. "You make me sick." He swallowed hard, lifted his chin and boldly met her gaze. "I will not, repeat, will not, work for your uncle, for you or your boyfriend."

Overwhelmed with resentment, Ben forced himself not to yell, breathed heavy and shoved his hair aside. "I have to go." His broad shoulders heaved as he sighed. *What have I done?* New anguish seared his soul. Once out on the pavement, he sprinted towards the hotel. *She hurt me once again.*

The dazzling inn stacked with folks in and around the corridor was noisy when he entered, and the elevator attendant stuffed him and way too many other guests inside the tight space.

"What floor?" The usher rumbled on as he pressed buttons.

Ben was so near a young woman; her hair grazed his nose. Thankfully, she smelled nice. His cell phone vibrated in his pocket. He snatched it and noticed Tori's number. *This will be interesting.* "Hello," he answered when he stepped away from the elevator.

"Ben, I saw how agitated you were. Please listen for one minute."

He closed his eyes as his heart raced and moved with unhurried purpose. "Tori, there's nothing else I can say."

"But I love you. While George was with us, I couldn't share my true feelings. Stay, please! I'll be desperate if you don't."

He shook his head at her piercing fake words. "I may be vulnerable, but I'm not naïve. You leave me no choice but to change my plane ticket and fly home."

"You have to stay. Don't you still love me?"

"Stop." He halted at his room and slid his back against the door frame until he reached the carpet. "I do not want you to contact me again."

"But, Ben."

"Tori, I thought after nine years you'd be a different person and our visit together, well... it started out way wrong when I saw you on the street kissing your fiancé. How could you? You know what... it doesn't matter anymore. Goodbye." He pressed the end button and blocked her number.

* * *

Where to search for a house? Caroline skimmed the newspaper's real estate section. Here's one on Water Edge Way. It will be convenient to Mom and Dad's. She reached inside her bag for her phone and dialed the number. "Hello. I'm calling to find out if your residence is still for sale."

"Hi there, I'm Marlene Simpson."

"So, your home is available?"

"Yes. Would you like to come see it?"

"I'd love to come." Caroline spun her car into a fast-food restaurant's parking lot, grabbed a pen and paper from the console to write the directions. "I have time this afternoon around three o'clock."

"That will be fine."

The nice lady spat off directions and Caroline wrote as fast as her fingers allowed. "Bye now, I'll see you at three." She checked the road for traffic and pulled her Mercedes onto the highway. What did Pastor Luke tell us last Sunday? Pray for everything, then listen for the answer? *Lord Jesus, hear my plea. Will this be the house for us? Help me be able to afford it. Thank you for going ahead of me and guiding my footsteps. Amen.*

Her prayers were becoming more real each time she prayed since going to St. Luke's Baptist Church on Grand Avenue and it felt good. Now to wait for an answer.

Upon finishing up her phone conversation with the woman named Marlene Simpson, she found her compact in her red and gold makeup bag and powered her nose. A quick glance at herself in the tiny mirror, she scrutinized the woman staring back at her. Her hazel eyes looked spunky and her complexion looked smooth. She slid her fingers across her cheeks to blend her makeup.

Now, at 27, she reflected on the good things in her life, her two adorable children, her family and her restaurant. She'd worked hard at Olli's for her dad since she turned 15. He'd established the eatery before she was born and from childhood through her teen years spent many an hour hanging out while her mother did tons of paperwork. Never in a million generations did she imagine she'd run Olli's and have 51 percent ownership. *Thanks Dad and Mom.*

A quick glance at her watch gave her the time and she thought, what the heck, a quick drive by the potential house would be adventurous. Without a second thought, she did a 360 in the road and drove towards Water Edge Way. A few miles down, across from Penobscot Bay, she turned onto the street. The immaculate neighborhood with freshly groomed lawns and no trash along the way would be a perfect place to live. As she drove closer to the address given, she slowed the car to a crawl and took in the beautiful sights and parked in front of the house, stayed a minute or so, then drove towards town. Her chest rose as she thought of her living in that residence. *It can be a happy place.* She pictured her children running and playing on the front lawn.

The stop light in front of Olli's brought her back to reality. As she waited for the light to turn green, one more time, she replayed the words of her father the day he handed over the keys to the establishment, 'Be an authoritative boss while managing Olli's.' *But what is an excellent business owner if she degraded her workers?* She sucked in a quick breath as she iterated her own statement, "Treat employees with dignity and respect, always pitching in to help, from making salads, to emptying the trash, to washing dishes, and being a waitress, it didn't matter if it needed to be done. I will be there to complete the task." With the words out of her mouth, she smiled and remembered her goal from day one, to gain loyal personnel and maintain the highest reputation the restaurant had had since it opened and not run through employees like her father had done. *Keeping happy employees makes me happy.*

The memory of last evening gladdened her thoughts as she parked and went inside the building. After a decent hand washing and putting on their small aprons, Penny and Harry got involved with wrapping napkins around the silverware. She chuckled at Harry's folding technique.

Her cell phone resounded. With quickness, the handful of things she'd carried from the car flew onto a table beside her and she pressed the talk button. "Hello, Caroline here, may I help you?"

"Can I talk to you for a second?"

"Eli, you're not supposed to call me. End of story. Whose phone are you using?" Her mouth dropped. *I can't believe him.*

"I'm on Tony's phone. You'd remember him from high school."

With a deep sigh, she flung her hair and ducked into the pantry closet. "You've got two minutes."

"I'm leaving Camden."

"What? Are you for real?" She could barely control her gasp of surprise.

"Yeah, I wanted you to know that I'm moving to California. My friend, Tony's father, has offered me a position at his company."

"I hear you."

"Can we bury our past and be friends?"

Irritation grew within her. "Are you asking me to forgive you?"

""Well, yes. Caroline, don't breathe a word. I will leave and never bother you again plus, I'll send you child support payments when I get established. The kids deserve it."

What in the world? It's just a pile of nonsense. Just words. She shook her head. "I can't accept any money from you. Your intentions might be good now, but I'm sure you will demand things in the future."

"Okay, Caroline, but when you receive a check, cash it."

"Don't bother, Eli." She shrugged dismissively. "Nothing more could make me happier than to see you change, but I realize that will not happen. You need to face facts head on. Why don't you make your first task be abstaining from alcohol?" Tears stung her eyes, and she threw the phone inside her pocketbook. "Lord, take away my memory of him."

Their last encounter flooded her mind. 'Don't do this, Eli,' she remembered shouting. 'You're drunk. Please don't hit me.' Did he listen? He pounded his fists to her face on the front lawn of their house, then kicked her repeatedly in the stomach after she fell to the ground. As he continued beating her, Penny and Harry tried to pull him away. Eli slammed Harry to the grass hitting him on the side of his head while she watched helpless. His drunkard self... Fresh tears streamed upon her face.

She clinched her teeth as she replayed Penny's screams for him to stop. Her neighbor, Lauren Castle, called the police. She landed in the hospital for three weeks from the injuries she sustained and didn't go back to Olli's for two months.

I hope Eli *never returns.*

*   *   *

Chloe was right. Every memory of Tori rushed to the forefront of his mind with unwelcomed frankness; she dated people behind his back, broke into his dorm room, took things and lied to him continually. *That's when she must have put the ring I'd given her in the back of my photo album.* His fingers brushed against his cheek. Worst of all was the day after class when he returned to his dorm to find his roommate David with Tori almost naked. David apologized, but as he recollected, Tori denied anything to do with David and tried to convince him it was just his mind thinking such horrible things. Breathless with rage, her last remarks he recalled before today, spewed from his lips, "David and I weren't together, it was just your imagination." Tori, in all her ravenous glory, was still a gorgeous beauty, but that didn't change her or make her nice. In fact, she was still a devious, conniving and heartless person. As he relived the many hurtful things about her, a hint of sadness hovered around him. *She wasn't worth it then and not now.* Another bad mistake.

"Hi, this is Ben Matney. I need to switch my ticket."

"Yes, sir. I can do that for you."

He rattled off his date of birth, address, voucher number and told the customer service representative he needed a flight into Portland, Maine.

"Sir, we can get you on a flight in an hour and a half. It leaves at 10:45 p.m. with arrival time at 3 a.m. eastern time. Can I book it for you?"

"Yes, that's perfect."

Praise God he hadn't unpacked. He turned off the lights in his suite and went to the front counter of the hotel. After a bit of a wait, he approached the guy in a royal colored vest behind the desk. "Hello. I'm in 304." He slid his room key across the smooth surface. "I need to check out."

"No problem, sir." The attendant punched the keyboard on the computer, then looked at him. "But, sir, you have seven more nights with us."

"My plans have changed." He gave the man a grim stare.

"I see." The desk clerk punched more buttons then looked up. "You're all set. I canceled your reservation."

Anger abated somewhat under the warm glow of a nicely dressed woman who greeted him when he turned to leave.

"Have a nice evening." A genuine smile outlined her face.

"Thank you, you too." He put his duffle bag across his shoulder and walked onto the foggy street. The scent of grilling steak filled his nostrils, making his stomach rumble. *I could eat.* Dinner on the plane was his only choice or would it be breakfast? He strolled to the edge of the walkway and spotted a taxi down the street barreling in his direction. He waved it down as it passed.

The yellow cab screeched to a halt.

"Hey. It's you," Ben conveyed to the same cab driver who'd dropped him off a few hours earlier.

"You need another ride?" He turned his body and glanced in Ben's direction.

"Believe it or not, yes. I'm heading back to the airport." His eyebrows rose as a glint of a smile passed his lips.

"Hop inside. I'd be much obliged to drive you." The cab driver popped the trunk.

Ben dropped his luggage in the rear then jumped inside. "Thank you." His mouth went tight and grim as he thought of the nine-hour flight home. His body tensed as he tried to relax. He guessed it was from all the embarrassment he'd been through. *What a day.* He decided not to phone Chloe but instead go see her when he returned, telling her everything. A visit with the newborns sounded great. I wonder what she named them.

6

As the sun peaked the bright blue skies, Caroline circled the ad in the paper several more times and glanced at her watch. They'd be early to Water Edge Way. After her wonderful viewing the day before, this second visit with Mrs. Simpson, and the kids in tow, should confirm and reassure her strong feelings that this was the right place to live. It was love from the moment she stepped through the threshold. Caroline gazed at the reflective rays along Penobscot Bay when she turned onto the narrow street. "There's the house." The adorable white sided home with black shutters is a perfect spot for her and the twins. She eased the Mercedes to a slow crawl and parked alongside the property. *Pictures.* A quick snap here and there, she took 20 plus photos of hopefully their new residence.

"I love it, Mommy," Harry unbuckled his car seat.

"I dreamed us getting it, Mommy." Penny put the window down, held her hand against her forehead and stared.

The neatly groomed yard had a nice stone walkway that led to the front porch. Small shrubs perfectly lined the path. Skillfully stacked against each side of the steps were moist green plants bursting from the snow packed ground. In the spring she could plant red and yellow tulips with gaillardia sun devils rising up behind them. *It will be breathtaking.* A smile crossed her lips when the sweet old woman, Mrs. Marlene Simpson opened her door. "Hello there."

"Hey, Mrs. Montgomery. You are prompt and have brought your children." She smiled.

"This is Harry and Penny." She ran up the steps and shook Mrs. Simpson's hand. "I'm excited we're purchasing your home. It's fantastic."

"You are so sweet, dear. Come, sit beside me. We are having such a nice day, aren't we?" Mrs. Simpson pointed to the blue rocking chairs.

"It is a lovely day." Caroline moved to the middle chair. "Mrs. Simpson, this may be blunt, but since yesterday, and after seeing your lovely home, I have a question." A slight grin shone on her lips. "Will you reduce the price of your home by $25,000.00?" Her heartbeat started racing.

Mrs. Simpson squeezed her brow. "I'd have to think on it." The ole gal shook her head.

"It is a lot to ask, I know." Caroline twirled her hands together. Harry ran from the yard and jumped on her lap. "My twins and I are trying to find a safe neighborhood to live. $25,000.00 less is all we can afford." She blinked and gazed at the blue water across the street. "The bay is gorgeous from here."

Mrs. Simpson picked up Harry's hand. "You like the place, do you?"

"Yes, I love it."

Penny was lying on the snow just below the front steps. "I love the house too, Mommy."

"I will miss living here. My husband and I lived here for over 50 years."

"What happened to Mr. Simpson?"

"He got sick ages ago." She wiped at her tears. "We lost him on a Tuesday."

"I'm sorry, Mrs. Simpson."

"Getting old is for the birds. We lose our loved ones, get stiff as arthritis takes over and you fall asleep without warning, but you didn't come here to hear my complaints or woes, you want to know if I'll take less money for the house." A quick grin crossed her lips. "Why, if I may ask, are you moving?"

Caroline jumped and the kids hurried behind the rocking chair she was sitting in when a dog meandered up to Mrs. Simpson's rocker. "Whose dog is this?"

"Oh, that's Max." Mrs. Simpson pet the top of the dog's head. "He lives several doors away. When he wants a snack, he knows where to come." A chuckle escaped her. "Back to my question, dear Caroline, tell me why you're looking for a new place to live?"

"My kids and I have been staying with my parents and we have to move…." Caroline sucked in a profound breath, "My father gave me an ultimatum."

"Is that so?"

"Yes ma'am. Your home is what I'm looking for." She closed her eyes and revisited each room in the adorable house she'd seen earlier. When she opened them, Mrs. Simpson was again holding hands with Harry.

"Caroline, I'd love for you and your twins to live here. I'll accept $25,000.00 less."

Thank you, Lord. That was the answer she was seeking. "Much appreciation, Mrs. Simpson."

"Will you meet me at my attorney's office to sign a contract?" Mrs. Simpson drew near Caroline and hugged her. "What do you think Mr. Harry?"

"You are nice to give us your house." He grinned from ear to ear.

Laughter broke out among Caroline and Mrs. Simpson. "Maybe we can meet tomorrow at my lawyer's office?"

"That will be great. I will have the earnest deposit."

"Let's call Mr. Felker."

They set a meeting for 2:00 p.m. the next day.

"I'll see you then," Mrs. Simpson announced. "Bye-bye Mr. Harry and Miss Penny. It was good to meet you."

Tears rolled across Caroline's face as she praised Jesus for her answered prayer. "Mommy why are you crying?" Penny reached up and touched her shoulder from her car seat.

"I promise, Penny, these are happy tears." She wiped her face as she continued along the street. A few minutes later, Caroline pulled her car in front of Harry and Penny's school, wished them well, watched them hurry inside and drove on to work. *I need to save my money.*

* * *

The commercial flight to Portland, Maine landed right on time the next morning. Ben collected his luggage from baggage claim and meandered to the parking garage. Still in disarray, Ben's Jeep awaited in Section, 15-C. *There you are.* He dug for his keys and hit the unlock on his key fob. Nothing. *What?* He hit the thing again. Oh, no. The Jeep didn't come to life. He slung his bags onto the pavement and stuck the key inside the lock. It opened with no problem. Next, he put the key into the ignition and turned it. Dead. He tried it one more time. Nothing. AAA is open 24/7. He pulled the hood latch and got out to inspect. He knew diddly squat about engines but took a gander, anyway. The battery cable may have come off. He leaned in to get a closer view.

"Hey, Dude," yelled a teenager as he got near the Wrangler. "You can't get your Jeep started?"

Ben spun around. "No. It's dead."

"I've got jumper cables in the back of my truck. Let me get them."

"I'd sure appreciate that."

"You look tired."

He was observant making Ben laugh. "I guess you can tell that I've been up most of the night."

The young man put his hands in his pockets. "I just dropped off my dad. He's flying to California this morning." He turned to Ben, "I'm going to get my truck."

Ben watched the boy walk up the aisle. Within a minute, headlights shone bright. A flash of humor crossed Ben's face when he eyed the sooped up white Chevrolet Avalanche with huge tires pull up beside him. "I can't thank you enough," he stated when the teen got out of his vehicle.

The young man snatched the jumper cables, popped his hood and clamped them onto the battery, then stretched them over to Ben's Jeep. "Okay, get in and fire it up." He glanced at Ben.

Vroom. The Wrangler came to life. He reached inside his pocket and rummaged for a few dollars. *What the heck.* "Here you go, Bud, for your trouble," and handed him his wad of cash.

"For real? Thanks, man." The grin on the boy's face was priceless.

"I couldn't have gotten out of here without you."

"Thanks, Mister."

Ben watched the teenager speed through the corridor to the exit ramp. He watched the kid's taillights until they disappeared into the night. He backed out of the parking space and followed in the same direction.

The trip back to Water Edge Way was becoming a nightmare as his eyes kept closing at their will. From singing to stopping at a convenience store and buying a box of cereal to munch on, to hanging his head out the window, sleep was what his body kept insisting. A couple of hours home turned into three. Relief soared through him as he rolled his Jeep into the driveway. He left his belongings behind and took off running to his bed that awaited him. With a commanding pull, off came his shirt and pants. He fell into bed asleep before his head hit the pillow. When he woke, he turned and eyed his clock on the nightstand realizing he'd slept until the next morning. *Man was he ever tired. I slept over 26 hours.*

* * *

"Chloe?" Ben questioned the voice on the other end of the phone when she answered her phone.

"Hey, Ben. How's your trip? I'm glad you called. My curiosity was getting the best of me."

"It's a long story. I'm not in London."

"Where are you?"

"Home. I flew back a few hours after I got there." He rolled his eyes as he heard her laugh.

"You're kidding me, right?"

"No. I wish I were. I was planning to stop by and tell you what happened and see the babies."

"Gosh, I'm so sorry."

A chuckle floated from his throat. "Don't be sorry, Chloe, you were right."

His phone buzzed. "I have another call, let me call you back." He gazed at the number. Who could that be? After adjusting his eyes, he peered at the phone number a second time. "Hello."

"Ben? Ben Matney?"

"Yes." He propped himself on his pillows and laid still in his warm bed.

"I'm Natalie Fields from Jasper County Child Protection Services. Early this morning, an intruder broke into your brother's home and shot him."

"What?" A sudden wrench of pain shot through his chest. *Bradley hurt?*

"Yes, sir, someone shot him."

He sucked in a quick breath. "Where's my mother?"

"I don't have information regarding your mother. I'm sorry."

"Wait, a minute, may I please speak with Bradley?" This news jumbled his mind.

"Mr. Matney, Bradley is on his way here from Jasper County Hospital."

Perspiration beaded on Ben's forehead and his palms moistened with sweat. "Whoa. Can you repeat what happened?" He sat straight in bed.

"Hold on, Mr. Matney, I'm getting Captain Fink for you. He has more facts than I do."

Silence. He looked at his phone. The call dropped. She hung up on me. *Good grief!* Deep breath, calm yourself. Another vibration brought his phone back to life. It was the same number. "Yes," Ben answered in a low voice.

"Mr. Matney. This is Captain Paul Fink. My apologies for not calling you myself."

Ben flung the covers off his body and stiffened as a nauseating gut twisting sensation invaded his stomach. He grabbed his belly, then squeezed his temples to relieve mounting pressure. *Lord, Jesus, help me handle what I'm about to hear.*

"First thing this morning, as I understand it, a robber shot your mother and brother. Bradley will be fine. He received two flesh wounds to his right arm and shoulder. The hospital has released him to our care, and he's headed this way."

"Thank God he's okay. And my mother?"

"She sustained multiple gunshot wounds and is in surgery."

"How serious is she?" Queasiness struck the pit of his stomach a second time.

"It's bad, Mr. Matney. I've got a phone number you can call to get an update on her status." He read the number. "Mr. Matney, the incident upset Bradley, and he is asking for you. He wants you to come home."

"Captain—." Ben shook his head. *I can't remember.*

The man replied, "Fink."

"Captain Fink, I'll get on the first flight to Washington."

His mind wandered to his mother standing at the kitchen sink back home, washing dishes after breakfast every day when he was a child. She kissed his and Bradley's foreheads and sent them to catch the big yellow school bus. While they were away, she tidied up their two-story house then hurried off to the local food market where she did their payroll and accounts payable. He and Bradley walked to the store after school and waited for her. Most days she exited the building at 3:30 p.m. on the dot. Those fond memories rolled straight to his heart. Alexandria, Virginia was a safe place.

"Mr. Matney?"

"Yeah, I'm here."

"Let me give you my cell number. Call me as soon as you land. I'll swing by and get you."

Ben saved the captain's number and googled the same travel agency that booked his flight to London.

He stilled as he held for his travel agent. *Coffee.* He needed coffee. Stiff and feeling awkward, he walked into the kitchen and made himself a cup of brew. Without a hesitation, he sipped the hot beverage as he stood gazing into his neighbor's backyard. *What is Clancy doing?* He opened his back door and shouted, "Clancy, you need help over there?"

"Yes, I do."

Rigid or not, Ben sprinted off his back porch and jumped the low fencing that separated their properties. Clancy, not so bright, had tiptoed to the top of his ladder with a chainsaw straddled to his back.

"Good grief. Are you trying to kill yourself?" Ben wiped the bottom of his feet.

Clancy hung onto the tree. "No. I'm trying to cut this limb for the misses."

"You ain't no spring chicken anymore, get down from there!" Ben held the ladder.

"Thanks, Boy."

"You got a rope? We can pull it down instead of you trying out your acrobatic skills."

"That's a smart idea. Let's go find one."

Ben followed Clancy into his garage. They found a long rope coiled against the back wall. "Here's one we can use."

"Yes, that will work. I'll go up the ladder this time." Ben climbed with the huge rope strung over his back and circled it around the branch. "Okay, Clancy, when I tell you, tug hard on the rope."

Clancy moved up against the tree and waited.

"Okay, pull," but the limb didn't budge. "Let me come help." Ben slid down the rails of the ladder and, together, they tugged the heavy-duty rope. Seconds later the limb was on the ground.

"Stay off your ladder."

"I will."

"Hey, listen, I'm headed out of town. My mom's in the hospital."

"I'll say a prayer."

On the snow-covered path to his yard, he bent to the ground and rubbed Clancy's dog. "Take care of the old man, will you, Max?" He smiled at the dog. He retrieved his coffee cup and walked around the side of his house. The water was radiant against the sun's rays along the bay. He released a deep sigh. *Lord, please help my mom. Please get her through the surgery. Be with Bradley.*

He'd forgotten he was on hold with the travel agent. It'd been 20 minutes. "Geez," and ran inside the house. He grabbed his phone, refilled his cup with coffee, then headed back outside.

"Hello. Sorry for the long wait. This is Katie Brunson; how can I help you?"

"I'm Ben Matney. I need to book a flight to Washington, D.C. from Portland, Maine as soon as possible."

"Let me check the flights."

"Thank you." He tired from the constant waiting.

"Mr. Matney, I can get you on a flight at 2:40 p.m. this afternoon."

He twisted his wrist watch – 9:48 a.m.

"So, may I book the flight for you?"

He ran his free hand through his hair. "Yes." After reading the woman his credit card information he couldn't take his eyes off the calm water. Minutes passed, Chloe popped into his thoughts! He pressed his recent calls menu and tapped her number. "Chloe."

"Hey, Ben. I thought you'd be here by now."

He watched a flock of geese float near the shore of the bay. "Chloe, I got terrible news just now."

"What is it, Ben?"

"An intruder shot my mom and brother early this morning."

"Oh, my goodness."

Ben walked to the mouth of the bay. "Someone broke into their house and shot them. I have no other details."

"How did you find out?"

"A Captain Frick, I mean, Fink called me. I've got to fly to Virginia."

"Listen, Ben, don't worry over the bakery. Mitchell put a sign on the door. Do you have a flight out?"

"Yeah. It leaves at 2:40 p.m. Listen, I need to hang up so I can call my buddy, Trey, and see if he can drive me to the airport, plus, I want to call Mrs. Whitehurst to find out if she can work if I'm gone longer than a week. Also, I need to talk with Kandice before I leave." Ben smoothed his t-shirt. "It was good to talk with you. You always make me feel better."

"Ben, I'll be praying."

"Thanks, Chloe." *How could this have happened?* Bizarre couldn't describe what he'd been through since yesterday and today was even more unreal. Weariness engulfed his soul. He had no intention of permitting tears. He must be strong. A gruffy sigh escaped him. *You've got to do this.* He dialed the number Captain Fink gave him. "Hello. My name is Ben Matney. I'm calling to get details on my mother, Emily Matney."

"Yes, Mr. Matney. Let me get you the latest information. Please hold a moment."

Ben put his phone on speaker, laid it on his bed and hurried into the bathroom. He opened the shower door and turned on the hot water, knowing it would take a few minutes for the water to heat up.

"Hello, Mr. Matney."

"Yes, I'm here." He ran to the bed and picked up his phone.

"Your mother is in ICU."

"Can you give me any details?" With a quick tug, he yanked off his shirt.

"Your mother sustained wounds in her stomach, right thigh, and left shoulder. She came through her surgery well and her vital signs were in the good range when I last checked. The doctors informed me they had to remove part of her stomach."

"Wow. I've already made plans to fly in from Maine this afternoon. Upon landing, I will come to the hospital. Can you tell me her prognosis?" He fought hard against the tears he refused to let fall.

"The doctors will go over everything when you get here. Be thankful, Mr. Matney, she's stable. It could be worse."

Ben stood at his bathroom mirror in front of him and stared at his deep blue eyes. *Pull through this, Mom.* He tipped his chin upward and slid the palm of his right hand over his unshaven chin and cheeks. His mouth twisted as he pulled open the small drawer under the counter to find the electric razor his mother sent him last Christmas. Tears formed across his eyelids as he pressed the start button. He couldn't hold them in any longer. He moved the rotating blades in circular motions over his face and wiped his tears with his free hand. With one last gaze, he whispered to himself, "I'm going home." Smooth to the touch and satisfied he'd done a good job, he placed the razor inside the drawer, then jumped into the hot shower, letting the water soak his back. He washed his hair, squeezed conditioner into his hand and ran it through his hair and let it sit two minutes. Upon a quick scrub on his face with facial soap, he then picked up his shower brush and washed his body. After he rinsed his hair, he raked his hands through and through it again to make sure no conditioner residue remained.

Clean from his shower, he wished he could have washed away the heavy burden he felt for his mom and brother. *Leave it at the altar.* That's what his pastor repeats every Sunday, but he wasn't at church. *God, take this burden from me.* Upon turning off the water, he snatched a towel off the rack and ran to his bedroom to dress so he'd be ready when his friend Trey, who was driving him to the airport, picked him up.

It'd been five years since he set eyes on his baby brother. He may not recognize Bradley who turned 17 two months earlier. No matter what, when saw him, he'd pull him into a hug and tell him he loved him. Immediate thoughts flew to this mother. *What if she...*

Without a second thought, he pressed Kandice's number. "Hey, how are you?"

"Hey, Ben. I didn't think I'd hear from you."

"Yeah, well, my plans changed and I'm on my way to Washington, DC."

"For real?" Kandice sighed.

"Someone shot my mother and brother this morning. My brother is fine, but my mom is in ICU."

"Gee, Ben, I'll be praying for them."

"Thanks. If I'm not back next week, hopefully Mrs. Whitehurst can help you at the bakery. I got to go. I'm flying out in a few hours."

"Stay in touch."

7

The sweltering temperatures for the middle of January were extreme for his liking and the forecast called for storms throughout the day. Would cooler temps be on the way? *It's 55 out and the snow has almost disappeared.* Trying to ignore the beads of perspiration forming against his eyebrow, Ben crossed his lawn and stopped at the edge of the road as a strange sensation overcame him. *Mom!* He pulled his carry-on bag away from his shoulder, dropped it to the ground and moved toward the shade of a nearby oak that looked inviting to relieve the beaming sun from his back. He stiffened and grabbed his gut when a sudden pain inundated him. Should he go back inside the house? *It's just nerves.*

His neighbor, Mrs. Simpson and Clancy Chambers' dog, Max, were amongst a group of people in her driveway, laughing, hugging, and from where he stood, enjoying a grand reunion. He squinted and stared with curiosity when he spotted a gorgeous woman gathered among the rest. Something was vaguely familiar about her. *I think I've seen her.*

"Ben," Mrs. Simpson shouted and waved, "come greet your new neighbors."

"New neighbors?" He checked for traffic then crossed the street and hugged the silver headed sweet lady. "Hi, how've you been?"

"Meet Caroline Montgomery, she's the one who is buying my house," she announced as she stepped sideways to allow Caroline to be the center of attention.

Not holding back, and with every ounce of courage, he breathed deep and spoke, "I remember you. It's a pleasure to see you again," and took her hand into his. As their hands touched, a prickle tingled his spine.

Caroline held onto his grip. "Hi there. It's nice to see you. You live across the street?" A grin arose upon her lips as a frown appeared.

A quick flashback he'd never forget; the moment he first laid eyes on her when she stepped inside Camden Bakery. A smile tipped his lips, "Yes." He stood gazing and went dumbfounded for words to say. He gazed into her eyes and blurted, "How were your brownies?"

Her straight white teeth shone bright when she drew a few inches closer. "The brownies were wonderful and, how was your spaghetti?" Her eyes deepened as she focused on him when a sudden squint appeared a second time, "I thought you were taking a trip out of town?"

A blue Tesla came rolling at a fast past towards them. "I am on my way now and, let me say before I leave, the spaghetti was fantastic, the best in town." He paused and watched his friend, Trey, park his fancy car. "I'm glad we'll be neighbors," he smiled then ducked from the crowd and waved goodbye one last time to Caroline who didn't take her eyes off him.

Trey's car window rolled downward, and he poked his head out, "Is everything okay over there?"

"Yes, all okay. I was meeting my new neighbors," he wiped his face then ran his fingers through his hair.

"Is that right?" Trey scanned the folks milling in the yard. "Is it the older couple?"

"Uh, no, it's the babe standing beside them in the dark blue dress."

"Ooh, I should get out and introduce myself," his friend unleased his seatbelt.

"Stay in the car," Ben struggled to keep an even relaxed tone. "I'll be right back; I need to get my overnight bag." He took off and grabbed the item and returned to find, no other, but Trey, shaking hands with

Caroline. *No way! He always gets the girl. Not this time.* Girls flocked to him, he guessed, because of his charming charisma.

Caroline dropped Trey's hand when he approached. "Hello, again," she grinned.

"I see you met my friend, Trey?" He shifted in between them.

"Yes, he introduced himself."

Caroline's two small red headed sweet children bolted from the door and Ben dropped to his knees. "Hi there, Harry and Penny, how are you two?" He welcomed them into an embrace.

Trey took a step backward as his mouth tumbled open, "You have kids?" He averted Caroline and stared at Ben, tossing his head towards his Tesla.

"Yes," a gleam appeared on her face. "That's Harry, and here's my sweet Penny," Caroline affirmed as she stepped next to Ben and put her arm around Penny's shoulder.

Penny leaped from Ben and fell into Caroline's cuddle quickly, then turned to him. "I 'member you, you gave me the best cupcake in the world."

"Me too!" Harry shouted as he playfully frolicked on the front porch steps.

Trey continued his mad dash to the car and shouted over his shoulder, "It was a pleasure meeting you and your children."

Ben tilted his head, then regarded her eyes, "Um, when I get back, can I take you out to dinner?"

"That sounds great."

He ran his hand through his hair and put a loose strand behind his ear. "Will you give me your number?"

She laughed, "I guess you need it, huh?"

"I do," he replied as he retrieved his phone from his pants pocket and saved her number.

"Have a wonderful trip," she put her arms around the shoulders of Harry and Penny and held on tight.

He didn't want to leave her. "Trey's waiting." Their eyes met one last time, "I've got to be going." He shuffled his feet, turned and hurried away as the gorgeous girl, he hated to leave behind, waved one more time. He got to the Tesla, slung his bag into the backseat, then hopped inside.

Trey hit his shoulder. "Geez, Bro, you don't need a woman with two children."

Ben rolled his eyes, "I guess neither do you since you retreated like a wildcat when her kids came out of the house."

"Heck no, I prefer my own children, thank you. She was a splendiferous darling, but I would never want to inherit her problems, especially twins, if you catch my drift."

With a snap, Ben's mouth shut, stunned by Trey's bluntness and sat quietly for a minute, then in a low voice, he breathed, "Her children are pretty darn terrific, in my opinion." He opened his satchel and pulled out two granola bars, "You want one?"

"Sure, thanks," Trey accepted.

From meeting Caroline a few days ago to now finding out she'll live across the street broadened the smile that had already surfaced. "It will be wonderful having her as my neighbor."

"You got her number, didn't you?"

Ben tapped his phone, "Yeah, I did," as his grin widened in approval.

"You can call her while you're waiting to board your plane."

"Not a bad idea, thanks." He tried to avoid his friend's view of him, turned and faced the window to hide his sneer that still beamed.

"You've fallen for her? I see that look in your eye."

"No, I haven't." *I have.* "We only met each other a few days ago."

"Tell me about the girl from London," Trey raised his eyebrow poking for answers.

"Tori?" He wrenched. "As soon as I landed in London, I was starving, so I found a place to eat across the street from my hotel, and while I was waiting on my food, I noticed Tori outside the window from where I was sitting. And, get this, she was with another guy. The next part I still can't believe."

"Tell me."

"They stopped and kissed right in front of me."

"Are you kidding?"

"I wish I was." His jaw clenched and his eyes slightly narrowed. "I wanted to be sure it was her, so I followed them and guess what? It was Tori."

"Geez, man, that's awful," Trey sped beyond the speed limit as they raced to the airport in Portland.

He cast his eyes upon the bay as they passed over the bridge. "Tori's intentions were to convince me to move to London and work at her Uncle's restaurant."

"So, she lied to you?" Trey waved his hand in a gesture of dismissal and stared at him.

"I'm so ashamed," Ben stiffened abashed as he readjusted in his seat. "I should have never gone, and I know now, girls of that sort, never, ever change."

Trey exited the interstate. "We need to get some sodas for the ride," and pulled into the first service station on their right. "I am so sorry she treated you terribly. So... how long have you lived in Camden?" A muscle quivered his jaw.

"As long as you have, maybe a little longer, why?" He questioned, amazed at the constant diversions.

"I remember now, we met at Harvey's Gym right after you moved here, and I'll get to the point."

"I wish you'd hurry up." He was irked by Trey's cool, aloof manner.

"You have dated no one since I've known you."

"Well, there has been little to no time for that sort of thing and guess who reminded me of that when I saw her at the hospital?"

"Chloe."

"Yep, you sound just like her."

"There's that gal at the bakery, what's her name, you could take her out."

"Kandice?" He gritted his mouth tight.

"Yeah," Trey laughed as he got out of the car. "You want to come inside?"

"Yeah, I'll go inside and get something." Ben unbuckled his seatbelt and opened the car door, halting at the pump and sneered at Trey. "About Kandice... we've been to lunch a bunch of times and usually sit together at church when she's there."

Trey frowned at him. "So, do you have feelings for her?"

"Gosh no, she's more of a sister than a girlfriend and besides, she has a boyfriend back home."

Together, they walked inside the store, picked out a few snacks, opened the drink cooler, retrieved two cans of soda and hurried to the register. "I'll get this since you're driving me," Ben pulled his wallet from his hip pocket.

"I appreciate that," Trey took a deep breath, "You know, Ben, it's hard to find the right one."

"Can we finish this conversation in the car?" He ran ahead of Trey and slammed the passenger side door and waited. Once they were out on the highway, Ben let it spill, "Gosh, Trey, I know it's got be hard finding the right girl, believe me, I've had nothing but bad gone to worse since I started dating." He shook his head from side to side.

Trey set the cruise control to 80 miles an hour and sped up the road. "Sit back and relax, my friend."

"I think my mom and brother will have to be my main priority now, dating... well," he slapped his friend's shoulder, "I might fit Caroline into my plans." He lifted his arms in the air and shrugged his shoulders.

"How is your mother?"

"She's in ICU. They told me they had to remove part of her stomach and she had to have an extensive repair done to her leg."

"Ooh, and your brother? What's his name?"

"Bradley." His head swung and he laid back against the headrest. "He's fine, thank God, I know you will flip out, but I think they should move to Camden with me."

"Yeah, I'm with you, I think that's a great idea." Trey leaned his hand on the seat behind Ben's shoulder.

"I'll pack them up and put mom's house up for sale."

"What will they think?"

He hesitated, blinking with bafflement, "I am sure neither of them will want to move here and when I suggest it, it's going to send my mother through the roof."

"Did you notice your hands trembling?"

He fisted them and nodded. "I guess my nervousness is showing."

* * *

Was Ben, Tori's boyfriend? He has the same name. The speculation hit her like a ton of bricks hitting concrete and shattering. "That's crazy!" A few days later and after her father handled a cash deal with Mrs. Simpson, she stood alone in the front lawn of her new home and watched the moving truck pull away. The image of Mr. Matney captivated her when she looked across the street at his house. His blond hair against his olive complexion was so handsome, "And, those deep blues, oh my," made her melt. He was tall, just the way she liked a man. What a coincidence he was going to be her neighbor! *Was God sending him to rescue her and her kids?*

"Mommy, hurry, come inside with us," Penny yelled from the porch.

"I'm coming," she hurried from the indented spot in the snow where she had stood for a long while.

The three-bedroom home with pine floors were original to the house and had withstood pounding of feet for many years. Well kept, their glossy shine glistened in the sun when she stepped inside Harry's room. "It's a wonderful room, Harry," with crisp light blue walls, perfect in every way for a boy.

"Me stay in here," he ran to her embrace, "and, Penny can stay in there," he pointed across the hall.

"That will work," she hugged her small boy.

"There you are," she found Penny running down the hall. "Where did you go?" Caroline asked as they entered the yellow bedroom.

"I had to tinkle."

"Harry just picked out his room, is this one going to work for you?" Penny ran, opened her arms and twirled around, "I love this room." They continued and walked further along the hall and into the master suite. "It's nice back here, and look at this big bathroom, I love it." She stayed an extra second to peek inside all the cabinets in the spacious tile floored lavatory.

Penny ran to her, "I love your room, Mommy."

"Me, too."

Her father strolled in, "Caroline, I need a word with you."

"Yes, Sir," She answered as she moved to where he was standing. "Thanks for going with me to the lawyer's office and allowing me to pay you instead of having a mortgage."

"I thought it would be better that way so you could move in right away and it would help your mother. Oh yeah, don't let Eli find out you've moved here."

"I'll try, Dad." Why did he have to ruin her day? How could she stop Eli from anything? "I forgot to tell you, he called last night on someone else's phone and informed me he was moving to California."

"I hope he's left," she affirmed.

"Yeah, me too." Her dad's tender expression amazed her.

"You might have a nice neighbor when you get settled, huh, Caroline?" He smiled.

"How do you know that?"

"I don't, but you could ask Mrs. Simpson," he gestured and squeezed her tight.

"You're funny, dad," she dropped her arms and breezed through the house, looking for the kitchen. *That's a great idea.* Her cell phone rang, "Will you excuse me a moment," hurrying out the side door. "Hello."

"Caroline."

"Eli, I've told you a hundred times you can't call me," she stopped on the front steps of her new home.

"I'm on my way to California and wanted you to know."

"That's wonderful, I've got to go."

"Wait, I need to tell you something."

"What?" Her lips thinned into a flat line.

"I've gotten myself into trouble."

She released a stifled breath, "I can believe it, but why are you telling me?"

"I need $2,000.00 today."

His words were nothing new. "Eli, I don't care to hear this." Her mouth took on an unpleasant twist.

"I've got to have the money for my plane ticket."

"Get off the phone, Caroline," her father announced as he stepped up behind her.

She put her hand into the air and waved him off, then whispered, "Sorry." She grinned and touched her father's arm.

"Eli, you know there's no money in my piggy bank for what you want and there never will be," she sighed with a groan.

"Do you remember the condition you were in last summer? Well, that's what will happen again if you don't get it for me."

"Don't you dare threaten me! I'm calling the police." She disconnected the call, opened her purse and threw her phone inside and flung herself into her father's arms. Squeezing her eyes shut, her mind rushed to her hanging on to dear life and lying in a hospital bed as Eli's words hammered at her insides. I *can't let him scare me anymore.*

"How much money does he want?" Her dad inquired.

Not hiding it, she lifted her eyes, "$2,000.00 to be exact. Not only that, he is demanding it today," the words tumbled with edginess.

"That boy has lost his mind, and... I think it's time to call the police.

"You won't give him the money, will you?"

"It's for his plane ticket to California, for God's sake."

"If you give it to him, he will only give me an ultimatum for more."

"Give me the phone number."

"Dad, please... don't call him," she spoke as her pulse raced.

He didn't listen and dialed the last number on her phone as she froze. Her legs began to wobble as perspiration beaded on her forehead. *I need to get off my feet.*

"This is David Gladden, put Eli on the phone!"

Caroline quickly moved to the steps as a sick feeling overcame her as she listened intently to her dad.

"Eli, David Gladden here, where are you?" He continued and his voice rose with anger, "You are insane."

Caroline stared at her father and mouthed, "What is he implying?"

David waved his hand and brought his index finger to his lips. "I'll see you in Portland. No, be at the entrance, I'll find you." He ended the call. "Sorry, honey, I wanted to make sure I heard his every word," he voiced, then winked at her.

"I am not following you," she replied and forced her hand to stay on her hip.

"I'm leaving to find Eli and give him the money."

"This scares me, what if..."

"I'll take my chances." He halted, spun around and grabbed ahold of her arms as tears streamed down her face, "Honey, this could finally bring him to stop bothering you and the children."

"Portland is a long way," she squeezed him tight.

"I'd better be moving, so I don't miss him."

She scrutinized him as he wiggled his wallet in his back pocket, "He asked you for the $2,000.00?"

"Yes, and I might give him more."

"No, Dad."

8

The airport traffic was grueling as Trey zigzagged in between the cars that caused an inundated nauseous feeling to his stomach, "Please stop weaving in and out of this traffic, I could upchuck."

"I thought you were in a hurry," he laughed and slapped him on his upper back, "Oh, you'll be fine."

"Not at the risk of throwing up," Ben bowed his head and held his hands over his face.

Trey cackled and his eyes narrowed on him, "You look queasy."

"Don't laugh, I get motion sickness easy, okay?"

"That's hilarious." Trey pulled the car over onto the side of the road. "I'm sorry... but it's funny."

He couldn't help but laugh at himself, too, when he gazed at the pure pleasure on Trey's face. "Would it give you utter joy to see me throw up?" Ben cocked his head sideways.

"You're a trip." Trey turned his head and stared at him, "I've never met anyone like you in my entire life," and he continued to laugh.

Fifteen seconds later, Trey pulled back onto the road after he made sure Ben was okay. With a slow go through bumper to bumper traffic, 20 minutes passed before they finally approached the departure lanes. "Thanks for the ride," Ben paused, "I'll keep you up-to-date," he yelled through the car window.

"I hope it goes well."

Ben smiled, "I'll catch up with you when I get back, thanks for bringing me."

"Sure thing, buddy, hope you get better."

He hurried inside the terminal to find the check-in desk straight in front of him. The only thing, the line was super long. Waiting had always been a test of his patience and today, well, he was in for it. To his surprise, the people in front of him rapidly moved through the line. "Hello," he handed the desk clerk his voucher when it was his turn.

"How are you today?"

"Fine, thank you."

"You're all set. Have a wonderful trip," responded the nice woman behind the desk.

"Thanks," Ben replied, and he made his way to the waiting area for flight D378A. A mass of people occupied almost every seat. He glanced over to the windows and one empty chair was available. After he grabbed it, he made himself as comfortable as possible, because he had a 50-minute wait before he or anyone else could board the plane to Washington, DC.

Ben nodded towards a nice dressed man who occupied the seat beside him when the guy looked in his direction. "Hey," Ben acknowledged. He pulled a bag of chips from his bag and pried it open with his fingers. The man's cologne filtered to where he was. "You want a few chips?"

"No, thank you, I just had lunch. Where are you headed?"

"Washington. My mom's in the hospital."

"Oh. I hope's it's not too serious."

"Well..." Ben tipped his head, "I really don't know how she's doing."

"Oh, my goodness, I'm sorry."

"Thanks," Ben munched on the chips until he finished the bag.

"I didn't mean to pry," the man spoke up after a few minutes.

"Oh, it's okay... someone shot my mother early this morning."

"Good grief," the man turned in his seat, "that's terrible."

"Yeah, and the robber shot my brother, too, but he'll be fine, thank God."

"I'm Eli," the man announced.

"It's nice to meet you, I'm Ben Matney. So where are you headed?"

"I'm starting a new job in California."

"That's cool. Can I ask what you do?" Ben inquired as he shifted his bag under his feet.

"I manage grocery stores."

"Oh?" Ben squeezed his brow.

"Yeah, have you heard of the grocery chain B&B?"

"No, I can't say I have."

"I used to be their regional manager and traveled 20 states for a good while, but it became too much so... I quit." Eli started to play with the zipper on his piece of luggage.

Ben picked up his canned soda and took a gulp as he listened to the guy rattle on. "I'd hate a job that required a lot of traveling."

"I missed out on raising my kids," Eli replied sadly.

"Wow, it's so taxing, isn't it?" Ben put his soda in the cup holder then folded the chip bag and put it into his satchel.

"I liked my job, but I messed up and lost it."

"I thought you said you quit."

"Well, it's a long story," He turned and faced Ben. "They fired me, to be honest."

Why is this guy spilling his guts? "Wow, that's too bad."

"If you want to call it that." Eli glanced at this watch. "Nice talking with you, but I've got to meet my father-in-law at the main entrance. I'll catch up with you on the plane."

* * *

A Deja Vu moment? Weird, but as he gazed out the porthole of the Delta jet descending to land, for one second, he had to remember where he was going. *Wow,* amazing how things can change within a few hours. Glued to the tiny window, the trees were mere sticks poking out of the ground and the houses he scrutinized, were mere matchboxes. As he gazed upon the ground below, more and more buildings came into view so it must have meant the plane was getting closer to Washington.

His heart ached to be with Bradley. *Will the care facility allow him to leave?* His mind boggled with questions over his mother and brother, and he wanted to be on the ground. After a quick view of his watch, he realized the flight only had a few more minutes in the air. As he sat in the small seat gazing at the chair in front of him, he couldn't, for the life of him, remember the last time he was home. Five years? He wondered. *Wow, how time flies.*

"This is your captain speaking; we will arrive shortly, thank you for choosing Delta Airlines."

Cloudy skies greeted him and the 80 plus passengers. *There's the guy I met.* He exited the plane and tried to catch him, "Hey, Eli," Ben shook his head as he watched him in a frenzy with his plane ticket in hand, run in the opposite direction from the exit signs. He m*ust be in a hurry to catch his next flight.*

Ben grabbed his phone from his hip pocket and dialed Captain Fink's number, then scanned the bottom of a small slip of paper and read the hospital's phone number. *Lord, I pray my mother is okay.* A flicker of apprehension coursed through his veins as he got the captain's voice mail. "Captain Fink, Ben Matney here, please call me," and he repeated his number a few times. He rubbed his stomach to rid the sudden pain that riddled him, put his phone inside his pocket and fiddled through his bag for an antacid pill. He grabbed one, pulled it out and popped it into his mouth. A fast-food restaurant was to his right and to his surprise there wasn't a line. With quick feet, he dashed to the counter and greeted the cute girl behind the counter. "Hello, may I get a bottle of water and a hotdog?"

"Sure thing, sir, that will be $7.00, please."

He handed the girl his debit card and within a few seconds he had his food. He readjusted his bag on his shoulder and headed to the exit. As he stood waiting, he bit into the hotdog and sipped his water, while his phone vibrated in his pocket.

He gently placed his hotdog on the bench and retrieved the call.

"Ben?"

He hurried and swallowed, "Hello." He pulled the phone away from his ear and spied the number.

"Captain Fink here, you landed yet?"

"Yes, about ten minutes ago."

"Do you need to wait on a bag or two?"

"No, I only brought my shoulder bag for this trip."

"Well, I should be there shortly."

"That's great, I'm outside waiting. You can find me by the main entrance, oh, Captain Fink, I have on a white sweater and blue shorts. You can't miss me."

"See you in a few."

Ben finished his hotdog and drank the rest of the water. *Things are about to change.* He ran his hand across his sweater. Life as he knew it may never be the same. But his priority... family. *Help me Lord, to understand, and help me be willing to go the exact mile for Bradley and my mom. Please help us through this tragedy.*

A white Tahoe pulled up beside him and the passenger window rolled down. A dark-haired man asked, "Are you Ben Matney?"

Ben flung his hair and secured his shoulder strap. "Yes, Captain Fink?"

"Yes, it's nice to meet you, hop in."

"Thank you."

"No problem." The captain held out his hand and shook Ben's, "How was your flight?"

"Great, and before I forget, thank you picking me up." He opened the back door and put his bag on the seat, then got in the front.

"You bet. We're going to stop and pick up your brother before we go to the hospital," Captain Fink added.

"I was hoping you'd tell me that, thank you." Ben's insides were rioting on whether he should ask the captain about his mother. Surely the guy knows something, should he ask? *What the heck,* "Do you have any information on my mother's condition?"

"I'm glad you asked, I just got off the phone with the hospital, your mom is holding her own at the moment and I'm sure she will be better once you get there."

"Is she awake?" Ben gasped.

"She was an hour ago."

"That's wonderful news," he replied as he wrung his hands together as he tried to regain his wits, but tears wet his cheeks. He sighed, "Sorry for the tears," Ben wiped his fingers across his face.

"You need not apologize; I can imagine the worrisome emotions spinning inside your head right about now. I enjoyed meeting your brother earlier today. He seems to be a great young man. From the little time I spent with him, he had his head on straight."

Ben took a deep breath, "That's a relief, it's been so long since..." another tear welled in the corner of his eye, "Well... let me put it this way, I can't wait to be with him." *Get a grip. It was becoming harder by the second to hide his sentiments.*

"He will be eager to see you."

"I hate these circumstances, Captain Fink," Ben responded as his mouth thinned with displeasure.

"Your mother is progressing and doing better than expected."

"Oh?" Ben frowned not trusting the words out of Captain Fink's mouth as he wanted to see for himself before trusting a complete stranger's optimism. He stared and wanted nothing more than his mother to come through unscathed, "How long will it take us to get to where Bradley is staying?"

"I'd say 15 minutes. What do you do in Camden, Maine?"

"I'm a baker."

"That is an interesting career, how do you stay so thin?"

Ben laughed, "I don't have a clue."

Captain Fink slid his hand down his torso, "I love sweets as you can tell."

"Huh, you're not overweight."

"I could afford to lose a few pounds," Captain Fink announced as he continued along the road.

They approached a familiar sight when they drove across the 11th Street Bridge. It brought back fond memories from Ben's childhood. Time reversed to the moment he, his dad and Bradley in a stroller, were walking across that same bridge and Ben had their Basset Hound, Motley, in tow. He tried to keep up with their fast-paced father but failed. 'Hurry,' his dad yelled behind him, 'You are so slow.'

'It's not me, it's Motley,' he remembered. His brow wrinkled in an amused acknowledgment of just how slow Motley was. Without trying, his face lifted into a smile as he took in the view of Washington. *I loved that dog.*

"What's funny?" Captain Fink asked.

"I was just thinking back to when I was a kid and my dad fussed at me on this bridge."

"You want to share?" He tossed Ben an inquisitive shrug.

"My dad, Bradley and I crossed the 11th Street Bridge almost every day when we were little and, he fussed at me and our dog, Motley, to hurry us up. We lived near the bridge and went to school a few blocks away. My dad had us walking everywhere because he was a fanatic about us getting exercise." An uncontrollable laugh escaped, "That dog was so slow."

"What type of dog was he?"

"A Basset Hound."

"They can be slow," the captain replied. He slowed the vehicle to a crawl as the flow of traffic stalled.

"Yep, and Motley was the slowest. I know he hated me pulling him along," he grinned.

Captain Fink turned the large white SUV into a rounded driveway and stopped, "This is where Bradley is staying."

"Do you want me to stay in the Suburban?"

"No, come in with me."

They entered the building and the captain pointed towards a row of chairs.

"Have a seat, I'll be a minute," he touched Ben's shoulder.

Time went by as the second hand clicked around the huge clock on the wall in front of him and before long, an hour had passed. A frown creased his forehead as he paced the small room. Without warning, the swinging doors beside him opened and a lanky, sandy blond kid rushed to him. "Bradley!"

"Ben." The kid collapsed against his embrace and held on for dear life.

"Bradley." They sobbed as they held each other.

With gentleness, Ben pushed at Bradley. "Let me look at you." He couldn't believe how tall and handsome Bradley had become. "Wow, you've grown into a man since I've seen you."

Bradley tried to smile as tears rolled upon his face and he grabbed Ben to himself again. "Have you seen mom?"

"No, I just got here. We're going together. Are you okay?"

Bradley let go, lifted his shoulders and touched his arm, "I am, but sore in places. I got a huge cut on my shoulder, but they stitched it up at the hospital." He wiped the tears from his face.

"What happened?" Ben put his arm around him.

"Ouch."

Ben grimaced, "I'm sorry," and let his arm fall to his side.

"Mom and I had just gotten into bed when I heard something at the back of the house. I screamed her name, hopped up and ran into her room. Glass was breaking and things were falling. Mom told me to get on the floor when two guys rushed in and shot us. It scared me to death. I couldn't help Mom. They took the money that was lying on Mom's dresser and shot one more time."

"Did they say anything to you or Mom?" Ben gazed into his much younger brother's eyes.

"No, they were talking between themselves and yelling at each other to hurry and get out."

"How much money did they get?" He glanced at Bradley as a frown crinkled his brow.

"I think she had $50.00 on there, I'm not sure, we can ask her when we see her."

"No, that's okay, we won't worry her with that."

Captain Fink drew near to them. "I got everything completed and Bradley is free to go."

"You said completed?" Ben scrutinized the captain's words.

"Yes, I got Bradley released to your care. I need a few signatures on these documents." The Captain waved the papers in his hand.

"Uh..." what to say. *This is happening so fast.* Ben took the papers from the captain, turned them over, and scanned for signature lines. "Do you have a pen?"

"Here you go," The captain obliged.

"Ben, what does this mean?" Bradley pulled on Ben's forearm and stopped him.

"I'm not sure, but, I'm willing, whatever the papers say." Ben started to read the documents. "Awe, it doesn't matter what they say, I agree to take care of you."

"Thanks, bro."

"The documents give you power to take care of Bradley as long as needed," Captain Fink blurted.

"I will be his guardian or something to that effect?"

"Yes, that's correct."

Ben looked at Bradley, "Are you okay with me signing this?" He waited.

Bradley lifted his hands in the air, "I don't have a clue."

"If your brother takes care of you, you won't have to stay at the Juvenile Home."

"Okay, I agree, please sign the papers, Ben."

All eyes were on Ben signing the legal documents. "So now what?" Ben looked at the Captain.

"I will have this filed at the Family Clerk of Court's office today. You will have custody of your brother until further notice. Now, let's go visit your mom."

"Come on, Bradley." By tacit consent, they both turned and followed the captain from the building. "Did you get your stuff?"

"I had nothing with me."

The cool night air blew against Ben's face as they walked across the parking lot. He turned on his heel when they stopped outside the captain's SUV. "Bradley, you want to sit up front?"

"No, I'll sit in the back," and opened the door.

He watched his baby brother take an abrupt step toward him after the captain ducked into the vehicle, "Ben... I so glad you're here. What's about to happen?"

Ben clinched his jaw, "I'm not sure, little brother. Do you believe in prayer?"

"What?"

He managed a tremulous smile, "You heard right, Bradley. I still pray every night and, I remember when you used to kneel with me beside my bed and beg to finish the prayer each night."

Bradley ducked his head, "I remember." He stepped closer and their shoulders touched, then Bradley glanced upward, "Ben, I haven't prayed in a long time."

"Well, little brother, now is a good time to start. You know as well as I do, Mom needs every prayer she can get." Overwhelmed by the unknown, Ben stayed quiet during the drive to Mercy Hospital.

* * *

Bradley pressed the elevator button once. He'd followed Ben through every horrid corridor until they found Elevator B. The smell did not differ from any hospital he'd been in, no matter where, they reeked HOSPITAL.

"Press three," Captain Fink announced as the three of them stepped into the elegant elevator.

Bradley and Ben's eyes met but no words were spoken between them. When the doors slid opened, Captain Fink held his foot against the elevator door, "I hope it will work out for you. I've got to be going, good luck."

Both Ben and Bradley shook the captain's hand, "It was nice to meet you, thank you for your help."

"Sure thing, I hope your mother will recover."

Ben stepped away and approached the counter. "Hello, I'm Ben Matney and this is my brother, Bradley. Our mother, Emily Matney is one of your patients. They told us to ask for the doctor on call."

"Yes, sir, give me a moment." She smiled. "You may have a seat in our waiting area over there," she pointed them in the right direction.

"Thank you." With slow feet, the two rounded the corner where multiple chairs were waiting for occupants. *Empty.* He touched the soft blue fabric of the first chair and took a seat. "This is a nice hospital."

Bradley sat beside him and nodded.

Stone faced, Ben spilled it, "I'm here for you Bradley, no matter what happens. My prayer... that you and mom will carry on as normal. But if it doesn't..."

"That's my prayer too." Bradley breathed deep and rested his head against the wall. "I'd like to say a prayer for Mom now." Bradley bowed his head, "Lord, Jesus, help our mom. We're scared for what the doctor will tell us. Please let her be okay and help the outcome be a positive one. Thank you, Amen." He touched Ben's arm and noticed tears streaming from his eyes. "I haven't seen you cry since dad died."

"I'm so touched by your openness and willingness to pray."

"Mom taught us how to pray, remember?" Bradley picked up a magazine from the table.

"The family of Emily Matney," Ben heard a voice ring out.

Ben jumped up and ran to a man in white scrubs standing at the edge of the room and Bradley followed at his heels, "I'm Ben Matney."

"Hello, I'm Dr. Hudson." The doctor held out his hand.

Ben shook his hand, spun around and put his hand in the middle of his brother's back pushing him forward. "This is my brother Bradley."

"It's nice to meet you both. We have a private waiting room right around the corner. Why don't we go in there so we can talk?"

A few feet away, they entered a light blue room with a round table and six chairs around it. Ben, along with Bradley and the doctor sat at the dark mahogany table. Unable to withhold the question that killed him inside, it flew out of his mouth, "How is our mom?" His chest rose, and he held his breath until the doctor looked at him. He felt he would drown in a pool of fear that he was plummeting under. He grasped for air. *Help me, Lord.*

The doctor held his gazed with Ben, then turned towards Bradley, "Your mother will pull through this."

You think? "Are you certain?"

"Yes, I believe so, however, she will have a long recovery ahead of her."

"Can you explain and give us the details of her injuries?" Ben twisted his hands together.

The doctor opened his file and plundered through it. "Her stomach received a great deal of damage. We removed two bullets from her stomach, removed the damaged areas and repaired the puncture wounds she sustained." The doctor scanned his notes. "We also took out her spleen."

"Is she going to be okay without her spleen?" Bradley stared at the doctor.

"Yes, she will be fine." He smiled at Bradley. "A bullet severed her right femur, so we implanted a steel rod in her thigh."

"Will she be able to walk again?"

"I believe so, but how soon, it will be up to her."

"Good grief, Dr. Hudson, this sounds terrible."

"I am so sorry someone hurt her, but she has improved at an enormous rate over the last six hours."

Ben wiped his brow, "That's fantastic." He leaned forward, "Can she have visitors?"

"She can, I'll take you to her room. Your mom is a fighter."

"Thanks, Dr. Hudson." They followed the doctor through the corridor and down two hallways. "Here's her room," the doctor tapped on the door and pushed it open, "She'll be ecstatic you two are here."

"Thank you." The room was quiet when they entered. Multiple tubes and wires were hanging from her, making it appear that she was worse than he had imagined since speaking with the doctor. Dr. Hudson checked her vitals and pushed several buttons on a machine beside her bed and wrote something in his folder. "She is doing great," waved at them and exited.

Ben moved towards the bed and Bradley inched up beside him, "Mom?" He whispered, "Bradley and I are here."

Her eyes fluttered but didn't open.

"Mom," Ben repeated in a soft whisper.

"Let her sleep," Bradley interjected.

"Awe, lets wake her." As he leaned to get a closer view, her eyes opened.

"Ben?" She rolled to her left and blinked several times.

"Hey, Mom." He reached for her hand and squeezed it.

"What in the world? Why are you here?"

"I had to come, for you and Bradley."

She scanned the hospital room and locked eyes with Bradley, "Honey, are you okay? Come over here."

Bradley pushed past Ben and reached for her. "I'm fine, Mom, the question is, how are you doing?"

She squeezed her eyes shut, "I'm not so good at the moment, my head is hurting."

Bradley laughed, "What about your leg and your stomach?"

"I must have a lot of pain meds in me, because I have no pain except for my head, it's throbbing."

Ben eased to the other side of her and pulled a nearby chair close beside her, "Bradley and I will stay with you for a while. Close your eyes now and get some rest."

Emily tried to lean forward in the bed, "When is the doctor coming by to check on me?"

"He left a few minutes ago."

His mom scanned the room a second time.

"Do you need something?"

"I'm thirsty," She touched her throat.

Ben picked up her cup of water and held it to her mouth.

"Thank you." Emily sipped the liquid and took the cup from him and sipped more, then placed it on the roll around tray in front of her. With force, she finagled the bed covers from around her. "When can I leave here?" She stared at the two as tears flooded her eyes, "I don't want you and Bradley to worry over me."

"Mom, you can't help what happened. The doctor told us you will most likely have a lengthy recovery."

She pursed her lips, "I can't help but think of your job in Camden. How can you stay here and not lose your job?"

"It's all good, Mom, Chloe is an understanding person. You need not worry and agonize as my job will be there when I return. Let's get you better first, then we can talk of things we might worry about. Better yet, we shouldn't worry, right, Mom?"

"Worry is a sin," her lips showed a slight smile, "But it's hard not to."

Ben focused on Bradley's worrisome stare. "Little brother, you need not worry either, God's got this." He prayed under his breath and believed God would send the right answers.

9

As winter was at a standstill with constant snowstorms, a wishful thought of spring with budding branches from lilac trees entered her mind. Various shades of lavender and blue, brought a smile to her face. She counted four lilac trees across her back yard. Her eyes captured other hardwoods along the bay and as she took in the view, she hoped they would turn bright vivid colors, as well. A colorful spring may be coming by the end of April.

While unloading the dinner plates from the dishwasher, her brow squeezed, *did it snow overnight? I didn't notice that before.* She hurried to the door, pulling it open, realizing more than five inches had tumbled to the ground. "Wow!" Her driveway and sidewalks weren't even visible. *Scrapping walkways and the driveway?* Not a task she'd contemplated, but in the coming days, for certain, it would go on the list of weekly chores. *I've never done that before, and we need a shovel.* "Harry, Penny and I can make a game out of it," she laughed at herself.

She made herself a cup of hot cocoa, slipped on her warm cozy boots and with mug in hand, moseyed out the front door to enjoy the beautiful scenery. A thin layer of ice had settled on the steps, so she cleared a spot to sit.

The view of Penobscot Bay at daybreak was breathtaking. Gratification filled her heart as she sipped her java. As she breathed in the crisp air, Harry and Penny burst from the front door. "Hey, you two, what are you doing up so early?" Pit-a-pat on the stone floor, she heard their bare feet rushing to her.

"It snowed," Penny shouted and slipped down the steps and into the fluffy white slush.

"You don't have any shoes on, Penny, get back up here."

"My toes are freezing," Penny dashed and jumped onto Caroline's lap and knocked her cup out of her hand while Harry retreated just inside the door.

"Hold your horses, prissy." Caroline grabbed her into her arms and wiped at her wet feet, "C'mon, I'll get you a towel and dry you off. The snow is pretty, isn't it?"

Penny grabbed at her toes, "I love it," and jumped down.

Caroline collected her cup, held the door for Penny and hurried to the back of the house.

Standing in the middle of the bathroom, Harry brushed up against her legs, "We got an idea, Mommy."

"You do?" Her mouth edged into a smile. Penny pounced around after her feet were dried off and followed Harry and her to the kitchen. "Are you two hungry?"

Harry nudged himself close beside Caroline at the table.

"Yes, I'm starved. Mommy... you need a dog."

"A dog?" A chuckled rose within her. "I haven't had a dog in years, Harry, um... since I was seven?" Caroline pulled three bowls from the cabinet, filled them with cereal and milk and the three of them ate quietly for a few minutes.

"Please, Mommy, please," Harry blurted, "Can we get a puppy? We will help you give it a bath."

Penny got up from her chair, ran to her mother and began to roll her fingers through her mom's reddish locks. "Yes, don't you think we need a dog?"

"That's not a bad idea. What kind should we get?"

"A big dog to protect us," Harry proclaimed as he opened his arms wide then picked up his bowl and sipped the remaining milk inside.

"Let me get you some juice," Caroline poured each of them a cup of orange juice.

"Can I have a piece of toast?" Harry shifted in his chair.

"I want one, too," Penny remarked.

"I'll fix us all a piece." With quickness, Caroline popped three pieces of bread into the toaster and grabbed the butter and grape jam from the fridge and placed them on the table.

"I'll start a search for a puppy today. It's a great idea," she declared as she brushed her hair away from her face.

"We want to help you pick him out," Penny announced as she stood gazing through the back glassed door. "One like that dog... the one running through his yard."

"Let me see," Caroline hurried to the door and glanced across the way, "That's a Labrador. We met him when we first saw the house, remember?"

"Yes, I like him, can we get one like him?"

"I don't want us to get a dog that sheds, honey."

The three munched on their toast and sipped their juice while they discussed the different types of dogs they could get. Caroline gazed at her watch, "It's getting late, we need to start your bath water, c'mon."

Harry slid off a chair and ran down the hall and into the bathroom.

Caroline ran the water for their bath and into the tub Harry and Penny went. After a good scrubbing and their hair washed, she wrapped them both in a towel and each ran into their bedrooms. "Penny, pick out something to wear while I help Harry."

"Yes, Mommy."

Dressed and readied Caroline grinned when Penny appeared in the kitchen dressed exactly in the same outfit she'd chosen for Harry, a red school shirt and navy pants. "Good choice, Penny," she touched Harry's shirt, "You two match. We are out of time," she remarked when she spied the clock on the stove.

"Why are we in such a hurry?" Harry asked.

"It will take me a little longer to drive to your school since we moved." Penny picked her toast up and chewed a bite. "I'm glad you're finishing your breakfast." Caroline laughed at the way Penny continued to leave the bread in her mouth, nibbling it away until the last bite disappeared. "You are too funny, young lady."

"Did you think about what kind of dog we can get?" Penny asked after she took a big gulp of her juice.

"Run brush your teeth."

Penny and Harry took off and ran to the bathroom.

A dog... Could they really handle a big dog like the one across the road? Yes... the bigger the better. A huge grin surfaced. He or she would be perfect security for them, "And... I hope it barks really loud."

"What are you saying, Mommy?"

"Oh, I was thinking about our dog."

"I can't wait for us to get one," Harry patted his mom's arm.

The path to the car was a slushy mess and she was glad the kids had on their favorite boots. Again for the billionth time, as she scooted the car towards the elementary school, to own a dog crossed her mind. "We need an aggressive dog, one that loves children, but hates strangers."

"Yeah, what kind is that?" Penny asked.

Caroline's brow squeezed tight, "I don't know, but we'll find out." *Where to look?* She pulled into the school's driveway.

* * *

Ben had decided what would be best for his family, now to present it. He opened the cabinet beside the sink in his mom's dilapidated kitchen where an ancient refrigerator, stove, and dishwasher were on display. If any of his friends visited this place, it would embarrass him to no end. But... once a upon a time, it was a nice home, he remembered. *They need to move, plain and simple.* Was he trying to convince himself? "Bradley, where does mom keep the coffee filters? *No response...* Bradley?" He stepped to the edge of the den. "Did you hear me? Does Mom have any coffee filters?"

"She keeps the extra ones in the laundry room."

"Thanks." He slid his socked feet across the slick, worn floor and opened the rickety louvered doors. "What in the world?" His eyes doubled in size at all the stuff piled inside the tiny space.

Bradley poked his head in. "Yeah, I don't understand it myself."

Mounds and mounds of canned goods, cleaning supplies and paper products were from floor to ceiling. "When did she start stock piling?"

Thirty or more coffee filter packs were amongst hundreds of cans of food, laundry detergents, boxes of noodles, and bags of dog food. "Bradley, why is there dog food in here? You and mom don't have a dog."

"Yeah, I know. Do you remember mom's friend, Freda?"

"The lady who lives across the street?"

Memories forever embedded his mind from his childhood. Their neighbor, Freda, was their mom's best buddy and for as long as he could remember had them over for dinner every Tuesday night.

"Yeah, that's her. Anyway, they got all excited about some meeting to learn how to coupon, and that's when it all started. She cleaned out the laundry room one day and has been stuffing junk in there ever since."

"I wouldn't call it junk, but what's up with the dog food? I don't get it."

"Me either. She told me about a month ago that she had to buy a certain brand of dog food, so she could get six tubes of toothpaste free."

"Geez." His frown turned into a laugh, "I hope you have clean teeth, show them to me," he laughed.

Bradley squeezed his eyes closed and parted his lips. His straight teeth were white as puffy clouds in the sky, "Bro, I brush my teeth twice a day."

"You brush them twice a day because mom fusses until you do," he scowled.

"How'd you know that?"

"Because she yelled at me, too." Ben caught a glimpse, through the back-door glass, at his father's old truck in the garage. "Have you driven pop's truck?"

"Heck, no. That old heap of bolts needs to go to the dump."

Curiosity rose within him. "Where's the keys?"

"I guess there in the kitchen drawer, why?"

"Let's find out if it'll crank." Ben rushed and pulled open drawer after drawer and searched, but no keys were found. "Where else can they be?"

"In mom's room," Bradley announced. "Do you think it will crank?"

Bradley's eyebrows rose, "I have no clue."

"Why not try? C'mon, help me look for them."

They both raced to the back of the house and into their mom's room. "Bradley, this room is still messed up from the break in."

"Yeah, it is."

"Where did they break in?"

"I guess in the basement, I didn't check. Let's go look after we find the keys."

Ben pulled opened the top dresser drawer. A small bowl was on the left-hand side holding several sets of keys. He rummaged through each one and picked up a key with the emblem of Ford embedded on the top. "This is it." He handed the key to Bradley.

"I bet it won't start," Bradley blurted.

Ben's mouth opened, "What if we work on it until it does so you can have something to drive to school."

"That would be super cool." A gigantic smile etched Bradley's face. He led Ben to the basement. At once, they both saw shatter pieces of glass. They gasped at the same moment. Ben moved towards the broken pieces on the floor. "Look at the window," he pointed.

"Should we try and get that fixed?"

"Yeah, we'll fit it in our schedule."

"You sound like a businessman," Bradley punched his arm.

"Well, I kind of am one," he snickered. "Race you upstairs." They both ran and made their way up to the garage.

Bradley had grown into a handsome, muscular young man. That weightlifting class at his school he'd heard about was working. Bradley's hair was as blond as his own, he was a few inches taller and much better looking. Ben watched as Bradley jumped the three steps to the cemented garage floor. Shelves full of odds and ends lay against every wall. The dimly lit dungy space needed major repairs. The cobwebbed, dusty dark green long bed Ford pickup had sat in the identical spot for 12 years.

Their dad, Franklin Matney dropped dead from a heart attack when he was 15 and Bradley seven. So many times, before he'd left home for New York, he had wanted to back the old truck out of the driveway and take a long drive, but something deep inside would never allow him that pleasure. His dad was a gentle and loving man. Never raised his voice to him or Bradley and he had spent a many hour playing ball with them, or he'd teach them how to fix something around the house. Not a day went by that he didn't spend time with them both. *He will smile down from heaven when he sees Bradley driving his truck.* "Go ahead, start it."

Bradley stuck the key into the ignition and turned it. The ancient engine tried to start but failed. "I bet the battery is weak," Ben expressed.

"Yeah, you're right. After we go visit mom tomorrow morning, why don't we get one and get something to repair the window downstairs."

"Sounds like a plan." Bradley stretched his arms upward as they re-entered the house, "I'm getting sleepy."

No matter the cost, together they would get this truck running. *I hope the old thing will make it to Camden.* "Not you, you never get tired as I recall. Boy, how times have changed. I remember when we'd be up in our room for the night, you'd never go to sleep first and throw things at me when I was sound asleep."

Bradley laughed, "You remember that. Are you going to sleep in your old bed?"

"Sure, why not?" They went upstairs and into their old room. "It hasn't changed a bit." Ben approached his closet and pulled opened the door. Things he had left behind were still in the exact spot. "Wow, nothing's been moved since I left."

"Yeah, Mom wouldn't let me touch your things."

He picked up an old box of photos and sat on the edge of his bed. "This will keep me busy for a while." He plowed through the pictures of him and his friends, along with photographs of his father, him and Bradley. "Look at these pictures of us," Ben tossed a couple of them across the bed as a smile crossed his lips. Forgotten memories rushed back. "Here's a picture of you and me during that horrible snowstorm when we made ten snow men and dressed them all in different clothes."

Bradley grabbed it away, "We had so much fun, didn't we?"

Ben laughed. "You laid in the snow and about froze to death. I recall that, but did I threaten you to help me finish building those snowmen?"

"Yeah, you told me you'd break my arm if I didn't help." Bradley leaned across the bed and punched his brother.

"Did you ever tell mom?"

"Nope, never did."

"Thanks, Bro."

Laughter broke out as they continued to go through picture after picture until the pile was stacked back into the same box from which they came. He and Bradley had a great childhood together. Bradley got comfortable on his bed and looked at his phone while Ben found a washcloth from the linen closet. He marched into the old pink tiled bathroom, washed his face and neck, brushed his teeth, and laughed when he opened the drawer and saw 10 new toothbrushes inside. He made his way back into the bedroom where Bradley was fast asleep. He threw a small pillow and hit him in the stomach, "Night." He tossed a lazy-eyed glance at him, then rolled over.

"Night," Bradley whispered.

He prayed and thanked God for his baby brother. A smile gleamed into the dark room as he laid his head on the pillow. *Thank you, God, for Bradley.*

* * *

Showered and ready the next morning, the brothers drove the 20-minute ride to Mercy Hospital in their mother's new Dodge van. "When did mom get this nice vehicle?"

"Last fall." Bradley pushed the radio button and sought his favorite station for them to listen to.

Minutes later, Ben slowed the vehicle to a crawl, and turned into the parking lot of the hospital, stopped at a guard shack and rolled down the driver's side window.

A man stepped out and waved his arm. "Where you are going?"

Ben, with a low voice, "We are here to see our mother."

"What floor is she on?" The guard asked.

"The seventh."

"Have a nice day." The weird-looking man gestured them past. They parked and hurried inside. After a quick tap on the door of 712, with caution Ben pushed his way inside. They found their mother sitting in a recliner. "Mom, wow, you look so much better today."

Bradley leaned and kissed her forehead. "Hey, Mom."

"Are you okay, Bradley?"

"Yes, I'm fine." He felt his shoulder. "Right here, above my arm, is a little sore, but nothing major."

"I'm so glad," his mother declared as tears filled her eyes. Sadness was clear from the sudden changes of her facial expressions.

"What is it, Mom?" Ben slanted towards her and put his arm around her shoulder.

"The doctor told me a few minutes ago that I will need therapy for a year or more."

"Mom..." Ben released his firm grip and pulled a chair closer to her. "Bradley, sit down." He bit his bottom lip. *Here goes.* "You and Bradley are gonna have to move to Camden and stay with me. It's the best scenario for us."

A frown surfaced upon his mother's face. "We can't." Tears began to form at the corners of her eyes.

He grabbed her shaky hand, “I can get Bradley registered at Camden High School and I’m sure we can get a good physical therapist for you there.”

No words, just tears poured from his mother’s eyes.

Bradley stood and started to pace the pale blue room with a huge picture window, “I’m not moving.”

“Bradley, Mom... it will be okay.” He jumped up and stood by Bradley. “My house is small, but it will work.”

Bradley pounded his fist into the wall. “You’ve lost it, Ben. I can’t leave my friends, I won’t go.”

“You can make new friends. Mom...”

She shook her head as tears continued to wet her face. “I don’t want to go either.”

“Bradley and I will get dad’s truck running so Bradley can drive to school. I’ll get as many people from your church to help us pack up everything and close up the house.”

A bewildered stare grew on his mother’s face. “This is just too much for me to handle.”

“Your neighborhood is no longer safe.”

“It’s been getting worse for a few years now. It’s bad, just terrible.” She bent her head, “To be honest, I’ve wanted Bradley out of there for a long time but couldn’t afford to do it. What will we do with the house?”

“Close it up for now, then sale it when you’re better.”

“That’s the only house your father and I ever lived in.”

“Mom, because of our circumstances, we have no other options.” He turned and looked at Bradley. “You’ll love Camden.”

She glared at him, “This is our home, Ben.”

“I know and I’m sorry, Mom, but... Camden is a nice, peaceful place and you will grow to love it there, besides,” he reached for her, “I will be there.” He stepped backward after he hugged her and dusted at his shirt then, lifted his arms in the air. “I will take care of you and Bradley.” He sat on the soft cushioned chair beside her bed.

Bradley tipped his head towards the ceiling as a tear surfaced and fell against his cheek. "I've got to get out of here," he mumbled and ran from the room.

"Wait," Ben yelled. He leaped from the chair and took off after him and stopped him at the elevator. "Please try and understand this." He grabbed his brother's arm. "I've got to keep my job in Camden."

"I don't like your plans for me, let me go. I'll talk with you later." The elevator door opened, and Bradley stepped inside.

"Please don't be mad." Ben stared at his brother until the elevator door closed. A nurse was with his mother when he returned. "Mom, I'm leaving." He leaned over her and kissed her cheek. "I'll be back, I need to catch up with Bradley, and I'll talk with your doctor about you being transported to Camden." He looked at her from her door, waved, then hurried down the hall.

The elevator wouldn't open fast enough. He eyed the door to the stairs across the hall and took off and flew down seven flights. When he reached his mother's van, Bradley was leaning against the hood. "Hey, I'm so glad you're here," he smiled and tapped Bradley's shoulder. "Listen, there's no other way I can take care of you and mom; you both must live with me in Camden."

"At your house?" Bradley thrust his hands into his pockets, but no other words escaped him; just intent stares given as tears fell from the his eyes. He jumped behind the wheel of the van when Ben unlocked the doors. "I'll drive."

He tossed a stern glance at his brother, "Are we going to the car-parts store? And... the answer to your question is, yes, my house."

"I guess I won't have much of a choice about moving."

"No, I wish it were different."

Bradley drove approximately two miles and turned into Henry's Auto World. He parked the van and together they entered the store, got a cart, and hunted for the battery department.

Bradley touched battery after battery. "Which one should we get?"

Ben read the details on the one in front of him, "This one looks good." He lifted it off the shelf and put it in the cart.

It was their turn at the register. The clerk rang up their purchase. "Your total is $127.33." Ben's eyes met the clerk's.

Ben swiped his credit card in the machine and waited for the approval on the screen.

"Here you go," the clerk remarked as she handed Ben the sales receipt. "Come back soon, thank you."

"Thank you," he politely bent his head and headed to the door.

Bradley heaved the battery off the counter and rushed it to the van, "Thanks for holding the door."

"You're welcome," Ben ran past Bradley and opened the back of the van. "I know that's heavy."

Bradley blew out a deep breath once he heaved the battery into the rear. "How much do those things weigh, anyway?"

"At least 40 pounds," he lightly punched Bradley's shoulder, "I'm glad it's your back instead of mine," he laughed. "Did you hurt your stitches?"

"No, not at all."

The drive back to the house only took a few more minutes. They shared small talk of old memories of their childhood on the way and a giant smile etched Ben's face as he lifted the garage door and propped a broom handle against the edge to hold it open. "Dad never got that fixed, huh?"

"Nope. I'm glad you remembered to put the broom there or it could have hurt one of us."

Ben moved over to his father's toolbox and searched for a wrench to loosen the battery cables from the old battery. "Here we go. This is what I'm looking for." He pulled the tool from the bottom and rubbed at the soiled grease and grime.

"I'll do it." Bradley grabbed the wrench and went straight to work on it.

Ben observed Bradley's handy work. "You're a pro at this."

"I take auto shop at school. We've changed out a heap of batteries."

"I didn't know that. I was apprehensive about getting this old thing running. I can tell you've been in shop class..."

Bradley's eyes gleamed. "We can get this truck running."

They worked through the day and made four more trips to the same place for spark plugs, belts, and an alternator then stopped by a hardware shop and picked up a piece of plyboard. "You ready to try it again?" Ben asked.

Bradley crawled from under the truck and sat in the driver's seat. "Here we go."

Vroom. The truck started. "This is fantastic," Ben hit the side of the truck with his hand. "I know dad would want us to get it running again."

"Let's take it for a drive."

"Yeah, let's do, but before we do, let's cut this board and nail it in the window."

"... then go tell mom," Bradley grinned from ear to ear.

With a steady hand, Bradley cut the board after Ben supplied the measurements, The handy skill saw was found on a shelf near the back door. "I knew that ole thing would work," Bradley confirmed.

Upon finishing that task, they went back to the truck, "You ready to try it out?" Ben glanced at Bradley.

"Sure am." He turned the key and it started for the second time. Bradley put the truck in reverse and backed out of the driveway, then pulled at the gearshift and slid the old Ford into drive. With a slow go, he pushed the accelerator and the green, long bed truck, purred along the two-lane street. "It needs a new set of tires."

"Yeah, it's bumpy. When we get to mom's room, I'll price some on Google." He hoped the truck would help Bradley want to make the move. "The truck has got to make it to Camden."

"Oh, that's right." A weird frown surfaced on Bradley's face.

When they entered their mother's room, the doctor they'd seen earlier was with her. "Hey, Dr. Hudson," Bradley shook his hand.

"Can I talk with you about transporting my mother to Camden?" Ben stepped closer.

"Uh, sure." The doctor took his clipboard and opened it.

The three, Ben, Bradley and Dr. Hudson stepped into the hall. "Can our mother be discharged and travel to Camden, Maine?" Ben asked with a stern face.

"It will be all right to move her," the doctor replied as he rubbed his white stubby beard.

Something within him wanted to explain himself. "My job is there, and I need to get back as soon as possible." He pursed his lips, "The sooner the better, actually."

"Uh... I understand your situation." The doctor shifted his footing.

Ben folded his arms. "We will need your help to set up everything, also... and, we must find her a doctor. I hope you can help us find one."

"My staff will be more than willing to arrange everything."

Should he press the question? He had no choice but to ask. "Now for my next question, how soon can my mother leave the hospital?"

"I think she will be ready for discharge by the weekend, if her vitals are reading good and she's still progressing."

A sigh of relief escaped Ben. "That's great news. Thank you so much, Dr. Hudson."

Dr. Hudson held out his hand and shook Bradley's hand first and then grabbed his. "My office is down the street at 1303 Merlin Avenue. When you come in, ask for Pam Brighton, she's my office manager. She will handle everything for you. Our office opens at 8:30 a.m. and you can contact her then."

"All right. I'll be in first thing in the morning. Thank you again." The three of them went back inside their mother's room. "Mom, it looks like you'll be ready to check out this weekend if all goes well."

"That is wonderful news."

"The doctor is giving us permission to move you to Camden and he is helping us find you another doctor there."

Ben and Bradley drove back to the house. Packing, packing, and more packing had them exhausted by night fall.

* * *

Caroline's cell phone vibrated in her purse. Again, it vibrated. Not stopping, over and over someone called her number. *All right already!* Too busy to answer as she was trying to get the lunch regiment situated, she let the constant buzzing continue. She became infuriated with the buzz, dropped what she was doing, hurried across the room, reached inside her purse, and stared at the number. *It must be Eli.* After tossing the phone back inside her bag, she picked up a dry erase marker and wrote instructions on the board next to her office door.

"Ms. Caroline, I keep hearing your phone going off."

"Yeah, I just looked at it. I didn't recognize the number and they're not leaving me a message." She repeated every detail for the lunch crew in her head then read the board of instruction a second time. *It's good.*

"Someone must need you if they keep calling."

"I guess so." She raced to the opposite side of the restaurant and rummaged back through her purse. Her phone had 20 plus calls from an unknown number. *Why didn't they leave a message?*

"Hello, hello, anybody there?" She heard a low voice from across the way.

Caroline rushed to greet whomever it was. Two police officers were standing by the hostess stand, and she hurried over to them. "Good morning, sorry we aren't open yet, but I'd be more than happy to seat you. Can I get you both something to drink?" She leaned under the counter of the hostess stand and picked up two menus.

Navy blue uniforms were so impressive to her. Both men wore guns on their belts, along with handcuffs. The shorter of the two men came nearer. "Is Caroline Montgomery available?"

"I'm Caroline Montgomery." She backed away a few steps.

"We're here to inform you, Mrs. Montgomery, that someone killed your husband, Eli Montgomery this morning."

Stunned by the officer's words, her feet wobbled, and she felt lightheaded. "I need to sit down." The abruptness of the officer's words was harsh. Why didn't he ask her to sit or tell her they had bad news before blurting the dreadful words? Was that the way they dished out news to loved ones of dead people around Camden? Her brow creased as tension started to mount.

One officer hurried to her side and grabbed her arm. "I'm sorry, Mrs. Montgomery."

Her head filled with many questions. "How did it happen?"

One officer pulled a piece of paper from his folder, looked at it, then held it out for her, "Here's a copy of the police report."

She took it from him. "Thank you." She rubbed her temple and scanned the report. She stopped at the word 'shot.' As she lifted her head, she felt their eyes on her. "Officers, I'll be fine. Thank you for informing me of this horrible news."

The shorter officer sat across from her, "Mrs. Montgomery, your contact person is Officer Matthews. It's written at the bottom of the report." He reached across the table and pointed to the name. "He'll be able to give you further information if you have questions. Again, we're so sorry for your loss."

Her phone rang again. "Thank you. Will you please excuse me?" She stood with her phone in hand. As she continued to walk towards the rear of the eatery, she pushed the answer button. "Hello. Who is this?"

A slurred voice cried, "Eli's dead."

"You're the person who's been calling my phone repeatedly?" She held the phone a little tighter against her ear.

"Yes, Eli's dead."

"Who is this?"

"Margaret," she announced.

"How did you get my phone number?" Her free hand balled into a fist. A hot flush rose as sweat started to bead on her forehead.

"Eli gave it to me right before he died and told me to tell you he loved you."

A grimace crossed her brow and as the seconds passed, she softened. *He didn't love me.* He never knew how to love. Tears crept upon her face and in a subtle voice, she asked, "Can you tell me what happened to him?"

"Yes, we had just come out of the house when a car pulled into the driveway. Several men in the car asked Eli if he had their money."

Did she want or need this awful news? "What money?" She rolled her eyes and patted at the sweat on her forehead.

"He owed money to a man named Derrick. Anyway, Eli walked up to the car, dug into his pocket and handed a guy in the front seat a pile of cash. Without warning, the back window rolled down, someone pointed a gun out the window and shot Eli in the head. It was awful. He lived only five minutes afterwards."

A horrible pain inundated her stomach. She felt as if she would throw up at any second and gripped her mid-section. "Thanks for the information." With a shaky hand, she calmly laid her phone on the table beside her. When she glanced up, she noticed the officers were still standing by. With appealing eyes, she repeated the woman's exclamations, "That was a friend of Eli's. She told me what happened."

"Here's my card, Mrs. Montgomery." He placed it beside her phone. "If you need anything, please give us a call."

"Thank you." She waved goodbye, pulled her legs up onto the chair, wrapped her arms around them and cried.

10

Looking at the calendar on the dingy wall next to the rear door of his mother's home, brought fond memories of her checking what was in store for her family each day. She made sure he and Bradley, along with their dad, never forgot any of their events. He slipped over, flipped through its pages in search of the date, Saturday, January 16th, the day that drastic changes were indelible. No one had penned anything on the spot, so with a quick hand, he withdrew the marker from the holder and wrote 'moving day' in the space.

His reflection of the mirror on the opposite side of the kitchen drew him to it and he glared at the man that stared back at him. A little closer in, he rubbed at the creases between his eyes and peered at the wrinkles against his forehead. The squint lines that had formed made him appear so old, yet his smooth skin had a young appearance in places. He was a mess. Was it worry over the last few days that caused him to look worn out?

Blowing winds greeted him as he strode onto the stoop and he raked his fingers through his silky damp hair, then dropped his hand over his face. An ancient thermometer on a lamppost near the sidewalk read 23 degrees. It was so warm a few days ago. The sky above displayed brilliant blues, purples, whites and pinks. A sight he'd not seen before as the array of colors burst through the puffy clouds and it was as if he could reach up and touch them as they hung so low to the earth. As he took in the blessings of God, he then tried to block out the final look his mother had given him the night before.

Those painful stares would be glued to his mind forever and the deep hurts he'd caused continuously hounded him. He skipped the steps when he glimpsed a newspaper lying on the cold ground next to the garage. He moseyed over, picked it up and, as he flipped it around, his gaze landed on the front-page headline - Terrible Shootings Ravaged Timber Lake. "That's less than a mile from here." He shook his head, *that's a confirmation.* They'd be out of the neighborhood in fewer than two days. As he continued to read the article, he couldn't help but see his mom's face over and over in his mind's eye. When he reached the house, with a quick hand, he opened the glass-paned door with peeled blue paint and laid the newspaper on the kitchen peninsula and found the filter he'd left behind the previous morning, with three scoops of coffee poured in and started the final pot of java.

As he waited on his cup of brew, he grabbed his phone and dialed Chloe. Encouraging words from his friend, at this moment, was a must, "Hey."

"How's your mom?"

"She's going to be fine, thank God. We're headed that way on Saturday."

"I bet it's been tough with all the decisions you've had to make."

"Not too bad, I guess. Bradley and I closed the house and filled up a U-Haul. Yesterday afternoon, we stacked piles of stuff in the back yard that needs to go to the dump. I hope mom and Bradley's things will fit in my house when we get there. I'm telling you, that U-Haul is packed." He laughed. "Anyway, our plan is to be in Camden by Sunday night. Mom's neighbors are transporting her in her caravan. They're supposed to leave in a few hours."

"To think of you with your family living at your place is wonderful, yet you don't sound so happy."

"I cannot lie, I am a little nervous, but regardless of how I feel, the three of us are about to start a new adventure." *Change the subject.* "How are the babies?"

"They are wonderful. I can't wait for you to see how much they've changed already. Mitchell and I are so in love."

"That's fantastic." He fiddled with his cup, rubbing the rim. "I'll come and see you on Monday if I have a chance."

"Is your mother okay with the move?"

Could he utter the truth? A deep sigh escaped him, "I didn't give her much of a voice in the matter. She needs my help and Bradley can't take care of her by himself, plus, their neighborhood is a nightmare, so the answer to your question, she's not at all happy about it, but it is what it is." After a long pause, he snickered, "What we need now is a dog to complete our family," and let out an insignificant, but forceful laugh.

"You're too funny. I will pray."

"I'm glad, cause we're gonna need it."

"Have a good trip."

Whooshing out an exasperated breath, he uttered, "Okay, if everything goes as planned, I will be at the shop, start everything and open on time Monday morning, I promise."

"Gee, are you sure?"

"Yes." Was *he*? Could he drive ten hours and be at the bakery by 3:00 a.m. the following Monday? He prayed his dad's pickup would make the long drive. *Tires!* The truck needs tires. After hanging up with Chloe, he called the tire place they'd found on the internet the previous night. "Hello, I need new tires put on my truck." He rattled off the model number and gave the person on the other end his credit card number. "Yes, I'll be there soon." He checked on Bradley, who had fallen asleep in the truck, ran back inside, poured himself another cup of coffee, and turned off the coffeepot. Without a second thought, he dumped out the leftovers, unplugged it from the wall, nestled it under his arm, allowed the glass pot to dangle from his other hand, and headed out. He pulled a towel from a stack right inside the U-Haul entrance, folded it around the pot and slipped both inside the trailer, locked it up and hurried to the pickup.

With the house emptied and Ben satisfied everything had been done, he phoned his mother on his drive to Tire Mart. "Hey, you sound great." *To think... the excitement in her voice was a promise of her embrace of the move?* Spectacular!

"I am so much better today."

"Guess what?"

"I have no clue, tell me."

"We are stopping at Tire Mart to have tires put on dad's truck."

"I can imagine the old thing needs them, huh?"

"Yeah, that's right." He stared at his snoring brother as a huge grinned surface. *I wish I was fast asleep.*

"Oh, Ben, before I forget, the doctor left a few seconds ago and cleared me to leave today."

"That's great, Mom."

It was happening. Could he cope once he got back to his regular routine? "I'm about to pull off from the house. Bradley and I'll be there shortly to help you to your van and load up your things."

"All right. See you then. I was wondering... has Bradley ever threatened to leave home?" He whispered not to wake his brother.

"No, why?"

He gripped the steering wheel and covered his mouth to muffle his voice. "He just announced to me that he was leaving." The phone went silent. "Mom?"

"I'm here. Please try to talk him out of staying."

"To win him over is my goal. We'll talk when I get there, he's waking up." A struggle he'd face head on. He somehow, in some way, had to convince Bradley to leave, no matter what.

"Were you talking about me?" With a sudden pull on the passenger door handle, he yanked it open.

"Yeah, to mom." Ben's adrenaline pump through his veins, "Stop... will you talk with me?"

Bradley opened the passenger door, rambled to the porch and plopped down, "I'm listening, but, before you spill it, can I say something?"

"Shoot."

"Kayla, my girlfriend, said I should go with you."

Ben's head tilted slightly, "I wasn't expecting that."

"Me either and right before I took my nap in the truck, she told me I wasn't welcome to stay at her house, and then, you won't believe it... she hung up on me."

Ben touched his Bradley's shoulder. "Wow."

"I'll miss her and my friends."

Nothing more needed to be said. "Hey, I got us a hotel room for the night." He pulled on his shirt, "I'm hungry, do you want to get something to eat or wait a while?"

Bradley hurried inside the house as Ben followed. He opened a kitchen cabinet, "The place looks so much bigger empty." He moseyed into the living room. "I'm a little hungry, too, we can eat now if you want. What time will we leave in the morning?"

Ben followed his every step then peeked out the back window. "We've got to get all that junk in the backyard to the dump this afternoon." He turned and faced Bradley, "And... I want us on the road by 6:00 a.m., if that's all right by you?"

Bradley smiled as he lifted his brow, "I knew you would say that."

"Funny how people never change, huh?"

"You think dad's truck will make the trip?"

"Yeah, it's running great, like a purring kitty cat. My concern is going through the Taconic Mountains."

"Do you want to grab a pizza? How about that place?" He pointed to his left, twisted and watched Bradley steer their father's truck with ease. "Are they open this early?"

"Yeah, they don't ever close." Bradley turned into the eatery's parking lot.

"They have a drive-through?" Ben inquired.

"Yes. They sale pizza by the slice, combos, you name it." Bradley stopped the truck behind two cars in the line at the drive-through. "You want to eat inside or take it to go?"

Ben lifted his forehead, then combed his hair with his fingers. "Let's get it to go so we can spend more time with Mom."

They waited and inched forward in the drive-through line. Ten minutes passed. "Do you still love pepperoni on your pizza?" Ben questioned.

"Yeah, you've got a good memory."

Bradley slid his arm across the back of the seat. "That's what you like too, if I remember right."

"It's the only kind I eat."

A loud voice blurted from the huge menu sign, "May I take your order."

Bradley firmly spoke, "Yes… a large pepperoni and two cokes, please."

"Pull through for your total."

Ben reached for his wallet and pulled out a 20 and handed it to Bradley.

When the window opened, Bradley greeted the girl inside, "Hey, Trisha."

"Hello, Bradley, wow, I see that you got a new truck."

"Yeah," he glanced towards Ben. "This is my brother Ben."

Ben leaned over and waved, "Nice to meet you."

She waved, "You too. Let me make your drinks. It's $18.50."

Bradley handed over the $20 and smiled at the girl.

In less than two minutes the window opened a second time, the girl handed Bradley their change, cups full of coke, and boxed pizza. "Thanks, come again."

Bradley gazed at her and let his foot remain on the brake, "I'm moving."

"What?" She squeezed her brow, "You said you were moving?"

"Yeah, my mom and I are moving to Maine to live with my brother."

"Gosh, Bradley, have you told anyone?"

"A few people."

"Did you tell Kayla?" She pressed her hand against his arm.

"I told her and guess what? Her mom got mad or something and she hung up on me. I don't understand why she did that."

The car behind them blew their horn.

"I'd better go, I'll snapchat you later. Please tell Kayla I'm sorry." He pulled away.

* * *

The hospital room was bright, and their mother's bags were sitting in the corner when they entered. "Hey, Mom," Ben reached and kissed her forehead.

"Hey," she whispered. "Bradley!" A smile crossed her lips. "Thank God you're here."

"Hi, Mom." He drew close.

"I know what you're thinking, I'm not staying behind." He tapped her arm as he smiled. "You'd miss me too much if I did." Bradley leaned over Emily and brushed her cheek with his lips.

"That's so true, I'd miss you so much. You will make friends quick; you always have."

He stepped back, sat in one of the chairs and allowed Ben next to her. "We got a pizza. Do you want a piece?"

"No, that's okay, I had enough lunch."

The three chatted for a while, finished their pizza and 30 minutes later were interrupted when a nurse entered. "Hey, Mrs. Matney, I have your release papers for your checkout. We need you to fill out a few forms."

"Ben, will you help me with this paperwork?"

"Of course."

Bradley jumped and moved sideways and hugged his mother and blew her a kiss. "Love you, Mom."

Ben filled out the documentation.

"Thanks for that."

"You bet; you need to sign here." He smiled and stacked the papers after she put her signature on them and left them on the roll-around-cart.

Hugs, kisses and goodbyes were shared, then the nurse wheeled Emily to the elevator. They stayed and waited until she was loaded up in the van. "Thank you for taking our mom," Ben shook hands with the neighbor.

"We are looking forward to the trip," their neighbor replied. "We will miss having her as our neighbor."

Ben and Bradley waved to their mother and stayed on the walkway of the hospital a few minutes. They returned to the house and, together, hauled away 16 truck loads of junk to the city trash dump. Satisfied at what they'd accomplished, Ben stopped just shy of the front steps and took one last gander at his stomping grounds. He glanced at his father's old truck, Bradley's new ride pulling into the driveway for the umpteenth time that day. He ran to greet him. Was there any regret? He gazed at Bradley, "Are you good with the move, now?"

Even with freezing temperatures outside, Bradley brushed sweat from his brow, "Why do you keep asking me? I have no say in the matter, do I?"

"You're so mad." He glanced at him as he rolled his eyes. "Good grief, Bradley, can you muster a little compassion for our mom?"

Bradley followed him into the empty house. "Can I stay with my best friend, Gordon?"

"I cannot believe you'd ask that. You'd know Mom's answer is still no."

Bradley shoved his hands into his pockets and puffed out a vehement breath. "Mom never liked Gordon."

"Why doesn't she like him?" Ben's hands rested on his waist as his brother's statements overwhelmed him.

"She thinks he's a troublemaker and a bad influence."

"With the hard work we accomplished, I thought you were getting excited about the move tomorrow."

Bradley sucked in a deep breath, "You never asked me what I wanted."

"I'm sorry, but you don't have a choice. I have to look out for you and mom, now."

"I wish I'd hadn't brought it up, but it still doesn't change my mind."

Ben stared, "Wait a minute. You can't possibly want to stay here." He pulled his brother's arm.

"Thanks for helping me with Pop's truck, it means a great deal to me."

"Why'd you bring that up?"

"I was thinking I could drive away."

Deep sighs burst from him as he shook his head from side to side, "Don't be that way."

Bradley kicked at some dust on the floor, "One thing's for sure, I'm not at all happy. I do not want to move." His eyes softened, "Have you ever had a girlfriend?"

"A few, why?"

"Well, mine wants me to stay put."

"Oh, I get it." Ben stood and leaned against the peninsula. "Why, for God's sake, did you help me take all the stuff out of here, then?" He spun away, waving his arms. "You make me so mad."

Bradley shoved Ben backwards. "Kayla's begging me to stay."

"I thought she told you to go to Camden." Ben grabbed Bradley's arms. "Whoa... what am I gonna do with you?"

Bradley snapped Ben's hands away and sat on the step that led into the den. "Let me stay."

"Bradley, Bradley, Bradley."

"Can't you understand it from my point of view." He tucked his head to hide his grin.

"It's not that simple," Ben fought back as he inched closer.

"What if I disappeared?"

Ben moved in front of Bradley and pulled at his face, "That's selfish. Your move is not about you, it's for mom and don't forget it."

"I don't care," Bradley snorted.

* * *

Eli's dead. Mixed emotions tumbled through her.

"Excuse me, Miss Caroline, you're needed in the kitchen." Sharon, one of her chefs, poked her head into Caroline's private nook that overlooked the bay.

Caroline jumped. The place where her employees always came to find her, was her favorite spot. Only one small table could fit in the area and it was a retreat, or an adopted place where she allowed herself to be alone or rummage through paperwork.

"Something's wrong with the casseroles Mr. Z just pulled from the oven."

"Let's go see." Caroline made a b-line to scope out the trouble. A sour smell inched its way through her nostrils. "What is that ungodly odor?"

"It's the casseroles."

"Oh, no! We must throw them out."

Mr. Z surfaced from the pantry. "I'm sorry, Caroline, I guess the milk we used had soured."

"You guess?" She laughed, "The nasty scent is turning my stomach. What will we have for our special now?"

"Why don't we use one of our regular menu items, reduce the price and include a salad?"

"Mr. Z, it's been a while since we had the lasagna as a special. Wilbert, go change the chalkboard out front. Sharon, will you spray air freshener around the entire restaurant. That smell has got to go."

Wilbert, her number one cook, had the best handwriting in the bunch. With blue and green chalk pieces in hand, he hurried to the swinging doors that led to the dining rooms and stopped. "What price?"

"What do you think, Mr. Z?"

"Uh, how's seven dollars sound?"

"Great, that's reasonable."

A deep sign escaped her. What else could happen this day? Call and tell Dad and let him know what happened to Eli, but first things first, help Mr. Z make pans and pans of lasagna.

*   *   *

At 5:00 a.m., Ben tapped his watch to stop the alarm vibration. *Time to move.* He flung his feet to the side of the bed and found his jeans, flip-flops, and hat, and hastened to find a cup of caffeine *that he so badly needed*. He slipped the hotel key into his pocket and left. As quickly as the elevator opened on the main lobby, the aroma of java filled his nostrils. *It smells so good.* "Good morning," Ben greeted the person standing at the coffee bar.

"Morning, sir, hope your stay is enjoyable?"

"Yes, thank you." No cups for coffee were in sight.

"You need a cup?" The nice young woman asked.

"Yes. Two, please."

"I was just putting them on the counter, here you go." She handed him several cups.

"I appreciate it."

"Sure thing, anytime."

Upon filling the cups with the brew, with pondering steps, Ben rounded the corner to the elevators and pushed the up button. *11 hours...*

Ben zipped the keycard through the lock at room 314. When he entered, steam from the bathroom had seeped everywhere. Ben knocked on the door then stuck his head inside, "Bradley, I got you a cup of coffee."

"Thanks, I'll be out in a minute."

He sipped his coffee, grabbed the remote, and turned the noise box to the weather channel.

He couldn't wait to start the trip. "The weather looks good for our trip. Are you ready?"

"Let me brush my teeth."

"I'll wait for you in the lobby."

Ben collected his things and left the hotel suite. Downstairs, he moseyed to the coffee machine and filled two cups with coffee, then sat at an available table near the door. He waited and waited. Fifteen minutes passed. *Where is he?* He dialed his cell phone and let it ring until it finally went to Bradley's voice mail. He raced back upstairs to search. No Bradley. He'd skipped out. *What is that kid doing?* What was he supposed to do, leave without him? He grabbed his bag and scrambled to the truck. He drove as slowly as possible around the streets and looked at every person like Bradley's thin, tall shape. *This is crazy*. He called Bradley's cell a fourth time.

No answer. He ran his hand through his hair. Turning the pickup into the parking lot of a grocery store, he sat motionless. Heart pounding, he hit the old woodgrain stirring wheel. What to do? He didn't want to leave him. He dialed his number one more time. With fast finger movement, he typed and sent this text: *I hate what you're doing, call me ASAP. I can't leave you.*

Ben's phone came to life. "Where are you?"

"I won't go."

"Tell me where you're at."

"I'm across the street at Sweet Waffles."

"Stay put."

"I will not leave my friends."

"Do you have a place to stay?"

"I'll figure it out."

Ben spotted him sitting inside the small two-story brick restaurant. He slammed the brakes, shoved the gearshift into park, cut the engine and bolted to the door. Their eyes met as he slid into the booth. "Please don't do this. Come with me, not for me, but for Mom."

"There isn't anything there for me."

11

"Eli's dead." Her heart thrashed against her chest as her phone went silent. "Dad?"

"Yes, but... it's hard to comprehend what you said, honey, are you sure?"

"I'm certain, two police officers just left the restaurant that explained what happened."

A gasp, then a slight laugh escaped him, "I can't say I am sorry, gosh, that is the kind of news you want to hear, don't you think?"

"Dad!" She plummeted into the chair next to a bayside window, "I can't believe you."

"I speak the truth and from all that Eli did to you and the twins... it makes my stomach churn when I reflect on it."

Her lips pursed into a thin line. "We need to show compassion," she exclaimed and took a deep breath. "If you think about it, I'm glad I won't have to deal with him any longer, but I want us to be respectful and we need to pray for his mom."

"My sweet, Caroline, you always put yourself last."

Footsteps to her left halted. "Listen, Dad, I've got to go. Love you."

"Love you more," he replied.

Immediately after she hung up with her dad, her eyes trailed a man's feet all the way to his head and stopped when her gaze landed on his thick rimmed glasses. "Can I help you?"

"Hello. Are you the owner of this establishment?"

"Yes, I am, may I help you?" She stood and shook his hand, "I'm Caroline Montgomery."

He opened his thick folder and pulled out one single sheet. "Uh, I'm Danny Stanton, from Knox County Health Department to inspect your restaurant," he smiled a corky grin and allowed his yellowed teeth to glare at her.

Oh no, I don't need this today. "Where do you wish to start?"

"In the kitchen," he stated while making check marks on his form. "Looks great in here."

"I'm glad you approve." She led the fellow into the kitchen where her workers were busy preparing everything from salads, entrees, and appetizers for the dinner hour.

Thank God! Plastic gloves were on all her employee's hands. As the inspection continued, she pressed her shoulders against the cold and damp planked wall as her stomach did a flip-flop dance, all the while, scanned every move the man made. He opened freezers, refrigerators, and their main storage closet. He moved to each drawer, picked up silverware and cooking utensils.

He bent to the floor and rubbed his hand against it, "Hmm," he murmured.

Steady yourself, here he comes. "Everything good?" She smiled as he drew closer.

"For an unexpected visit, you keep a clean place, I must say." He continued checking boxes on his form, then grinned at her, "I'd eat here."

"I'd be happy to treat you sometime." She trailed the nice-looking gentleman as he meandered through the restaurant and made a few more stops until he reached the front. *Would you leave already.*

"I'd love to bring my wife back and take you up on that offer." He remarked as he continued towards the exit. "I'll write up my report and email it to you." He turned, "It was nice to meet you, Mrs. Montgomery."

Her curiosity was getting the best of her on how the restaurant scored. "Did we get 100?"

He glanced at his form, "No, a 99."

"What? Are you kidding me?" She moved toward him and leaned to get a better look at the form on his clipboard.

"I saw a small sticky glob of something in your closet."

"If I go clean it up, will you change my score?"

"Sure."

"Can I get you something to drink while you wait?"

"That won't be necessary. I'll take a seat over here and wait for you," he went a few steps and yanked out a chair.

With rushing feet, she found a bottle of spray cleaner and a rag, flung the closet door open and squatted on her hands and knees to inspect the floor. She couldn't find a thing to clean and to her naked eye, it was impossible to see anything. Back and forth she rubbed the floor with her hand and finally, at the back, her hand touched a sticky spot. Goodness, *it's the size of a pea.* In less than ten seconds the area was cleaned.

"I see you got it," the inspector announced, who stood over her.

Startled, she jumped to her feet. "I thought you would've waited by the tables."

"I forgot to make an inspection of your drink machine."

She watched him scratch out a mark on his form, cross out the 99 and write a 100 at the top.

"You've got one of the cleanest restaurants I've ever inspected." He showed his teeth as another smile appeared.

"Thank you." *Now will you please leave.*

"Have a great day, Mrs. Montgomery." He ripped the top sheet from his folder and handed it to her, "You deserved the 100."

"Thank you. Have a pleasant day," she replied and followed the guy to the exit as her mind tumbled to the shattered memories of her and Eli. The longer they were married the more horrible her days became. She went to her nook and allowed herself tears. Eli was dead and there wasn't a thing she could do to change it.

* * *

Ben's trip was long and exhausting but his old man's truck did great. The 11-hour trip lasted a little longer than expected since he had to stop for gas three times. He grabbed fast food at each stop and got to Camden upon the skies turning dark. He'd talked to Bradley on his cell twice. He tried to reason with Bradley about the move to Camden. "Bradley, please come. I need your help."

With a slow go, he creeped into the back yard with the truck, stopped, opened the back bed and unloaded what he could fit into his medium sized storage shed, locked it up and found his key to the back door. After a quick flipped of the light switch, he unloaded the rest of the stuff into the TV room, the laundry area, his brother's new room and his mom's new room. "I hope they like this place." He lifted his brow at what he'd accomplished and went to find himself a bottle of water.

Without hesitation, he mustered a bit more strength and hurried to the mailbox, collecting the week-old deliveries from inside. Hurrying, he dashed inside the house, sat at his kitchen table and rummaged through each piece of mail. Nothing out of the usual was among the stack, just advertisements and the like. He tossed the junk in the trash and put his power bill on top of the fridge with the rest of his monthly bills, then moseyed into the den to catch up on the news that had started five minutes before. As soon as he got comfortable, he heard someone pull into the driveway. *It must be mom.*

Hustling to the door, he pulled it open and saw his mom's van, driven by her neighbor, Mr. Moody, who'd volunteered to bring her to Camden, easing to a stop. With quick feet, he zoomed off the porch to greet them, waving. "Mom, how was your trip?" He greeted Tommy and Marsha Moody through the rolled down van window.

"Exhausting, but the Moody's were so helpful."

Ben shook Mr. Moody's hand, "I appreciate you bringing her."

"We drove a couple hundred miles each day and stayed in super nice hotels," Emily cheerfully announced. "Marsha helped me shower, get dressed. You name it, she helped me. I owe her big time."

"Emily, you'd do the same for me if needed," Marsha replied.

"Mr. Moody, I have a hotel room reserved for you and Mrs. Moody for the night. How much do I owe you for your hotel stays and your other expenses?"

Mr. Moody pulled him to the side, away from the women. "Not a thing, my friend. It's our ministry. We love your mother and wanted to help."

"Can I at least reimburse you for your airline tickets for your return trip, plus your expenses?"

"That won't be necessary." Mr. Moody put his hand on Ben's shoulder. "Like I said, this is a ministry for us. Our flight home is free because of my military status. But, Ben, we will have to leave your mother's van at the airport.

"Yes, sir, that will be fine. If you wouldn't mind, will you please call and let me know where you park the van, so I'll know where to pick it up?"

"You bet," Mr. Moody patted Ben's shoulder.

Ben gave them the address of the hotel and wished them on their way. "Have a safe trip home."

After Mr. and Mrs. Moody were gone, Ben turned towards his mother, "I'm gonna have to pick you up and carry you into the house."

Emily remained still as Ben struggled with her luggage, "Your place is adorable, I love it."

He reached for her and scooped her small frame into his arms. "You don't weigh a lot, do you?"

"A whopping 92 pounds, thank you," and grabbed his neck.

A little way up the path, Ben readjusted his arms, "I gotcha, Mom."

"Ooh, be careful, honey." Emily kissed his cheek. "I can never repay your generosity."

With gentle hands, he sat her in her wheelchair that awaited her on the porch. "Here you are."

"Where's Bradley?" She asked once she got shifted and comfortable in her chair.

He grimaced at the question. "He's not here, Mom."

A frown furrowed her face. "Is he out with new friends, already?"

Just tell her. "No, Bradley stayed in Washington with Gordon."

"Ben, no." She covered her face with her trembling hands.

He opened the door then wheeled her inside. "I'll show you your room once I get your luggage situated." After he settled her in her new room, Ben sat at the foot of her bed. "Mom, about Bradley, I left him, I'm sorry."

"You did what?"

"I did, Mom, I left him. I hope you understand," he replied as he sucked in a sharp breath.

"You should have called me and let me talk to him. Maybe I could've talked sense into him."

"I wish I would have now, but it's too late. I contacted Gordon's mother once Bradley finally gave me her number and informed her that school here starts next week. She was so understanding and said she'd try and have Bradley here by then. I'll get him registered this week. Did you ever meet Gordon's mother, Janice Gunter?"

"No, I never have."

"She seemed nice, Mom, and she told me she'd convince Bradley to move."

"Do you believe that woman?" She stared with protruding eyes.

"That's just it, I do. Why don't you?"

"I don't disapprove of her, it's her boy I dislike. He's wild and a bad influence on Bradley."

He could feel a scowl surfacing on his face. "Why aren't you fond of him?"

Emily huffed, "He got caught speeding on the school grounds, then was arrested for drinking at a school party after a football game." She lifted her arms into the air. "Your brother also told me he got two in-school-suspensions for being tardy. That sort of stuff happened with him all the time."

Ben blew out a pent-up breath. "Mom, the kid could have learned his lesson."

"I hope Gordon's mother can convince Bradley to come to Camden. This upsets me to no end, and another thing, Ben, why did she offer to bring him, anyway?"

How could he convince his mother that it would work out when he wasn't sure himself? "I'm not sure why she offered, but, Mom, my only choice is to trust her. She thought it would be fun to bring Bradley."

She peered at him with a puzzled look, "Are you serious about this?"

"I guess we will have to wait and see what happens after they get here. Janice, that's Gordon's mother's name, said she would keep me up-to-date."

"Bradley had mentioned her before."

After pouring a cup of coffee for each of them, Ben took their cups and put them on the table, then pushed her wheelchair into the living room.

"Do you need me to help you onto the couch?"

"Thanks, I'm a bit sore," she heaved.

Ben helped her onto the couch and sat close. "Oh, before I forget, I got you a new doctor here in Camden and your doctor's office helped me find a therapy place. You have a doctor's appointment at ten in the morning and a physical therapy appointment at noon. A lady from Camden Adult Home Services will be here at 8:00 a.m. to help you get ready."

"Is it expensive for them to come?"

"Not too bad, don't worry, Mom, we don't have a choice. I'll be at the bakery, so I hired this company to help you until you can dress yourself. They will drive you to your appointments and get your prescriptions, etc.... plus, take you to the grocery store, if need be."

"Gosh, Ben, I never thought of that." She pulled on her hair and put it behind her ear. "If Bradley were here, he could help me".

"It's okay, after he starts school next week, he should be able to take you places." He touched his mother's arm. "Let's keep our fingers crossed that Bradley will come." He didn't want to push the issue. "I'm getting tired. Are you going to catch the news?"

"Yes, I think I will," she laughed, "You remembered that I love to watch the news channel?"

"Yeah, that's all you liked to do when we were growing up." He reached for the handles on her wheelchair in front of him, "How well can you maneuver this thing?"

"I don't have any practice, so we'll have to see."

After a final sip of coffee, he pushed it to where she was sitting, "Mom, will you be able to get in it by yourself after I go to bed?"

"Let me try to see before you disappear."

"Ben stood by and gazed at her determination as she sat straight up.

"Here goes nothing."

With a firm grip on the chair he pushed it forward, "I'll help you," he remarked as he grabbed her arm.

"No, stand back," she announced with a firm voice.

He let go and grasped her chair and held it so it wouldn't roll backward.

"I told you to get away. What will I do when you're not here?" she replied as she locked the wheelchair's brakes and slid to the edge of the sofa. She forced herself up on her good leg, and with a quick hop into the chair she jumped. "That wasn't hard." A huge grin arched her lips.

Ben's cell phone rang. "It's Gordon's mom, I'll be right back... hello." He answered and hurried outside then stepped off the porch.

"Ben, first things first, how's your mother?" Janice asked.

"She's doing great. Much better than I could have imagined. What's up with Bradley?"

"He doesn't want to move there without Gordon."

That kid gives me a headache. "Gosh, I don't know what to say."

"Gordon needs a change and it would do them both good to move from here and heck, I may just move myself, then you wouldn't have to deal with Gordon staying with you."

Ben rubbed his neck, "You'd do that?"

"I need to conjure up a plan, find a job there and sell my house. Her words trailed off and nothing was said for a few seconds.

"Are you there?" Ben waited for a response.

"Yeah... to tell you the truth, I just remembered, my ex and I were warned about buying a house on this side of town when we moved to Berry Farm. I hope, if I decide to sell, it'll be quick."

"Well whatever you decide, I am willing to let Gordon stay with us."

"I thought through their first semester, if not longer."

"It would be easy for Gordon and me to move, we have no ties to the area. No family here, and as for my friends, well, I can keep in touch with them anywhere."

"It sure would make my life a lot easier."

Janice laughed. "I know it would."

"Where is your ex now?"

"He moved back to Arizona and another thing that would be positive if I moved, is... I'd be much closer to my parents who live in New Hampshire."

"Did you grow up in Washington?"

"No, my ex and I both attended George Washington University. We met our sophomore year, fell in love and got married, you know the story." After a quick breath, "I miss our early days. We were happy for the first three years, plus the two we dated."

Ben's brow squeezed together. "So, why did you get divorced, if you don't mind me asking?"

"I'm sorry, that's a story I don't care to share with anyone, ever again. Gordon is the best thing that came from my soured marriage." She took a deep breath, "Let's just say, you don't know someone until you live with them."

"Wow, I'm sorry."

"Don't apologize, I'm really glad it's over."

Ben swapped his cellphone to his other ear. "Can I ask when your divorce was finalized?"

"Seven months ago."

"It may be a good change for you to move here," Ben remarked.

"That's what we need, I think."

Ben started to shiver. "Stay in touch and keep me informed of your plans, okay?"

"I will. Thanks for calling."

After he ended the call with Janice, he ran back to the house and found his mother asleep in her chair and tapped her shoulder, "Mom, do you need some help to get into bed?"

"I think I can manage, but if I can't, I'll holler."

He stepped back to give her some space. "Mom, will you please try and keep an open mind about Gordon."

"I'll try," she responded as she readjusted herself and propped her leg on the coffee table. "Will you put a pillow under my leg?"

After a quick snatch of a pillow off the chair, he gently lifted her leg and put the soft cushion in the exact spot needed, then looked at her, "If Gordon is similar to his mother, he's got to be a super kid." He stepped behind her wheelchair. "I'll push you into your room when you are ready."

"Oh, stop babying me, that won't be necessary, I want to watch the news before I turn in," she reacted as she rubbed her leg.

He didn't understand why his mother hated Gordon, but he was sure she had her reasons. He was positive she'd feel different once she met Janice and got better acquainted with Gordon, he hoped. "Night, Ma." He leaned and gave her a kiss on the cheek. As soon as he stepped inside his room, he prayed under his breath, *Lord, help mom to heal quickly and help her to see a different side of Gordon, a likable one, Amen.* Jauntily, he cocked his blond head to one side then to the other in front of his bathroom mirror, *All I want for her, Lord, is healing and to find peace here in Camden. Help her get along well and meet new friends.*

After he finished in the bath, he dropped onto his bed and flipped on the TV. Identical to his mom, he turned on the news. Several minutes later he snatched the covers away from his body and headed to the kitchen. When his feet hit the den, he saw his mom steadily rubbing her leg, "Is your leg bothering you?"

"Yeah." She picked up the bottle of pills from the glass-topped table beside her. "I'll take one of these," she remarked as she shook the bottle, "It should help."

"I forgot something... I need to tell you what Gordon's mom shared with me."

"Is it bad?"

"No, not exactly," he abruptly turned. "Bradley doesn't want to move here without Gordon coming with him."

A frown grew across Emily's face. "What, are you joking?" She pulled herself up in her wheelchair and banged her hand against the armrest.

"I promise it will be okay. We don't have much of a choice if we want Bradley with us."

"I needed some water," She pushed on the wheels of her chair and eased to the other side of the room. "I did it. This crappy thing is already getting on my last nerve."

"If I know you like I know you, you'll be out of it in no time."

"I sure hope so."

After a deep, steady breath, Ben stepped towards her, "I can get you water."

"No, you go to bed, I cannot depend on you for every little thing, I'll get it."

"Okay, Miss I Can Do It All," he smirked.

She pushed herself further and with a final thrust of the wheel, stopped at the kitchen counter where paper cups sat beside the sink. With an awful bounce, she flipped on the waterspout, held herself against the counter, withdrew a cup from the stack and filled it up. "That wasn't so bad."

Ben held back and let her manage. *Here goes*, "Mom, Gordon is coming with Bradley to stay with us and I hope you're okay with that."

"What in the world?" She threw her free hand into the air.

"I understand that you despise Gordon, but that's all I could get worked out. He will go to school with Bradley and I will get them involved in the youth group at church, plus spend time with them every evening after work. The bakery closes at five and I don't work on the weekends." A frown creased her brow and a deep sigh resonated from her.

"What's wrong?"

"I don't like this, and I am afraid you're only asking for trouble, you wait and see. Gordon will continue to lead Bradley down the wrong path." She shook her head.

"Mom! That's why I will get involved."

"I hope you're right," she rolled her eyes.

"Let's drop it, please, I'm going to bed. I've got to be up at 2:30 a.m. Night."

"Good night." Emily eased in front of the television.

Cherished memories of his childhood flooded his mind as he retreated to his room. He'd grown up with the best mom. She'd always tucked him in and when he was panic-stricken, all he had to do was call her name. She came running to where he was, and he and his brother never went without, and, for the most part, got what they wanted when they asked. A chuckle escaped him as he recalled their list, and it was huge, he remembered. As he readied himself for bed, he prayed the Lord would continue to heal his sweet momma. *Thanks, Mom for all you gave us.*

* * *

Not one sound was made by his mother during the night and it was great to see the lights shining bright in the bake shop when he drove past on the way to the car park the next morning. With quick feet, Ben made a dash to the back door of the bakery, fit the key into the lock and opened it. Wonderful aromas filtered the air. *Kandice!* A smile spread across his lips that his load would be easier. *Happy to be back.*

"Kandice?" He called when he entered, not stopping until he reached his workstation. After tying an apron around himself, he hurried to the front of the bakery.

"Hey there, I wasn't expecting you to be here today."

"Chloe called me and asked if I'd help you this morning."

Ben slipped to the entrance, opened it and yanked the sign off the glass that Mitchell had put up while he was gone.

Kandice flew to him and threw her arms around him, "I'm so happy to see you, how are you?"

"I'm okay... I've lived one nightmare after another since I left a week ago." He looked towards heaven as if to say thanks for getting him through the mess.

"Well, how did it go with Tori?"

"It didn't." He ripped out the words, sped to his worktable and grabbed a bowl.

"Whoa, so you don't want to talk about it?" Kandice stepped back and moved to her workbench.

"Let me just say, it was awful. I may tell you about it later, but for now, I'll pass." He took an abrupt step, grabbed a bag of flour and decided bagels would be first on his list. "Did you make any bagels?"

"No, I started on our orders for pick up today and was going to get to the other things in a little while."

"Okay, I'll fry up the donuts after I get the bagels in the oven." With a quick wipe to clean any residue from the bowl, he scooped six cups of flour and poured them in, then added the remaining dry ingredients and sifted them together. Upon finishing the mixture, he added eggs and milk, then kneaded the dough and formed them into individual pastries. He plopped three trays into the oven and turned on the timer for 22 minutes. While he waited, he whipped the glaze for the donuts that made them irresistible. A smile crossed his lips at how great the pastries looked when he checked on them in the oven. Without a second thought, he whipped up the donuts and fried three batches, then onto the blueberry, cinnamon, and plain scones.

The desserts and pastries at Camden Bakery were first-rate, their menu featured every kind of pastry known to man, and heavenly scents greeted patrons upon their arrival. On Monday's and Thursday's free samples were offered to customers. The previous owner's cake, Groove's Famous Cake with his killer icing; they received ten or more orders for the special cake each week.

As Ben put out cake samples by the front door for patrons, he thought of Chloe, then Kandice. Chloe was the one who made the best frosting in the shop. *Wonder how she's doing?* He'd have to check on her and the babies this afternoon, as promised.

Even though Kandice was less than six feet away, he wanted to avoid any conversation. When his tasks were completed, he spun around, "I'll be up front if you need me."

"Okay," Kandice gestured with a hand toss.

Eight minutes before 7:00, a handful of patrons were standing at the door waiting to get inside. "Welcome to Camden Bakery," Ben greeted them as he held the door.

"I'm happy you opened, I'm in a hurry this morning," one customer remarked.

"Sure, come in." Ben picked up an order pad and pen, "What can we get you?"

"I'll take an espresso with chocolate sauce and three blueberry scones."

His lips parted in a knowing smile, "Let me check to see how much longer the scones will be in the oven." He sped to the back and checked the timer. *Three minutes.* He pursed his lips. "Shoot." He returned with a tray of cookies and a tin of warm bagels, "The scones have another minute or two."

The customer stepped closer. "That's fine, I don't mind the wait, I'll sip my drink till then." He meandered over to the tables and took a seat. "Tell me," the customer yelled his way, "why are you in this profession? I mean, I can't believe you'd get up so early day in and day out to work at a bakery? I'm curious."

Ben laughed. "I guess it's in my blood, I never really thought about it, but I love this kind of work." He went to the display counter, "May I help you?" He took the person's order and hurried to check on the scones. It was the most popular item this morning.

Nothing else was shared with each customer as Ben rotated the trays and put out more trays. He ran to the back when the buzzer went off then returned with the scones for the man and woman, waiting at the register. He applied two tablespoons of warm glaze to their orders, wrapped them in a small sea-foam box, tied ribbons around their boxes and took the orders to them, "Here you go, sir, and here you are, ma'am."

"Thank you, how'd you know I wanted it to go?" The man seemed amazed.

"I had a hunch."

"Thanks again," he remarked and walked out of the bakery.

"Thank you for stopping in."

By 7:15 a.m. the front was cleared of people and Ben and Kandice filled the shop with every kind of scone, bagel, muffin and donut the bakery offered, and the last batch of blond brownies were in the oven.

Kandice had been a wonderful help to him. "Thanks for helping me this morning. I'm sorry for the discreetness about Tori. As usual, Tori was up to her old tricks. She had another man, her fiancé, with her when I saw her."

"Her what? Fiancé? Oh, Ben, I'm so sorry."

The bakery's bell rang out. "It was awful, we'll talk in a few, got to wait on the customers," he gazed at her, then dashed to the front. There, standing at the counter, was none other than Caroline Montgomery. "Good morning."

"Hey… Ben."

He couldn't hide the increased grin that had inched up his face, "Hi, Caroline. It's good to see you. Thanks for coming in."

"I have a confession. I asked Mrs. Simpson about you." Her face lit up.

"You did? What did she tell you?" The red leather coat against her slim body made her look even more attractive than the last time he'd seen her, and he couldn't help but stare. "Lovely coat."

"Thanks for the compliment." She ran her hand down the face of the smooth leather. "Mrs. Simpson said you had been a perfect neighbor to her."

"That was nice of her." His eyes met hers. "May I get you a donut and a coffee?" He caught himself before he spilled, *you're gorgeous.*

"I'd like to order a dozen donuts and a large cup of coffee with cream, please."

"You prefer the donuts mixed up?"

"I'd like that, thanks." She was careful not to touch the display case with her fingers. "I'd also like to get a half dozen of your apple fritters."

He reached for his plastic gloves and grabbed a box. After putting two chocolate glazed, four glazed, one rainbow sprinkle, two cream-filled, and three plain cake donuts in the box, he closed it and tied a ribbon around it. "Did you want the apple fritters inside the same box?"

"No, can you wrap them separate, please, sir?"

Ben collected the remaining pastries from the shelf, nestled them against one another in a small box, closed it and tied a ribbon around that box. "Here you go." He placed the two boxes on the counter. "I'll get your coffee." He stopped, "You said you wanted cream?"

"Yes, please." She scrunched her hair then fiddled with the seafoam green bow on the large box. "I love how you add a ribbon to all your boxes. It's a nice touch."

"Thanks, but I can't take the credit for that, the shop owner came up with that idea, way before I ever came here."

"How long have you been here?"

He glanced at her while he stirred in her cream, "Almost five years."

"It's amazing we've never met. I come in quite frequently."

He spied her beautiful green eyes, "I eat at Olli's at least once a week, sometimes twice."

"Fate has brought us together now," she blushed.

"You're right." He drew near and put the hot cup in her hand.

Her expression was so cute. With a quick sip, Caroline looked at him. "Hmm... this is just right, thank you." She presented her visa card and laid it beside the cash register. "Here's my card, I had it ready this time."

Ben laughed, "I'll get you your receipt." He punched a few buttons on the register, "It's $18.58." Lifting his hand, he swiped her card and handed it back as his eyes locked with hers, "It was nice to see you again."

She stopped just shy of the door, "I'll wave if I see you across the street."

Should he ask her out on that date he'd mentioned earlier? He followed, "Hey, about that date I mentioned a week ago, would you like go to dinner?" To his astonishment, the words tumbled out and it was too late to take them back. He glanced to see her response. *Will it be rejection?*

She spun around. "I'd like that. Oh, did I tell you I own Olli's?"

He stood at attention with his arms by his side, "No, you didn't. That's amazing. I love to eat there."

"Can you come and have dinner with me tonight?"

"I'd like that." He tried to relax his tightening jaw to hide his sudden delight that began to mount within himself. *Elated.*

"Is 7 p.m. a good time for you?"

"That's perfect," He agreed and backed off from any more conversation as he knew, from experience, that too much chatter was a turn-off, and by no means, did he want to mess this up.

She placed her coat over her arm.

"Hey, Ben," Kandice called from the back of the bakery, "your mother is on the phone."

Ben spun around and gave his full attention to Caroline, "I need to take this call."

"I'll see you later," Caroline replied and scooted out the door.

His body swayed. *Calm down.* "Hello, Mom?"

"Ben, I hate to bother you at work, but can you give me the phone number to the people who are driving me to the doctor?"

"Sure, I'd be glad too. Why do you need to call them?" As he stood by the counter, he noticed a set of keys were sitting next to the register. *These must be Caroline's.*

"I want to check on the time they're supposed to be here, so I won't worry."

"Sure, let me get it for you, hold on." Ben ran to his workstation and retrieved the number. "Are you okay this morning?"

"I'm doing okay. Now hang up and get to work, I hate to bother you."

"Yes, Ma'am." Ben shook his head and rolled his eyes. *Always a child.*

Into the shop returned Caroline. "I think I forgot my keys."

Ben lifted them into the air. "Are these yours?"

"I'm embarrassed." She grabbed them and leaned against the counter, "I'd lose my head if it wasn't attached," she laughed. Afterward, she took the lid off her coffee, "Do you give refills?"

"For you, yes." He took her cup and replenished it.

Caroline squeezed her brow. "I've got a few minutes to spare, can you sit down and have a donut with me?"

Ben gazed around the room. "Sure, it's slow at the moment."

"Is everything okay with your mother?"

He gave her an odd glance. "Is my mother okay?"

"Yeah, silly, she called you."

"Oh, yeah, she needed a phone number."

"Tell me about her, does she live nearby?" Caroline moved towards the tables and pushed back a wayward strand of hair.

Ben pursed his lips, "As of last night she does."

"That's odd," she retorted as she gazed his way.

"I know, it's a long story." He withdrew a chair and sat beside her. "I'll start by telling you a week ago today, a robber shot my mom and brother."

"You're kidding?" She stared at him with a stunned face.

"I wish I were."

"It happened in their home?"

"Yes, that's why I moved my mother here from the Washington, DC area. My brother and his friend will be here on Sunday."

"What happened?"

He could see the shock of discovery hit her full force.

"Someone was rummaging through their house. My brother ran to my mom's room to make sure she was okay when intruders rushed in and started shooting. My brother, thank God, was only grazed by the bullets, but my mom... she was shot in the stomach and her right leg."

"I am so, so sorry."

"All is okay now," He uttered and clenched his hands together. "She has a long recovery ahead of her."

"Wow, did they catch the guy?"

"I don't know. The police haven't contacted us about it. My mom had surgery to repair the damage she sustained."

"Is she okay?"

"The doctor informed us that she is doing way better than expected." The tenderness of her expression amazed him.

"How old is your brother?"

"Seventeen."

Caroline peered with an intensive glare, "Is your house big enough for a teenage boy and your mother?"

"Not exactly, but..." He shrugged his shoulders, "it will have to work."

Several people walked inside the bakery. Kandice appeared and asked if she could help them. *Has she been listening to our conversation?* He bit at his lip and fisted a shaky hand. "I've never been in a situation like this before, I mean, to have my mother and brother come stay with me. It's not going to be easy. I'm going to have to be a parent, sort of." He gave her a sincere gesture, "Thanks for listening." At that instant, he imagined what her reply would be.

She put her coat on the chair in between them but no words were exchanged as her eyes met his.

Ben jumped up, "I'll be right back," and slipped behind the counter. He poured them another a cup of java and like glue, he peeped at her every move. The navy dress she wore complimented her perfect figure and lovely reddish blond hair; hair that shone against the light that filtered through the windows. He made a quirky grin when she looked his way. *I can't believe she'd be interested in me.* After the lids were put on the cups, he hurried over to the display case, he excused himself past Kandice and slid open the glassed display door. He withdrew two donuts, one for Caroline and one for himself and placed the moistened pastries on a plate. When he took one last glance, she was standing at the counter, "I thought you might like another donut and a refill on your coffee."

"I'd love one but..." she dipped her head.

The warmth from her smile memorized him, "yeah?"

"I'd better not, but I want to tell you what Mrs. Simpson informed me about you."

He was astounded by her words, "What did she say?" His smile widened in approval.

"I promise it's good. She told me that you would be a great catch and I'd better start fishing."

"Oh, wow, Caroline, I'm flattered."

"I'm telling you now, the woman thinks the world of you, and you should stay in touch with her."

"I will. Maybe we can go together and visit her." Ben's face turned hot and his palms started to sweat, "Mrs. Simpson is a sweet person. I've spent a gazillion hours at her place, helping her with so many things, from cutting her grass to changing light bulbs for her and I even helped her fix a pipe under her kitchen sink. You name it, I've done it." His lips parted into a smile as he laughed.

Caroline's mouth fell open, "Did you get wet? That's what she shared," and burst out laughing a second time.

"Gosh, I was trying to forget that." His facial expression changed, "I'm gonna miss her, actually... a lot. Many a night as soon as I'd get home from work, she'd wave me over to eat dinner with her."

"She didn't mention that?" Caroline gave him an inquisitive gaze. "And I bet you accepted."

A chuckle bolted from him. "Yeah, almost every time she asked. Sometimes," he snickered, "she'd place weird stuff on my plate."

"Did you ask her what she was serving?"

Her smile made his insides melt. "I never did." A loud cackle escaped him, "I only gagged once."

Laughter filled the bakery.

"Hey you two," Kandice yelled. "You're having way too much fun over there."

"Kandice, I was telling Caroline about Mrs. Simpson's dinners she fed me."

"I see." The awkward gazes that came his way from Kandice made his skin crawl. *Why is she staring?* He stood and gathered the plates from the table, hurried to the counter and eyeballed Kandice, "Why the looks?"

"I'm jealous of her," she whispered.

Ben, with a gentleness, pulled her by the hand through the door that led to the back, "You're what?"

"You heard me," she blurted as she shifted her shoulders.

"Kandice, you've never shown feelings for me."

"I know that, but... when I saw you with her, I realized I loved you."

"Whoa, whoa, whoa! Sit on this stool, please, I'll be back." He hustled to the front where Caroline was halfway out the door, "You're leaving?"

"I can't stay," she responded. "I didn't realize you had a girlfriend."

He caught his breath, "I don't."

"Oh? I thought she just told you that she loved you."

"She did, but..."

"Dinner is off. It was nice meeting you." Then she turned to leave.

"I was excited about us getting to know one another and spending some time with your kids."

"Why?" She scrutinized with a commanding gaze on her face.

With a faint tremor in his voice as though some emotion had touched him, "I love kids, especially red headed ones and I fell in love with Harry and Penny the first time we met." He lifted his brow and shrugged his shoulders.

"Well, since you put it that way, do you still want to have dinner?" She slid her hands to her waist.

"I do." Ben eased behind her to the exit.

"For our first date, we won't invite Harry and Penny. What time can I expect you?"

"Is 7 p.m. still a good time?"

"Perfect, I'll see you then." Caroline turned at the door, "See you later," and let the door close behind her.

12

With quick feet, Ben blazed to the rear of the shop as he pondered Kandice's words; *I love you*. Once upon a time, she possibly could have been his girl, although she didn't show it. Why, he may never know. Thinking back, she was the only person he'd cared about being a newbie in Camden. As his mind burned with the memory of the first day they met, a surge of happiness soared through him while he tidied the shop. She was so beautiful that day, and still was, whether she loved him or not, he now didn't feel the same way. Confusion mounted as he racked his brain to recall an inkling of affection on her part, which was none. She never accepted any of his date proposals and to his recollection, he'd asked her over a dozen times. Pushing the mop to and 'fro on the tiled floors, anger overcame him, *why now?* He pulled the mop one last time and heaved a labored breath to stifle his rage.

Her cute self, with her small frame pulled on the mop handle. "You want me to wipe the counters for you?"

"Sure, that would be great. I'll help after I finish this and empty the trash cans."

Ben inched closer to her, "May I have a word with you?" He propped the mop against his left hand and leaned his chin on it. "Why did you say you loved me when you know you don't?"

Kandice turned off the hot water, "Because I was jealous."

"Jealous of Caroline, someone I barely know?"

"Yes!" She flung a clump of soapy suds onto his arms and shirt.

"Love me? That makes no sense, Kandice." He wiped at the bubbles that lingered.

"I shouldn't have said it," she yelled and rolled her eyes. "Can we drop it?"

"Stop what you're doing and come sit beside me." Ben, as a rambunctious puppy, dashed and grabbed her stool then tugged her away from the sink.

"Let me get a cloth to dry my hands." She snatched a rag off the counter and sat on the edge of the stool, "What?" She asked as she lifted her arms in the air looking shocked.

He narrowed his eyes on her, "Tell me the truth."

"It just came out."

"That response doesn't tell me a thing. Okay... answer this, then." Turning around on his stool, he got within inches of her face. "Will you be mad if I go out with Caroline because..." *Can he say it?* "The last thing I want to do is hurt you."

Her bottom lip protruded as she released a pent-up breath, "I really don't care if you go out with her" she huffed and swung her head to divert further eye contact.

He lifted her face, "Kandice?"

Tears trickled down her face, "No, Ben, I won't be mad." She slowly turned, "Please let it go?"

Ben's shoulders slumped, "Why are you crying?" Her precious blue eyes deepened and her dark hair against her tanned skin looked gorgeous. He slid his fingers across her face. "You're so beautiful when you're mad."

"Stop it," as she pushed his hand away.

The bell above the bakery's front door rang out, "Someone's here," Kandice jumped from the stool and ran to the front.

He followed and several customers stood by the cash register when they appeared. Together, they pulled scones from the case, made latte's and flavored coffees, and boxed up over four dozen donuts. Ben observed how great he and Kandice worked together. As he passed to get some napkins, he gently pulled her shirttail when she stretched to get more cups from above the cooler, "Thanks for being you."

"You too," she remarked as she re-tucked her shirt into her pants.

After the patrons meandered from the bakery, the conversation between them diminished and they finished tidying up the back of the shop. Together, without saying a word, they gathered ingredients for two carrot cakes, three batches of chocolate chip cookies, six dozen blueberry scones, and four dozen salted pretzels still to be made for carry out orders.

Ben shook his head, blinked a few times and squinted to get a better view of the recipe in front of him, but all he could manage to do was remember the words spoken from her lips. He pressed on and measured out each ingredient for the two carrot cakes. Excitement lit his face 30 minutes later when he picked up the pen from his station and crossed off the last dessert to be made for the day. Breathing in the rich aromas of the baked goods gave him a pleasant gratification. He moseyed to find him something to drink from his small fridge that sat beside his workstation. He withdrew an orange soda, twisted off the cap and took a long gulp, emptying half the bottle, then nibbled on a few remnants of the blueberry scone from a baking tin nearby.

"Ben, can you come up front?" Kandice's voice echoed throughout the shop.

After another swig of pop, he rushed to see what was needed, and as he rounded the corner, there of all people, was his brother. "Bradley," he shouted and reached, snagging him into a hug. A young man and woman stood next to him, which had to have been, Gordon and his mother, Janice.

"Hey bro," Bradley released him, "Let me introduce you to Gordon and Miss Janice." He shuffled his feet and turned towards them, "Miss Janice, this my brother, Ben," then pointed towards the boy, "this is Gordon."

No sooner had he shook Gordon's hand, he lightly picked up Janice's and held it against his own. "It's a pleasure to meet you. This is such a nice surprise. I wasn't expecting you guys so soon."

Janice readjusted her purse strap on her shoulder, "With all of us in agreement, we decided to leave early this morning."

"What time did you take off?" He gazed with an inquisitive stare.

"Close to 3:00 a.m.," she tilted her head, "Do you have a restroom by chance?"

"Yes, come on, I'll show you. Oh... my bad, I should've asked you guys... can I get you a coffee or something to eat, anything?"

Bradley followed with Gordon and Janice close at his heels. "This is a great bakery," Bradley remarked as a wide grin affirmed his likings and danced around every which a way. "Yum..." his gaze landed on the muffins behind the counter and he touched the glassed panel, "Ooh, I'd go for a few of those blueberry muffins, right there, they look amazing, also, how about a soda?"

Thrilled to no end that Bradley was in Camden, Ben could now focus on the matter with Kandice. "I'm glad you're here," and hurried away to get them some refreshments and something to drink.

Ben selected an assortment of doughnuts and muffins for the threesome, then pulled several cups off the top of the drink machine, iced and filled them to the brim with different fountain drinks.

"Why are you in such deep thought?" Janice asked Ben when she approached the table where he'd placed the muffins.

"I have a bunch of things to sort out, thanks for asking." *Caroline, Kandice, his mother, brother, and now you. You are gorgeous.* He took a deep breath.

Janice picked up a cup and sipped, then drew a chair from the table and took a seat. "Guess what, Ben?"

With a surprised look on his face, he responded, "tell me."

"I've decided to sell my house in DC and move here." She put her hand to her head, "Well... let me rephrase that, if I can find a job, that is."

"It's easy to find work in Camden, I promise you," Ben interjected. What do you do?"

"I've always been an office manager for a doctor's office. I pray I can find something in that field. Oh, before I forget, my realtor called a while ago and shared that she showed my house today." She moved closer to Ben. "I am ecstatic. I will keep my fingers crossed that I get an offer soon," she lifted her hands in the air. "You are such a nice-looking man."

"Awe, thanks." *Where did that come from?* A hot flash shot from his forehead to his feet and his face turned blood red, "I'm embarrassed." He blinked several times to regain his composure and took his fingers and pushed his hair behind his ears.

Clearing his throat, he leaned against the ice machine and folded his arms, "What made you decide to sell your house and move here?" He stole a glance at her stunning face.

"Bradley and your mother aren't the only ones who needed to get out of Washington."

"I see. Do you have a place to stay?"

"I took the liberty and leased a cute house a couple of miles from here. It's not too expensive and once my place sales, Gordon and I will be able to purchase something in Camden."

"If you don't mind me asking, what is the address of the house you rented?" He dipped his head.

Janice reached inside her purse and pulled out a small piece of yellow paper, "36 Captain's Way. We're gonna drive over there in a few minutes." She moved towards the door.

"That is two streets from where I live."

"That will be great for Gordon and Bradley."

"Yeah, its within walking distance."

"That is fantastic," Janice replied. "I'm a little worried about the shape it will be in, I sure hope it's going to be okay, because that's where we are staying tonight."

Ben quickly locked his eyes with her deep blues. "If it turns out to be a bomb, you can stay on my couch," he replied as he shifted his shoulders.

"I appreciate your offer, but if it's awful, Gordon and I will stay in a hotel." She retrieved a photo from her purse. "From what I saw online, it looks super cute. Here's a picture." She handed it to him. "Gordon, you want to help Bradley get his stuff out of the car?"

Gordon and Bradley leaped from their chairs. "Sure." They gathered around Ben and Janice.

"Wait, can I make a suggestion?" Ben asked and followed them onto the street. Taken back, he scratched his neck, "Is there any way you could take Bradley and his stuff to my house instead of leaving him here. I'm sure he won't want to stay until I get off work at 5:00 p.m."

"I didn't think of that," Janice hollered as she pulled open her car door. "Of course, we'll take him, or he can go with us to the new house."

"I'll be right back." Ben ran back inside the shop and grabbed a scrap of paper, "Let me give you my address," just as he gazed at his brother, "Mom will be so happy to see you. She should be home from the doctors after 4 p.m."

"Who took her?" Bradley squeezed his brow tight as a weird gaze appeared on his face. He took the paper from Ben.

"I had to get a transport service," Ben replied.

"It's my fault you had to do that, I'm sorry," Bradley apologized and with a soft punch, smacked his brother's back. "I'll take her from now on."

A huge smile appeared on Ben's face, "I'm really glad you said that. It will save us a lot of money."

Bradley smiled in return. "I can't wait to see her, how's she doing?"

"She's adjusting well and hasn't complained once, even though I know her leg and stomach have bothered her."

"Knowing mom, I believe it."

Janice shut her car door and moved towards them, "I hate to interrupt you two, but we need to meet the lady at the house in a few minutes. Bradley, c'mon, we'll take you home afterwards."

"I can't thank you enough for bringing him." Ben gently gripped Janice's hand.

"You are most welcome, I love your town, it's so nice here. Now, I hope our little house will be just as good."

Ben stepped a bit closer to Janice's car and hung onto the opened passenger's door where Bradley was sitting, "Listen, I could stop by and get Bradley about ten after five to save you the effort of driving him."

"That would be great, that way I can get unpacked and Bradley can help us move things in." Janice dug through her purse and pulled out her car key.

"Is the house furnished?" Ben questioned.

"Yes, thank God. We'll catch up later. It's nice to meet you."

Yeah, same here, I'll see you guys in a little while," and ran back inside the shop.

That woman was such a beauty. Just as pretty as Caroline, maybe prettier. He found Kandice standing at the counter. Her demeanor stunned him, and she was gorgeous, too. Ben pressed his lips into a thin line. What should he do about these three women? The woman in front of him just explained that she loved him. His hands began to clam up as he smiled at her. "You're adorable, but you know that, don't you?"

"Thank you," her eyes sparkled as she gazed at him.

"What kind of inquisitive stare are you giving me?" He stepped within inches of her. "You smell as good as the baked apples you just made," he snickered.

"Shut your mouth, Mister. These pies are for Mr. Goodman and they turned out great, c'mon let me show you."

A kiss? It crossed his mind. He had to find out if Kandice truly had feelings for him and a kiss... *maybe he shouldn't.* He had to know and with quickness stepped up behind her. The wonderful aroma of the baked apple pies cooling made his stomach growl. "They look amazing."

"They do, don't they?" She stalled to take a second glance.

Ben turned her around and embraced her with his arms, "Kandice."

Her eyes doubled in size, "What are you doing?"

He leaned ever so slightly and gently touched his lips to hers.

Her hands gripped his back and pulled his shirt with force, "Stop," she blasted and started to tremble. As soon as she stopped him, her body relaxed, and she fell against his chest. A quick turn of his face with her hand, she pressed against him and kissed him back, lingering for several seconds. Afterward, their eyes met, and her mouth parted, "I've waited a long time to do that," she marveled.

"You have?"

With tenderness, she brushed his cheek with her finger. "I never wanted you to know."

"Why? We could've been a couple."

Not answering, she remained still for a moment, then retreated to her table. "Why did you kiss me?" Pure shock manifested as tears swelled in the corner of her eyes.

"It affirmed my suspicions."

"Ben, you're the most attractive man I've ever been around, and you are so passionate. I can't help but love you." She stumbled to her stool, "I've got to ask you, though, and please don't be on the defensive… are you afraid to date?"

"Did you and Chloe get together and discuss me not dating women? And… the answer to your question is a big fat no!" He fled and marched to the front, "I will forget what you just said." Two customers were at the display case and three more entered the bakery as he rounded the counter, "I'm sorry for your wait, may I help you?"

One after another placed their orders and Kandice came and filled the drink orders, a caramel latte, double chocolate mocha, two hot chocolates and a black coffee. She rushed back and forth as she prepared the steaming drinks.

With an abrupt halt, Ben paused at the edge of the counter and watched her. *She's amazing.* With a smile, she handed the customers their cups, took their money and thanked them for coming in. Ben slipped to the rear of the shop and boxed up four dozen cookies, and another six dozen assorted cookies – nicely wrapped, three dozen donuts, eight blueberry scones, and he was done. "Please come again," Ben showed his gratitude as he placed the ribbon-tied boxes on the counter for the waiting patrons, "we appreciate your business."

Kandice approached his worktable, "We need to finish our discussion, I've thought about it and I can't help the way I feel about you. I've loved you from the first day we met."

"It's hard to accept what you're saying, because you've never hinted at that. Never shown one emotion for me." With a quickness he returned to his table.

She followed, "Now that it is in the open, we need to figure out what to do about it." She ran her hand along his arm.

Ben stiffened. *Tell her.* He focused on her petite stature. "I'm sorry Kandice, I used to feel the way you do now, but it's not the same, I'm sorry, I truly am."

"But you kissed me."

"The kiss got you to confess the way you feel, am I right?"

"Well... yes, but that's not a way to find out, Mr. Matney." She stepped up to him and hit his arm, "You shouldn't have done that," she smirked.

"I apologize. Do you recall when I asked you out over and over when I first started working here?"

"Yes, I remember. Those were the days that I could have said I loved you."

He turned to make sure she was in front of him, "But we didn't go out, and you refused my requests. Can you tell me why?"

"I made a huge mistake, but we did go to lunch a bunch of times."

"Yeah, as friends... you are my best friend and our friendship is something I've cherished. The longer we worked together, the more I realized we didn't stand a chance at dating, but my gosh, I couldn't have found a better friend than you. I love your personality, your contagious smile and the way you make me laugh."

Kandice grabbed his arms and held them firm, "I'm sorry I made the mistake of telling you I loved you, and I will not, repeat, will not mention it again." She turned away and grabbed her purse, "I've got to go."

"I hope this won't affect our friendship." Ben watched her leave and ran after her to the front entrance.

Kandice turned and they grabbed each other. "You are my best friend and I know we could never be a couple. I just realized that."

"I feel the same way."

As they held each other, they burst out laughing, "I pray we find our true love," Kandice popped the back of his head.

"I know we will. Go, get out of here."

He locked the door at 5:00 p.m., grabbed the array of leftovers and packaged them up for the children's home, as he did every day. He could drop them off on his way to Janice's to pick up Bradley.

As he was leaving, Kandice reappeared at the door, "Can we talk?"

"I thought we had it all settled."

13

Caroline had been on the run since early morning, she took her kids to school, picked up supplies for the restaurant, then drove home, cleaned the bathrooms, vacuumed the floors, and emptied the dishwasher. She checked off the last item on her list and headed out to meet five of her employees for their weekly deep clean of the kitchen.

As 7:00 p.m. that evening rolled around, her feet throbbed with pain from the horrible shoes she'd worn. Cute, but wrong for comfort and support. After a quick sit down on a stool beside the sink along the back wall, she wiggled her toes to relieve her agony and thought of Harry and Penny. With a quick dial of her father's cell, she rubbed at the sore spots and waited for him to answer, "Hey, Dad, how are the kiddos?"

"All is great over here and they're in the den with your mom watching a movie."

"I really appreciate you for picking them up from school today."

"After supper, I'll drive them home, get them ready for bed, and stay with them until you get here instead of you calling your babysitter."

"That is so kind of you, but it's not necessary."

"Uh, what's a dad for?"

"I love you."

"The same right back at 'cha."

Darkness settled upon the streets in Camden as the stars twinkled above and Caroline, along with the rest of her staff, worked steadily to ready orders that had been put on their, what she called, 'the rack.' With only a second to spare, she dashed to the front and spied all the patrons sitting at nearly every spot in the restaurant and scanned for her dinner date. On her return to the kitchen, she breathed in a deep breath of relief, glad she'd taken the suggestion of Mack, her favorite chef, to start the entrees early since they were already there to clean. With everyone's help, the evening selections were ready for the ovens by 5:00 p.m. and the dinner salads were waiting in the coolers with every kind of dressing poured into four-ounce cups and stacked inside the fridge.

Grace Haskins, the restaurant's main hostess tapped her shoulder while she was sorting through the desserts to put on display, "Miss Caroline, would you care if I ran across the street to pick up a prescription from Appleton Drugs? It shouldn't take too long."

One of those small pleasures she held in stride was to help wherever needed. Without any hesitation, she wrapped her arm around Grace, "Go ahead." Not a second went by and out to the hostess stand she went. A moment later she glanced at her watch, *Geez, it's after seven.* The realization that Ben was a no show messed with the good mood she'd been in the entire day. *To think he was coming* was a mistake and a disappointing notion flushed over her. *Man!* She held her chest to stifle her heavy breathing as she silently voiced understandable excuses of reasons he wasn't there. After seating more patrons that entered, she noticed the basket of silverware was almost empty. With agility, she hastened to the kitchen with the container, drew out the six that remained, set them on top of a new basket and noticed more people had arrived.

Upon taking three separate families to tables, an elderly couple approached the stand, "Two, please?" The gentleman requested as he stepped sideways to allow his companion to stand before him.

Caroline glanced at the transparent seating chart and with a marker, X'd out table number seven on the diagram and grabbed several menus, "I can seat you now," and turned with a sudden twist as she had forgotten their napkin wrapped utensils. She prompted them to follow her, "Have a terrific dinner," she stated after she sat them at their table.

Out of the corner of her eye, she spotted Ben Matney. *He came.* A spark of energy rushed through her bones and a chill spiked her spine. She bit at her bottom lip not to allow her eagerness to show and stood perfectly still as he approached. "Well hello, Mr. Matney, what a nice surprise."

Ben reached, offering her a hug. "My apologies for being late," he shrugged.

She leaned in as his arms embraced her, "It's okay, follow me, there's a special place for us," and led him to her little nook at the rear of the eatery. Most days she sat there with paperwork up to her eyeballs, but tonight they garnished the table with candles, nice wine glasses and exquisite dinnerware, "Here we are," she lingered for a reaction.

"Gosh, this is super."

She waited until he got comfortable, then looked him in the eye, "If you wouldn't mind, I need to step into the kitchen for a moment to see if things are running smoothly."

"Sure, go ahead," and waved her on.

With quick feet, she rushed to find her best employee and buddy, Tarsha. "Remember the guy, Ben, I was telling you about? He's here." A huge smile beamed and lit up her face. "There's no way I can hide my excitement." Her fingers covered her mouth, "He's so handsome, Tarsha."

"You are all bubbly inside, aren't you?"

"I want you to meet him." Caroline crossed the kitchen and followed as she put fruit cups in the cooler. "I adore his blond hair against his olive complexion. Ooh la la!" She shivered, "His eyes, oh, my, my...," and twirled on her feet, then released a shaky sigh, "are so deep blue. Good gracious, downright gorgeous is what he is."

Her friend grinned and a slight snicker escaped her, "That's wonderful, but you're making me sick," as she leaned over and hugged her. "I think you cherish him already, huh?"

"It's crazy, isn't it?" She forced herself to settle. "Will you work the front until Grace gets back?"

"Sure, I'll also bring out menus and be your server, how's that sound?" Tarsha nudged her, "Hurry and go out there."

"Thank you," she uttered. Thoughts of her and Tarsha sharing their personal, most inward feelings about every topic imaginable saturated her face with a smile and a burst of laughter escaped her. *She such a great friend.* Her skin tightened as her lips broadened. From the start of her taking over the management of Olli's, Tarsha had been her main sidekick. They slaved together in the kitchen for hours at a time, had become best friends and on top of that, she was the most excellent employee in the bunch.

Caroline stepped within inches of her, "I hope you adore Ben as much as I do. Even though I barely know him, he is so... um... gee, I can't put my feelings into words. Anyhow... I pray he's not like Eli." Her legs wobbled, "This makes me so nervous," She jutted her feet, slicked her hair into place and touched Tarsha's hand, "Wish me luck."

"I'll be out with those menus and..." with a smile, "I wish you luck," Tarsha reassured her.

As Caroline rounded the corner, she saw Ben standing near the picture window gazing out at the lights along the dock, "The view is lovely from here."

She drew near and paused by him allowing herself to gander from his oxfords, to his cream shirt and stopped when her eyes met his deep blue's. As she took in the gorgeous features of his face, she prayed under her breath that one day they could be a close-knit couple.

"I agree," he stated as he took in the lights along the dock. "The reflection against the water and boats is super nice," he sighed.

He smells heavenly. "Let's have a seat."

"I appreciate this," he conveyed as he moseyed over to the small space.

Caroline swung around and just before she withdrew a chair, Ben slipped by her.

"Ladies first," and took the armchair and pulled it away from the table, "I insist."

"Thank you," she gestured.

Ben brushed his hand across his forehead and moved his hair into place, "I love being here with you."

A blush reddened her face, "You've eaten here a lot, haven't you?" She asked and diverted her view and scanned the bay as a passerby went by.

"A million times or more," he stated. "This is my favorite place to have dinner, even when I have to get it to-go."

Tarsha appeared with menus and filled their glasses with water. "Greetings folks, what would you like to drink, a glass of wine or a beverage from the bar?"

"No," Caroline spoke first, "May I have a Coke?"

"I'll have the same," Ben glanced upward and smiled.

Tarsha laid menus down and exited.

"How do you have time to spare to eat dinner with me?" Ben questioned.

"Sometimes it's impossible, but today... my kitchen crew worked hard, and we prepared our entrees early." Her finger crisscrossed the menu. "Why am I looking at this?" She chuckled, "Our menu hasn't changed."

* * *

Lightning exploded through him when their fingers accidently touched as they reached for their glass. Their eyes met for a brief second and they stared at each other. *What is she thinking? Say something.* "What's your favorite dish?" He inquired as he picked up the menu.

"Without a doubt, the lasagna with mushrooms." She raised her brow.

"Mine, too," Ben studied the menu, "With mushrooms?"

"Yes, I love them."

Tarsha returned with glasses of Coke.

"Thanks, Tarsha."

He peeked at Tarsha standing at the table.

"Are you ready to place your order?"

Caroline spoke for them both, "We'll have the lasagna and add mushrooms. Also, may we have an order of cheese bread with our salads." She glanced his way, "Is the house dressing okay with you?"

"That will be fine," he replied.

Tarsha jotted down their order on her pad. "I'll check on you in a bit and bring you a refill."

In less than five minutes, Tarsha returned with cheese bread and a carafe of Coke.

"That was fast, thank you," Ben complimented.

"You're most welcome," and excused herself.

"Tarsha is a great friend of my family. I've known her my entire life."

"She seems really sweet."

"Yes, she is. I think she was 15 when she started working for my dad and agreed to stay on when I took over. She's so helpful to me and never says no." Caroline became quiet for a moment.

"You got quiet."

"I was trying to think of the exact word for Tarsha." She sat dumbfounded.

A frown surfaced, "Did you come up with one?"

"Dependable," she blurted, "Is the exact word for her and listen to this, she's never missed a day of work. My dad would come home and brag about how loyal she was."

Caroline leaned forward, "This is none of my business but, did you and Kandice get matters straightened out?"

"Not hardly, I cannot lie. I was shocked when she told me she loved me. It's still unbelievable, and I assure you, I had no clue she had that kind of feelings for me."

Her brow puckered, "Actions speak louder than words."

He licked his lips, "That's just it, she never said a word until you heard her tell me that."

"Well, I have another question."

"Are you a churchgoer? I mean, are you a Christian?" She fingered a loose tendril of hair on her cheek as his gaze intensified. "Maybe I shouldn't have been so nosy?"

"It's okay." He clasped his hands together, "Those kinds of questions are rare, and the answer to both is yes, Bayside Baptist Church is where I attend, and I love Jesus with my whole heart." He cradled his head against his palms, "I'd love to hear your story."

Caroline smiled, "I received Jesus as my personal savior when I was seven, and I rededicated my heart last year when I started attending St. Luke's."

It overjoyed him to learn of her Christianity, yet, he repressed a grin. "I visited St. Luke's when I first moved to Camden."

Caroline twisted in her seat, "Why didn't you stay?"

"I didn't know anybody that went there, so when my boss lady, Chloe Terrison, invited me to go to her church, I decided to switch, and I liked it."

"My pastor invited me to his church when he was in Olli's last Christmas and from all the horrible situations that had gone on in my life," she stopped mid-stream, rubbed her hand against her neck, then held her palms upward, "I loathe to admit this, but I backslid from God and left the church." She opened her napkin, "I'm so glad I went, and Penny and Harry love the children's program every week." Her fingers trailed her temple, "The people are so nice, and I've received an abundance of support from Pastor Luke, plus, he's a fantastic speaker. Visit with me sometime?"

Ben nudged forward, "I'd love that." He paused for a second. "Okay, since we are being personal with our questions, are you separated or divorced?"

"I hate to talk or even think of my terrible marriage." She glanced at him, "I'm divorced," she replied with a nod, then at once glanced at the floor to avoid making further eye contact.

"I apologize for bringing it up."

"Oh, it's okay. I thought I picked the greatest guy and was mistaken to think that our love would have lasted forever. The longer we stayed married, the more I grew to despise him." Her lips puckered with annoyance.

Maybe she would tell him how she felt as her expression changed. "You want to explain," Ben touched the sleeve of her blouse.

"What I experienced with my husband, Eli, was awful." Her response exploded from her as she folded her hands in her lap. "Are you sure you want to hear my horrible story?" She squinted, "It's not a pretty picture."

"Yeah," he retorted as he leaned forward. "If it's too painful, I understand, but a good rule my mom taught me," he tried to maintain his curtness, "is to always talk through your hurts and sorrows."

She sucked in a deep breath, "Sometimes it's hard for me to talk about those sorts of things."

"I totally agree."

"Eli and I argued over any little thing, even before we got married." Her mouth dropped, "He hit me... on our honeymoon. I didn't have a clue what to do, because, we were a million miles away from home, and, well," her hand flew up, "it felt that way. It was horrible. I ran and locked myself in the bathroom and stayed there until the room was quiet." She flipped her hair onto her back, "He was passed out and lying by the window when I found him."

"Oh, my."

He noticed her features shifting as a sadness entered her eyes, "I sat on the bed and watched TV forever and when he finally woke up, he repeatedly said he was sorry and my stupid self, accepted his apology. That day, I started praying he would never hit me again."

Ben listened as she fought through the cobwebs of her nightmare, "I hate this for you."

"I should have left Eli that horrible night, but hindsight is 20/20. We can't take back our mistakes but only learn from them." She drew in a sharp breath and shifted in her seat.

A different waiter brought out their salads. Caroline grabbed a piece of bread and placed it in on her plate then picked up the olive oil and drizzled it over her cheese bread. "Are you starving like I am?"

She smiled, tilted her brow and gazed at him as she placed her cloth napkin in her lap.

* * *

That face. She gazed into his gorgeous blues and let her mind wander to the merriment of them strolling along an old dirt road under shade trees, hand in hand, taking their precious time, as they watched her kids riding their bikes a little ahead of them and a sweet puppy following close behind.

"Caroline?"

She blinked and reality set in, "I was reminiscing."

"Yeah?"

She nodded. "Were you too busy to have lunch today?"

"Could you tell?" He laughed, "I nibbled on a few scraps from the baking pans," He slid his fingers down the front of his shirt and clasped his hand together, "May I bless our meal?"

"I'd love that," she remarked and dipped her head.

"Father, we are thankful for our food, bless us I pray, and watch over us, Amen." He leaned backward, "You look lovely tonight."

"Thank you," she returned the smile.

Ben swallowed a bite of salad but remained quiet. A smile surfaced between them at the same moment, she swallowed as he returned a piece of bread he'd held to his plate, "How long were you married?"

"A little over five years."

"Was he abusive the entire time?"

"Yes, and the worst of it was, he scared me." She blinked, "I've never told a soul about the way he treated me. I hid what he did until it was too obvious to hide. My father had his suspicions and continually asked me if Eli was hurting me, but… I lied." She moistened her dry lips. "When I found out I was pregnant with Harry and Penny, he became the nicest man and our marriage got better. I felt loved again, and his care of me was fantastic. Gosh, Ben, I couldn't stay pregnant forever."

Ben settled and relaxed against the back of his chair, "Where is he now?"

Caroline squinted as her demeanor flattened. "He's dead."

"What... I never expected to hear that, oh my gosh."

She lightly touched his forearm, "I know, right, it's hard to believe."

Ben stayed tight lipped, then stuffed a piece of bread into his mouth.

"It happened a few days ago. I haven't told Harry and Penny yet."

"Gosh, Caroline."

"I know, but one thing, I'm so thankful that God allowed me to have my kids. Quite frankly, they are the only good thing that came from my marriage with Eli."

"Your children are amazing." She gazed as he revealed his open admiration of them.

Caroline beamed, "I'm thrilled you think that." Her expression grew stern and her brow intensified. "Since I found out that Eli died, I've had moments, both good and not so ideal, of emotional outbursts." A grimaced escaped her, "I don't know if my crying is from me being happy that he is gone or a relief of not being threatened anymore. She cast her face downward.

"Probably both," he interjected.

"Something else I just thought of," her hands thrust forward. "When my father handed over his business to me, Eli went ballistic." A bridled anger rose in her voice. "He threw me against our patio furniture, then ran to me and repeatedly hit my face." A single tear fell upon her cheek, "I thought taking over Olli's was the greatest thing, but Eli couldn't handle it." She stopped and looked out over the bay, "There was never a night that we didn't argue and him throwing a punch at me. Harry and Penny had been outside playing that day and Harry threw himself in front of me. Penny jumped on Eli's back to try and stop him. He threw Harry against the fence and flipped Penny onto her back." She breathed a steady long breath.

"Did they get hurt?"

"No, thank God, but I landed in the hospital for weeks. When the doctor finally released me, Harry, Penny, and I moved in with my parents. Eli sold our house a few months later and kept the proceeds. I didn't care because he would've demanded my half anyway."

"I hate what you went through," he shook his head as his lips thinned.

Tarsha appeared with plates of steaming hot food, "Enjoy folks."

"Thank you," Caroline's temperament changed, "it looks fantastic."

As soon as Tarsha left, Ben picked up his napkin, "Can I ask how Eli died?"

"Someone shot him," She glowered and witheringly stared.

"Wow, that's just so unreal."

"I'm stunned, but from the horrible things I'd gone through, a burden lifted off me when I heard the news. That's bad isn't it?" Their eyes met.

"I don't think it is."

"My emotions have been like a rollercoaster; one second tears are falling down my face then relief soars through me." She swiveled, "Is it wrong that I'm relieved he's gone?"

"No."

"I'm so relieved that he can't beg me for money anymore."

"Wow. You aren't going to believe this. I met a guy named Eli at the airport when I was flying to Washington last week. I bet that was him, because he shared that he was meeting his father-in-law to get some money before we boarded the plane."

"Yep, that sounds like him. My father went to pay him off, well... a kind of a bribe, in the hopes that he would leave me alone once and for all," she remarked.

Ben dove into his lasagna, taking a huge bite and spied her chewing several bites of salad. Upon swallowing, he wiped his mouth with his napkin, "Thanks for inviting me tonight."

"You're most welcome. Our evening together is what I have longed for." She paused and briefly touched his forearm, "For a while, so... I thank you, too."

"No one would believe me, but I've longed for an evening like this, too," he replied.

She spied his handsome features every few seconds and tried not to be obvious. It was amazing to be sitting across from the best-looking man she'd ever seen, although she had an inkling that he wasn't aware of how handsome he really was. As she peered at him and beheld his utmost beauty, her wonderment of why he never married intrigued her? *Ask. Why not?* She couldn't afford to have another Eli in her life. "Why aren't you married?"

A huge laugh escaped him, "Goodness, I have never been close enough to marry anyone." He eased to the side of his chair, "Every girl I dated was on a mission to hurt me."

"Oh, come on, you've got to be joking. That's terrible."

"No, I wish I were. Nowadays, I stay busy at the bakery and try not to ponder on dating."

There must be more, she wondered. Her brow lifted when a flash of humor crossed her thoughts as she savored her Coke. "Tell me what they did to you?" *Was it that bad?* Maybe to him it was.

He extended his arm across the top of the seat beside him, "Gosh... where do I begin." He straightened himself and rested his elbows on the edge of the tablecloth. "My first girlfriend broke up with me because she adored my buddy more than me and, well..., the same happened with my most recent girlfriend." He pursed his mouth, "Good grief, she was unfaithful."

* * *

Her luminous eyes expanded in wonderment, "Wow, I can't understand why anyone would treat you that way."

Tarsha returned for the umpteenth time, "Excuse me, Caroline, someone is here to see you."

A frown creased her forehead, "Oh... who is it?"

"A lady by the name of Tori."

Caroline jumped up from her chair, "Tori Bailey?"

With a stunned look, Ben blurted, "You know Tori Bailey?" He paused then followed at her heels.

What is he doing? She stopped mid-stride, "Are you coming up front with me?"

Ben raised his voice, "Tori Bailey was the last girl who hurt me."

In the middle of the restaurant, Caroline turned and grabbed his belt loop. *This is unbelievable.* "Tori was my roommate in college."

They both stopped when someone called their names. Ben sprang backward as if a lightning bolt struck him, "Tori?"

"Ben, Caroline, you both look amazing," Tori hugged Caroline then turned to Ben.

Caroline ushered them to her nook. She hugged Tori and stared in disbelief. What in the world? *Be nice.* "Tori, what are you doing here?"

A sneer drew upon Tori's lips. "I wanted us to catch up and low and behold, Ben is with you."

* * *

Not believing what he was seeing, Ben turned from Caroline to Tori as his jumbled hurts, caused by Tori, overshadowed his thoughts. "I didn't think I'd ever see you again," his voice tremored with firmness.

Tori tugged him into an embrace. "How are you doing my sweet darling man?"

Caroline shot Tori a strange glare. "Whoa, what are you doing, Tori?"

He saw Caroline's strained view of what just happened.

"One of you needs to explain," Caroline huffed.

What am I supposed to do? He stiffened and shoved Tori.

Tori's brow squeezed, "Ben, how do you know Caroline?"

"We're neighbors," Ben bit his lip and grabbed Caroline's hand, "Thanks for the wonderful meal, but it's time for me to skedaddle."

Stunned, she didn't release his hand. "You need to stay and explain." She tightened her grip. "How did Tori break your heart?"

Tori interrupted, "Caroline, if you need to handle things, I'd be more than happy to walk Ben out, because I need to speak with him," she drew a step closer to Ben and brushed her body against his.

He stiffened and stepped two steps backward, as he held on to Caroline's hand, and angled to his left as their gazes met.

"Honestly," Caroline uttered; her smile disappeared as she released his hand.

Without a word, Tori shoved her palm against him and pushed him towards the door as a chill shuddered his being. He shifted his weight and whispered in her ear, "I will not talk to you about this."

When their feet hit the sidewalk, he stopped. He hated to admit it, but Tori was radiant in her red halter dress. "You have..." he pulled at his sleeve to check his watch, "30 seconds."

Caroline appeared without warning. "Wait right there." She stepped abruptly towards them, "Ben, Tori, you have a lot of explaining to do."

Tori looked at her, then towards Ben. "How do I make this any clearer?"

"We dated before you came to NYU," Tori blasted the information as she narrowed her gaze.

"What?" Caroline blurted as her voice broke in mid-sentence. "He's the Ben you dated in college?"

Ben's arms fell to his sides, then his hands slid into his hip pockets, "I am out of here. Tori, why don't you explain in detail how you hurt me." He hightailed it to his Jeep.

"Wait, Ben," Tori ran after him, "Don't make me beg."

Seconds later she pulled opened his Jeep driver's door. "Ben, listen to me."

"I told you a minute ago you had 30 seconds," and he tapped his watch.

"I have a better offer," She raised her fine, arched eyebrows, "I'd share it with you but here comes Caroline." She turned on a dime and watched Caroline coming towards them.

Caroline tried to catch her breath, "What are you trying to pull, Tori?"

Ben exited his Wrangler and leaned against the hood, "Wait Caroline," he stammered, then planted his feet, "I am not interested in Tori," he reaffirmed, twisted his wristwatch and gazed at Tori, "Your time is up."

Tori stuttered trying to get out words, then coughed as she drew in a deep breath, "What a tremendous misunderstanding," and reached for him.

"Stop right there," He threw his fist in front of her, "I'm done with you." He grabbed his key fob, "I'm really going this time," he turned and faced Caroline, "May I call you later?" He jumped inside his vehicle and rolled down the window.

Caroline nodded, "I guess, I'm confused."

"Tori can explain."

Just then Tori reached her arms inside his Jeep window, "Please move and live with me."

With a gentle nudge, he pushed her from the window, "You're going back to London without me. Do you hear me?"

Good grief. He'd never consider moving to England. The audacity of her. What nerve... to come all the way to the states and make such a ridiculous suggestion. What did I ever see in that girl? Her legs were so attractive. He cleared his mind of her and hoped Caroline would see right through her shenanigans.

He kept his affability, but breathed deep to settle his nerves. The conversation between the three of them caused a new anger against Tori. He knew he needed to leave all his relationships at Jesus' feet, and he prayed. *Lord, Jesus, if it is Your will, please open doors for Caroline and me. Help us have a lasting relationship and let our friendship be pleasing in Your sight. Lord, I couldn't be more grateful you brought her into my life.* As he remained silent in reverence to Him, the image of her adorable kids entered his thoughts. He already loved them and, as his prayer continued, he breathed that God would give him a chance to prove that love.

* * *

The curve of Tori's cheeks surprised Caroline. "Why are you smiling? You just tried to run off the sweetest man I've ever met." She hurried along the path to Olli's and didn't stop until she sat in her private space.

At her heels, Tori followed and patted her shoulder as she passed and withdrew a chair, "Now, now, Caroline, you don't stand a chance with my man."

Caroline picked up her glass, took a quick sip and swallowed the last of her drink. "I hope my feelings for him will flourish and I am certain, he is not, let me repeat, is not the least bit interested in you. He may have loved you once upon a time, or thought he did, but..." her expression stilled and grew serious, "he doesn't now."

The demeanor on Tori's face altered, "I couldn't care less if you guys are together, I just want him to work for my uncle." Her frown intensified, "I love my fiancé." She picked at her long fingernails, "I have the power to sweeten the whole thing, if he'd only listen."

Caroline put her glass down, "What sort of deal?" *She's lost her mind.*

"A free place to live for one and a hefty salary for another," Tori affirmed as she started to tap her foot. "Listen, I'll call you later."

As Caroline saw her friend exit, she smothered a groan, yet a crushing sensation captured her spirit. She leaned against the wall, put pressure against her temples and rocked her head to rid the mounted tension. She contemplated her next move and ran to the hostess stand, "What the heck, Tarsha," she yelled, "Can you handle things?" Not waiting for a reply, she flew to the door, stopped and peered for a response.

"I got this," Tarsha lifted a thump's up signal.

"Thanks, give me a few minutes." She scanned both directions and spotted Tori next to Ben's Jeep. *I thought he would have been gone by now and why won't she leave him alone?* She quickened her pace as she ran in their direction and slowed to a crawl within 20 feet from them. She saw Tori's mouth plowing at him. W*hy would she be fussing at him now? He couldn't be gullible, could he?* "Hey," she hollered as she converged upon them.

He merely stared as his mouth fell open, but no words escaped him.

"Why did you follow me?" Tori shouted at her.

Several people walked by and Caroline ducked her head as they passed, then regained her composure. "Why do you insist on hammering Ben with harsh words? I saw you going at him. Why do you still degrade people?" Caroline shifted her shoulders.

"Uh... that's not at all what I was doing."

"You were pretty darn nasty," Ben interrupted as he got out of his Jeep.

"Well, it's over."

Tori's jade eyes widened with astonishment as she hugged Ben's neck. "You know I adore you, huh, Ben? Imagine the two of us starting over but in a different place... like London."

Caroline's mouth gaped, "You just told me that you loved your fiancé."

Ben, with a sudden jerk, fled her grasp, then pulled on his knit shirt to straighten out the wrinkles. "Tori, my intentions last week were to rekindle what we had, but you messed up any chance of that ever happening."

Caroline jumped between them, "Ben, you went to London?" She pictured them arm in arm strolling the quaint streets as she gawked. Suddenly, he pressed his lips flat and squinted his eyes when their gazes locked with each other.

"It had been nine years since I'd seen her, so I decided to accept her invitation." Ben's shoulders shifted as Caroline stepped near him. "I planned to meet up with her after I got there and went to a nearby restaurant to grab a bite to eat. Just as I was finishing up my dinner, I saw her with another man outside the window where I was sitting. It stunned me when they stopped and kissed on the sidewalk. It literally shocked me."

Tori stared at them both, tight-lipped.

"My trip was a disaster," Ben remarked as he twisted and jeered at Tori. "She made excuse after excuse when I saw her in a bar across the road. It was like I was reliving my past."

"Really?"

"Yeah, I found her in my dorm room with my best friend, Edward, half undressed, I might add."

"I've changed, I really have," Tori shouted at them and pulled at her long black strands, bunching them together. "You didn't have to bring up Edward."

Caroline clasped her hands together, "You haven't changed a bit since our college days."

"I have, too." Tori started pacing up and down the pavement. "Oh, Caroline, I know you don't believe any of this," she pulled at her arm.

"Oh yes, I do, and stop pulling on me," Caroline jerked her arm and rubbed at the red mark made by Tori's fingernails.

* * *

A gust of wind blew through Ben's hair as he stood next to the curb. He shook his head as he tried to rid disturbing thoughts that began to race through his mind, "I found out later that you and Edward had dated for months behind my back."

"That isn't true." Tori jumped towards him even though her shoes stayed glued to the concrete.

They watched as Tori tried to hide her misery. Her fingers touched her chin, "I'm a klutz," she laughed then readjusted her footing, and was at him again, putting her hands on him, "You have to believe me."

Ben stepped away, then studied Tori with a sidelong glance of utter disgust on his face, "You strive on hurting others and what happened in London confirms that you are a selfish, conniving person."

Caroline swayed and moved within inches of Ben, "Wow! This is unreal."

"Wait a minute, let me defend myself," Tori gasped, then flung herself at Ben for the fourth time. "Please listen," she blurted as she rubbed against him.

"Tori, the answer is still... a big fat no! Stop your whining, you cannot convince me."

"How does a place to live for free and a huge salary sound?" She crossed her arms as she stood her ground and her teeth gleamed bright.

"You cannot bribe me with money." His right arm flew up, "Ladies, please excuse me," as he opened his vehicle door, started the engine and screeched his Jeep's tires as he sped down the street.

"Why do you always chase the sweet ones away?" Caroline peered at her.

"My uncle is desperate," she reciprocated.

"And... are you the least bit concerned and really care what your uncle thinks?" Caroline felt her eyes widen as she gritted her teeth.

Tori shrugged her shoulders in mock resignation, "I owe him big time."

Caroline's jaw dropped, and her head went blistery hot. As she brushed the sweat from her brow, she planted her feet, "I just bet you do. You haven't changed and I'll pray for you."

"What do you know about prayer, Miss Goody Two Shoes?"

Here she goes again. Caroline nodded, "You can't let things rest, can you? I gave my soul to Jesus when I was a child and rededicated my heart last year after the Eli incident."

"Yeah, when you were in the hospital, I bet."

"That's right. It's been hard, but I strive to live a holy life."

"You're serious?" Tori laughed.

"I am, and Tori, you can give your life to Christ." Caroline felt her skin turning hot a second time. "You make me so mad. We'd better end this conversation," and shoved her hands into the pockets of her jeans. "When are you leaving?" *Please say soon.*

"I'm not leaving until I get a yes."

"Tori, you're stupid if you think he'd go, how many times does he have to tell you?"

"A million," she blurted with a huff. "I don't care how long, but I promise you, his answer will be YES, wait and see."

14

Mixed emotions ran rampant as Caroline went through the front entrance of Olli's Italian Gardens.

As soon as she put her bags on the counter, Tarsha bolted through the swinging doors of the kitchen, "I've been waiting for you."

"What's wrong?" Caroline raised a brow from the concerned look on Tarsha's face.

"You will not believe this... Poppy's quitting."

Blowing out a labored breath, she murmured, "Oh no, why?" Things had gone so well with her employees. "Where is he?" Caroline asked with a sudden heavy heart yet proceeded at Tarsha's heels that led to the wash sinks.

"He was standing here two minutes ago," Tarsha uttered.

"Did he give an explanation?" She spun around for a response.

"No," she shook her head, "I bet you hate this."

"I do." Caroline spotted Poppy's bald head disappear through the rear exit. "Poppy, wait!" With pounding feet, she flew to the door to stop him. "Are you leaving me?"

He bent his neck and looked at the ground as though he was ashamed. "I can't work here any longer," and with a steady hand, swung around a metal box that was close by and plopped down on the smooth glossy surface. He drew in a slow breath as his mouth draped open, and with scrutinizing eyes, gazed at her. As he sat staring, his tears welled. "Things aren't good at home."

"I don't know what to say, Poppy. I'm sorry." Caroline's lips straight lined, nevertheless, leaned and hugged him.

Warmly, a slight smile spread across his lips. "The Mrs. needs help with our teenage boy." He stilled. "I can't give you a two-week notice." After a moment, he stood and stepped down onto the shadowed pathway.

"Is there anything we can do?" She followed him.

"I need my son back, not the creep that lives in my house."

"Ooh, Poppy." She dashed in front of him, "Listen, I will pray for you and your son."

Clumsily, he wiped at his lashes. "I appreciate that. We're gonna need a bunch of them."

A loud clash interrupted them, and Caroline stuck her head inside the kitchen "Is everything all right?"

"A-Okay. Rodney dropped a bowl," Tarsha's eyes met hers. "We will clean it up, no worries."

Caroline turned back to Poppy and leaned against his shoulder, "We'll miss you. Look here..." She waited for him to lift his head, "I understand."

"Thanks. Miss Caroline, you've been a great boss, and I have enjoyed working here." He walked to the end of the alley, threw up his hand and waved.

With slow steps back to the rear exit of Olli's, a huge disappointment not having Poppy around rummaged through her thoughts as she contemplated her next move. She tried to remember if he had ever mentioned his son before. With a squint, her mind reeled for a recollection. Nope, before tonight, he'd not said a word about him. Abruptly, she stopped and breathed a prayer: *Lord, please help Poppy handle the issues with his son and help the young man listen. I pray he turns his life around. Lord, grant it. Amen.* She released a pent-up breath, dashed in, grabbed a cloth and started wiping cheese sauce. "How did this happen?" She looked at everyone around.

Rodney, her night chef, hustled over, "It was me; I dropped the bowl." Thick cheese sauce was everywhere. "It slipped from my hand, Miss Caroline. I was being nosy about Poppy and not paying attention. My bad."

"Uh, it's fine, but help us clean the cheese off the walls," she retorted.

"Can I ask, is Poppy gone for good?" Rodney flitted to the stove and stirred several skillets of beef.

"Yes, I'm afraid so, his son is giving him trouble."

"I heard; Poppy told me everything about Frankie." He laid an oversized spoon on the counter, grabbed a cloth and started wiping cheese dip off the cabinets, then ran water over his rag, wrung it out and laid it down. "I need to add some onion to the meat."

"You just don't like to do this sort of thing, do you?" Caroline snickered.

"You know me well," he laughed.

He scooted from them, retrieved a knife and began the peeling process on the onions. "I'm afraid jail time is in that boy's future."

She shook her head. "Oh, my goodness, that's so sad. Rodney... Poppy never mentioned his son. As a matter of fact, I didn't know he even had a son. What did he do?"

Rodney adjusted his chef's hat, "Sold drugs out of Poppy's house. The police raided them at 5:00 a.m. the other morning and he's been distraught ever since."

"Poppy seemed fine; as I recall, he's been in a good mood lately."

"He probably tried not to think about it while he was here and put on a happy face."

"Yeah, you're right." She thought, "He must have gotten with the wrong crowd."

"Probably so," Rodney replied.

After they finished cleaning, Caroline moseyed over to the stove, lifted the lid from one of the huge pots and steam rose and tickled her nose as she gazed at the bubbling deep red sauce. "Smells good,

Rodney." She selected a small spoon from the bunch piled together and stirred the mixture, then scooped a little to have a taste. "Yum, this is great." Afterward, she stepped up to the sweets stacked on the cooling racks and wondered who could make their desserts from now on? As soon as that escaped her, Ben popped into her mind. *He can make them.*

"Miss Caroline, I see you spying those desserts? At the rate we sale our desserts, we will run out by tomorrow."

"You're right," she grimaced.

"Do you have anybody in mind to replace Poppy?" Rodney stepped closer.

"I'm trying to figure that out now." She looked at Tarsha, "If you need me, I'll be in my nook," and excused herself. She pulled up her contacts on her phone and pressed Ben's number. It rang twice. "Ben?"

"Hey, I didn't think I'd hear from you so soon."

She'd better get right to the point because Poppy's desserts would be a vanishing act by tomorrow. "I have a quick question."

"Shoot."

With a quick brush of her hair to the side, she found a pen and wrote his name at the top of her notepad. "My dessert man just informed me he couldn't work for me any longer and I was wondering if you'd like to make our desserts?" She squinted. *Please say yes.*

"That won't be a problem, you can count on me. Do you want to give me an order now?"

"Yes," She lifted her eyebrows, *Thank you, God.*

"What do you need?"

"First, let me explain how we do our desserts. I think you will like it."

"Sure."

"You probably know that we offer our plain cheesecake and chocolate coffee cake every day."

"Yeah. I've gotten both before."

"Our baker, Poppy, made four specials of his choosing each day and if you'd like to continue that, that would be great."

"So, what you're saying is, after we make the cheesecakes and the coffee cakes, we can choose whatever we'd want to make?"

"Yeah, and we would order two each of whatever you decide."

"Sounds wonderful."

"Would it be possible to discuss the details about pricing, etc., in the morning? I'm so darn busy right now."

"Sure, that won't be a problem, but let me go over exactly what you want; two cheesecakes and chocolate coffee cakes, then eight of whatever I come up with."

"You got it, and, before I forget, what time can I pick everything up?"

"I'll deliver. Is 11:00 a.m. in the morning a good time?"

"That's perfect." Caroline's cell phone buzzed in another call. "My babysitter is on the other line. I'll see you tomorrow."

"Okay, bye."

She pressed the swap button and switched the call, "Hey, Roxy, is everything okay?"

"Hey. The twins are sick. Harry has a fever and Penny is sneezing and tells me her tummy hurts."

"Oh goodness. Are you at my house? Is my dad there with you guys?"

"No. He's at home. I went by your folks a little after 7:00 p.m. and picked them up."

"You didn't have to do that."

"I know, but I wanted, too. Anyway, Harry and Penny want you."

Caroline looked at her watch. "Let me handle a few things here, then I'm on the way. I should be home in about 20 minutes or so. Thanks, Roxy." She hastened to the front of the restaurant and found Tarsha at the hostess stand. "Tarsha, hey," a smile surfaced when she scanned across the room and saw every table full of patrons. "That's a wonderful view," she expelled with a joyful sigh. "Darn, Tarsha, Penny and Harry are sick, and I need to go home." She turned and looked up at the tall woman, "Can you handle things?"

Tarsha's fingers flew down the reservation book. "We got this; your babies need you." A scowl appeared as she whispered, "Do we have enough desserts? Oh, before I forget, I want to hear about the commotion with your friends earlier.

"I'll be glad to fill you in." Caroline pressed her hand to her forehead, "For now, let's leave it alone, but guess what?" Not waiting for a reply, she let out the good news, "I'm getting Ben's bakery to supply our desserts."

Tarsha picked up a stack of menus. "You didn't waste any time finding someone."

"We need him." Caroline pulled at her watch.

"We certainly do."

"Are you all right with me going home?"

"Of course," Tarsha gave her a slight push.

"Thanks friend, I owe you one." Her smile deepened. "I'm so relieved," she sighed as liberation washed over her and scurried to find her purse.

Caroline zoomed from the restaurant, hastened to the car park, jumped into her Mercedes, started the engine, put the car in reverse and backed out. Turning onto the street, she fled like a bullet through the narrow streets and in five minutes flat, she pulled into her driveway. Not wasting a second, she dashed up the walkway. As she slid her key into the lock, the door flew open. "Roxy, how are they?" Once inside, she found Harry and Penny asleep on the couch and four blankets on top of Harry, "Geez, was he cold?"

"Thanks for getting here as quick as you did."

Caroline touched the blankets. "What's up with the covers?" She laughed.

Roxy giggled, "He kept complaining he was freezing, so Penny and I piled them on."

She eased up beside Penny and felt her head, "She doesn't seem to have a fever, then grabbed one of Harry's blankets and tossed it over her little girl. After tucking it under her legs, she nestled in between them and put her hand on Harry's forehead. "When was the last time you checked his temperature?"

"About an hour ago. You should probably take them to the doctor tomorrow."

"I will."

Roxy re-adjusted the pillows under the children's heads. "I'm heading out unless you need me to stay."

"You can go." She slipped behind her, "I don't tell you often enough, but I really appreciate what you do for me."

With a smile, Roxy turned, "I know you do."

Roxy slipped into her shoes, "I hope the kids will be better by morning."

"Me too." Caroline walked out and stood by the driveway until Roxy was out of sight then rushed inside, twisted the deadbolt and returned to where Harry and Penny were sleeping. For the fourth time, she touched Harry's forehead to check for a fever.

The sweet boy opened his eyes. "Mommy, you're home."

"Yes, I am, sweetie, how are you?"

"My throat hurts. Roxy told me I was hot."

She cracked a grin. *You are handsome.* "Let's see." She touched his face from one side to the other, "You are a little warm. If you feel bad when you wake up in the morning, we'll go to the doctor's office."

He put both of his hands on hers. "I be better, Mommy."

"Okay, but first, let me go find you something that will make your throat better."

She bit her lip as she went to find some medication knowing the cabinet was bare for a sore throat. I *hope we have something in the cabinet.* Touching every bottle, jar, and box on the medicine shelf, she was right, there wasn't a thing for his ailment. "Harry, Penny, we are going to have to go and get Harry some medicine." After gathering their coats and buckling them into their car-seats, she twisted and looked at them, "Mommy thinks we should get both of you a hamburger after we go to the drug store." When she glanced a second time, both were rubbing their eyes.

"Yay," Harry blurted. "I want cheese on mine."

"Me too" Penny added.

Traffic was murderous as Caroline moved along at a snail's pace for miles on end. Every time the cars stopped, she twisted and asked Harry if he felt sick to his stomach.

"No, me better," He replied.

After 22 minutes, they pulled into the Medicine Bin Drug Store and with a quick turn of the wheel, Caroline parked in the first available space. As they were getting out of the car, Caroline noticed thick dark clouds were looming near to the ground which was odd. She rushed the two inside and pulled a cart from the bunch that were stacked against the wall, picked up Harry and put him inside, "Penny do you want to ride in the cart?"

With a quick nod, she lifted her arms into the air, "Aha."

Not hesitating, Caroline lifted her sweet girl and sat her beside Harry. Up and down the aisles they went in search of cold medications. "Here they are," and threw three different bottles into the cart that aided in curing a common cold, a sore throat or/and sneezing. "Are you ready for your hamburgers?"

A smile appeared on sweet Harry's flushed face, "Me ready."

"Me, too," Penny hollered from the cart.

"Mommy thinks she will get a burger, too." They hurried to the check-out counter, paid the clerk, then left the store and Caroline drove to their favorite hamburger restaurant, ordered their burgers via the drive-through, and pulled into the first spot available.

With a quick unbuckle of her seatbelt, she hurried to the other side of the Mercedes where Harry was, found the bag from the drug store, opened the bottle of medicine, poured one teaspoon into the med-dispenser and handed it to Harry. "Will you please take this medicine?"

"Yes, Mommy." He squeezed his eyes shut. "Me don't like it." He swallowed the thick red liquid then shivered as his eyes blinked frivolously.

"Hurry, drink some of your juice to wash it down." She watched him take a big gulp. "That should be better now."

Huge tears fell onto his cheeks. “Me not like at all,” and gagged.

“Drink another sip of your juice.”

He sipped and drank more quickly.

Caroline unwrapped his burger and held it up to his mouth. “Take a bite.”

Harry took the burger from her and bit it. “It’s good.” A sweet beam surfaced on his face as he chewed. “I better, Mommy.”

“I’m so glad.” Not wasting any time, Caroline unwrapped Penny’s burger and handed it to her, then placed their packets of French fries in their laps and dashed to her side of the car and jumped in. “It’s starting to rain. Let’s finish our burgers before we go home.” They sat quietly for a few minutes. “Hand me your trash, please.” Both children obeyed. She wadded the paper, combined all the items into one bag, and rolled down the window at the end of the driveway trash barrel. “Do you think I can make it?”

“Try, Mommy, try,” Harry shouted.

With a quick hand, she heaved the bag and it landed inside the trash barrel. “I made it, yay.”

“You did it,” Penny clapped her hands.

“Okay, you guys ready?” Caroline pulled to the edge of the road and turned when the traffic cleared. Stopping and starting seemed to be the name of the game that everyone was playing as they made it through downtown and towards the house. When they arrived, a car was sitting in the driveway. “I wonder who came to visit?” Caroline squeezed her brow.

Penny rubbed the fogged-up window in the back seat. “There is a car here, Mommy.”

Caroline parked along on the street. “Harry, Penny, stay in the car,” but unbelted their car-seats. Out of the corner of her eye, she realized it was Tori who came to visit. “It’s a friend of mine from college, you can get out.” After helping them to the ground, she yelled Tori’s name.

“Hey,” Tori exited her vehicle.

Harry and Penny came up and stood right behind her. “Guys, please stay quiet.”

Tori bent to her knees, "You have grown so much, wow. Come here and give me a hug."

Caroline put her arms around them, "It's okay."

Harry shyly approached Tori and stood perfectly still as Tori encircled him with her arms. "Awe, you are such a nice boy."

"Thank you," he remarked.

"So, what brings you here?" *She's mighty persistent. I'll give her credit for that.*

"I need a place to stay tonight, do you mind?"

Caroline's mouth dropped open, "I don't think that's such a good idea… Harry and Penny are sick."

Tori scowled, "It's all right, I have other options."

Caroline picked up her children's hands, "So, did you schedule a flight back to London yet?" She gazed at her.

"No, I think I will stay a couple more weeks."

"Why do you insist on wasting your time?"

"Frankly, Caroline, that is none of your business."

"It is if you insist on hounding my new friend."

Tori burst out laughing, "You don't have a chance with Ben."

Caroline stiffened her shoulders, "Oh, yes, I do. As I recall, Ben told you he wasn't interested in going to London, remember?"

"I will change his mind." Tori squinted, "It's written all over your face that you want a relationship with him."

Caroline turned and eyeballed Harry rubbing his eyes. "Will you excuse me for a moment, I'll be right back?" Quickly, she unlocked the front door, pushed it open and walked her two children through the entrance. "Stay inside, I'll be outside with Miss Tori for a minute."

"Yes, Mommy," Penny obeyed and took Harry by the hand, "C'mon, let's go sit on the couch and wait for Mommy."

Caroline shut the door, turned, and found Tori on the porch with her hands on her hips, "I don't appreciate you saying that in front of my children. Ben is incredible, and I'd love a chance to date a nice man like him for a change, God knows I deserve it, but that's my business."

"Okay, okay, okay. I'm sorry I brought it up. But always remember, I had him first."

I could slap her. Caroline's stomach wrenched with anger at her words. "I've got to get inside. Don't bother Ben, you know his answer." That being understood, she walked to her door.

"I have no choice," Tori yelled.

Caroline spun around, "What do you mean?" Her eyes narrowed.

"If you must know, it's my fault my uncle is looking for a chef."

"What did you do, date him?"

"Yeah, we dated."

"Did you have an affair with him while dating someone else?" Caroline glared her, "Huh, Tori?"

"Yes, I got caught." A dumbfounded sneer appeared on her face. "So, to make amends, I told my uncle I'd find another chef to take over his kitchen."

"Ben?" She smirked.

"Yes, Ben, who else? He is the only person who could manage that heavy workload."

Caroline's insides began to shake, "You make me so upset." She readjusted her feet on the wet ground, "Your only option is to go back to London." She ran up the steps and into the house without saying another word.

* * *

As Ben drove down the road from Olli's after the fiasco with Tori, he was glad Bradley had wanted to stay at Janice's longer than anticipated. He dug in his back pocket for the slip of paper Janice had jotted her address on. She was one of the prettiest women he'd ever met. *Why hadn't Bradley warned him of that?* Many other things rummaged through his head as he got nearer to Janice's new abode; from Bradley's willingness to stay in Camden, to his newfound friend named Janice, to Caroline, to Tori and to Kandice. Could Kandice ever forgive him?

He approached the same annoying red light on Bayview Avenue that seemed to always be on red when he approached it. This time was no different. While waiting for the light to change, he plugged Janice's address into his GPS and noticed her house was only three miles away. The light turned, he zipped up the street and arrived at 36 Captain's Way in less than five minutes.

As he rounded the curvy road, the cute Tudor house with green shutters stood out among the rest. With a little paint, a good grass cutting and a trim of the hedges, the place would be nice. *I wonder how the inside looks.* He parked along a clear path and exited his Wrangler. With a quick tap on what looked to be a kitchen window, Janice turned and waved at him to enter as she opened the side entrance.

"Hey," she mouthed.

She is incredible.

Janice stepped sideways and greeted him, "Come in," and held the screen door.

"Nice place."

"It needs a great deal of tender loving care to bring it back to the way it was, come on in, I'll show you."

Room by room he followed and noticed the walls needed a coat of paint, new carpet was a must in the bedrooms, and a good polishing of the hardwoods in the kitchen and den would help the place look better. "Is your landlord making all these repairs?" He asked as they stood in the den.

"I think so. He informed me that some repairs were going to be done. One thing for sure, we are getting new carpet installed next week."

Bradley and Gordon were sitting on the couch watching TV. "Bradley, are you ready?"

The tall teen stood to his feet. "Yeah, I can't wait to see Mom."

"Thanks, Janice, for letting Bradley hang out." He stepped closer. "And, I almost forgot to thank you for bringing Bradley to Camden." He reached for her hand.

Instead of shaking his hand, she grabbed a hold of him and hugged him tightly. "You're most welcome."

Whoa! Her arms clung to him. Instead of pushing her away, he held her embrace. Her small frame was firm to the touch.

Bradley gathered his belongings, "I guess we'll see you later. Oh, before I forget, I'm taking Bradley for his school registration tomorrow, do you and Gordon want to come along?"

Janice frowned, "I'm going to have trouble getting him registered."

"Why is that?"

"I do not know where his birth certificate or social security card is, and we'll need them."

He grimaced. "Ooh! You're right."

"I haven't had a copy of his birth certificate since he was little."

"You can get a copy downtown and it won't cost much."

"I'll do that. Can you get both?"

"I think so."

Bradley stepped towards them, "Thanks, Miss Janice."

Ben and Bradley exited the house and stepped onto the patio with Janice right behind them, "Thanks again, Janice. Maybe we'll see you tomorrow."

"Okay, sounds good."

Ben and Bradley got in the Wrangler and drove a little way down the road. "How far do you live from here?"

"About a mile or so. Mom's going to be so excited to see you."

Bradley shifted on the seat. "I'm glad I made the trip."

"So... how you've been?"

"Good, since you left." He looked out the window. "I think this is a cool place, and I'm looking forward to starting at a new school."

"What have you done with Bradley, you're not him. You're a different kid and I like him."

Bradley cackled loudly. "I'm the same. I like it here."

Memories of them wrestling on the carpet in their basement as kids flooded Ben's thoughts. A glow glistened his face. It was amazing how handsome Bradley had become. Much taller than he was.

In their younger days, they were so closed knitted and inseparable, no matter what they did, they did it together. As Ben drove closer to home, he was determined to spend a lot of time with Bradley, he promised himself and *it will be like it was before.*

"What are you thinking about?" Bradley asked. "Why are you smiling?"

"When we were kids, we spent every waking moment together until I left for New York."

"Yeah, we did, didn't we? It about killed me when you left."

Ben stopped at a red light, "I never knew that."

"Funny how you never came back after you left." Bradley squinted as he stared.

Pure shock overwhelmed him. "I never really liked where we lived."

"And you think I did? We were stuck."

"We were, weren't we?" Ben shook his head.

"You should have taken me with you."

Ben pressed on the gas and sped through the edge of town. "I was in college, silly. Where would I have kept you... in my dorm room... under my bed?"

"I could have made it work," Bradley laughed.

The thrill of knowing his brother cared for him and that he missed him all those years, had him all giddy inside. "You never called once or told me any of this."

"I didn't know how. Let's please drop it. It was a long time ago."

"We've got all the time in the world now to hang out."

15

Before the sun was above the bay the next morning, a sigh of relief escaped Caroline the moment she touched Harry's forehead. *No fever, thank God.* She walked to the doorway of his bear themed, slate blue room. It was what Harry had asked for when they got down to decorating his choice from the bedrooms. From stuffed teddy bears, to a comforter with bears imprinted on it, she'd found two Yogi Bear prints for his walls. Harry beamed ear to ear at what they had accomplished. "Harry, it's time to get up. You need to wash your face and put your clothes on for school."

"Yes, Mommy." He stretched his arms and sat up in bed.

"Do you want waffles for breakfast?"

"Yay, I love waffles."

"Okay, I'm going to check on Penny." She slipped two doors down and much to her surprise, Penny was already dressed in her favorite outfit she'd picked out the night before. "I see you got up and put on your clothes, good job, sweetie." She bent and hugged her daughter. "I'll be in the kitchen if you need me," and ambled down the hall. In her new kitchen, she leaned against the edge of the French doors and took in the beautiful décor. The fresh, light gray walls contrasted with the black subway tile backsplash looked spiffy in the morning sun. Thanks to her church friend, Molly, her hanging pot rack, on the other side of the room was exquisite. Molly unpacked her copper cookware, decorated the kitchen and hauled empty boxes to the dumpster. Without her help, the place would still be stacked with boxes. *I need to buy her some lunch.* Her eyes followed the sun's rays to the bone colored tiles on the floor. She loved her new house. *Thanks, dad, for kicking me out.* She shook her head as she looked over the last tumultuous week, from moving, unpacking, the overwhelming news of Eli, the constant work at the restaurant, to the problems with Tori. Her lips suddenly stretched upward when her thoughts went to Ben.

A laugh escaped when she eased up to Harry who had made his way to his favorite turquoise stool at the kitchen bar. "I'm so glad you are feeling better."

He whirled around and jumped into her arms, "Me too."

"Let me make you a waffle, but before I do, take this medicine." After a quick pull of the drawer handle, she grabbed a teaspoon and poured the red cold liquid into the spoon and held it up to Harry's mouth.

"Get my drink ready."

"All right, hurry, swallow this so I can get it."

He squeezed his eyes shut, opened his mouth and swallowed. "It tastes so bad."

"I know." Within two seconds, his juice was at his fingertips. "Here you go."

"Thanks, Mommy."

Not wasting any time, Caroline opened the freezer, grabbed four waffles and put them into the toaster. Turning, she looked at Harry, "They will be ready in a minute. Do you want some syrup?"

His brow squeezed, "No, I want them plain."

After a quick pat on his shoulder, she turned and hurried back to the toaster. "They are almost ready," then she moseyed over to the back door to see if the morning paper had arrived. When she opened the sliding glass door, a burst of chilly air hit her face. *It's cold out.* "Penny run get your coat, you'll need it today, you too, little man."

Harry took off, "Penny, help me find my red hoodie."

"It's on the couch where you left it," she hollered.

Excitement rose in her voice as she slid across the tile floor in her socked feet. "Do you think it will snow?"

"Gosh, I hope not."

"Did you fix our lunches?"

A smile surfaced on Caroline's face. "No, you will eat the school lunch today, they're having chicken nuggets."

Penny jumped up and down, "Yay, I love their nuggets." Penny's bright smile radiated across her face.

"I know you do, sweetie."

With coats on, boots laced on their feet and book bags against their shoulders, out the door the three flew to the car. "It's even colder than I thought." Caroline frowned at the frost on the car's windshield. She hurried to the back, opened the hatch and found an ice scrapper and got busy working to clear the ice from the glass. Four little eyes were on her every move when she glanced toward them.

Harry mouthed, 'Can I help?'

"Stay in the car, I'll get it," and kept at it until the windshield was clear.

A playful thought grabbed her. She gathered the scraped ice and formed it into a ball. "Harry," she yelled, "Look this way," she laughed and threw the ice in his direction, laughing the entire time. If the glass wasn't in between them, it would have hit him square in the face.

Harry stuck his head out the window, sneering, "Mommy, you're funny."

Caroline jumped inside the Mercedes and drove to the kid's school. The car rider line seemed a little shorter, a lot shorter come to think about it. "What's going on, where are all the cars?" She eased into the large driveway and gazed at the dashboard clock, 7:39 a.m., "We're right on time, everybody else must be running late," and pulled close to the car in front of her.

"I think the fourth and fifth graders went on a field trip today," Penny blurted.

"Oh, that answers my question," Caroline folded her hands in her lap and waited for the school to open. "Did you guys remember to get your homework off the coffee table?"

"I got it for us," Penny announced.

"Good girl. Look, they're starting to get out of the cars. Love you two, have a wonderful day." She watched her prides of joy hurry for the entrance of the school. Their dad popped into her thoughts and left a kind of sadness in her spirit, but also a happy one. *Why?* Both her children had his eyes, mouth and nose. A frown surfaced between her eyes at the thought of telling them about their father. *I'll have to share that sometime.*

The first time she saw Eli in high school, he was so sweet and the best-looking hunk of the senior class. A freshman at the time, she had no idea when she fell in love, but was it love at first sight? She never realized what she would be up against three years later and it all started on their honeymoon when a slight... was it an insignificant hit on her face? Was she trying to make it less of an abused act? *I'm in denial?* She'd prayed day and night that the next time they were alone together, he wouldn't hit her because that's how often the abuse occurred. Every day it happened. To think on it now, his abusive hands were on her their entire marriage. That first slap, she should have run and never looked back, but as she relived every slap, kick and the like, all she felt was sadness for the once upon a time man of her dreams. Tears formed against the corners of her eyes. She was free and as she wiped her tear stained blue jeans, his death, though tragic, was bringing an end to her sadness. *Thank God he can't hit me again.*

Caroline rounded the corner to the back-parking lot of Olli's, parked the car and hurried to the door. She crammed her hand into her purse for the restaurant key. A man with a hoodie covering his head caught her by surprise with four large paper bags in tow. *Is that Ben?* She rubbed at her tear blemished face and proceeded to unlock the door. "Ben, hey, I wasn't expecting you so early."

"Hey," he lifted the bags, "I've got your desserts," and stopped when he got next to her. "Wait," he got in front of her, "Have you been crying?"

The man's sweet face gave her a chill. "Oh, they're tears of joy, I assure you." She shook her head and brushed her fingers under her eyes once more.

Ben followed her inside and placed the bags on a table. "I've got dozens of things to show you." He grinned broadly.

"You're amazing." *Will I be able to trust him?* His gentleness startled her. "Show me what you got," and held the door for him. "How long have you been waiting?"

"Just a few minutes." He pulled his sweatshirt away from his head and ran a hand through his hair.

This man is so impressive, plus pleasing to the eye. She stared at his broad shoulders as he unpacked the bags. His naturally tanned skin was perfect, and she loved his shadowy beard. Never had she remembered viewing eyes as pretty as his. "Have you been told how beautiful your eyes are?"

"Maybe once or twice." He was sure of himself as he unpacked two cheesecakes, two dozen brownies, two pies, two dozen muffins and two cakes. "I have four more bags in the car, I'll be right back."

"Are you for real?" With energy and a smile, he hurried to the door. Was she falling for him? Could or would he turn out to be like her ex-husband? *No one could be as cold and heartless as Eli, could they?* A confused state of mind hit her like a blast of wind. She would have to get to know him through and through. *Lord Jesus, have you sent this man into my life to rescue me?*

Ben returned with the bags. "I have Tiramisu, Apple and Chocolate Cream Pies, plus lemon squares."

"My goodness, what time did you get to the bakery to have this ready by now?" She was astounded.

"I got there a bit earlier than usual, I suppose," and a broad smile surfaced.

"So, Mr. Matney, how much do I owe you for these amazing desserts?"

He placed the last pie on the glassed shelf in the middle of her main dining room. "I spoke with Chloe about that."

"And?" Caroline scooted towards him.

"She wants this venture to be fair for both parties and wanted me to present to you a 65/35 percentage on each dessert."

"Quite fair, I think." Her mind started adding numbers. "I won't have any costs for ingredients or pay a salary for a baker. So, yes, it will be a fantastic deal for me."

Ben twitched his brow as she stared, "I'll take an inventory of what you have leftover each morning when I bring a new supply, pick up the left overs and bill you for what we sold."

She was certain by his willingness; they'd work well together. "You've got it all worked out, haven't you?"

He spun around, "It can be only a win-win situation," and held up his hand to give her a high five.

Her reaction was to hit his hand, so she jumped towards him and tapped it, "I'm super excited about this."

Ben reached into his back pocket and unfolded a piece of paper. "Here is a list of what I brought. Do you want to sit down and decide what each dessert will cost?"

"Sure." She unfolded her long flannel wrap she'd worn inside and laid it on the back of the chair beside her and straightened, "I need to turn on all the ovens in the kitchen, I'll be back in a sec."

"Take your time."

Ben Matney was a self-assured guy that she was so fond of. He was unlike Eli, and she need not to compare the two. Was the man in the front of her restaurant going to be her new beau? *I sure hope so.* Could she be brave enough to trust him? Three minutes later, when she returned, and with calmness, she watched him review the dessert menu board and took in his tall, manly frame. A chill struck her spine as she remembered how good he was with her children and as she observed him, she admired his blue eyes against his blond hair and thought how attractive he was standing there. To love him was the only thing that popped in her mind.

"You seem miles away," he stepped up to her.

"I was just thinking we need to change the dessert board."

"Do you have good handwriting?"

She laughed when her gaze met his, "I can't take credit for that great handwriting in front of you." From where she was standing, they both stared at the perfect chalked menu board. "One of my employees writes everything on the board for me. I'll have him change it when he comes in this morning."

Ben followed Caroline to her special nook in the restaurant where they'd had their first dinner together. "Take a chair."

He obliged and sat next to the window. Does $3.50 to $8.00 per dessert sound good to you?"

"Let's see." They hashed out the pricing for each dessert, crossing out prices and rewriting them. Finally, they decided that each dessert would range from $4.00 to $9.00 unless it was on special.

Elated, Caroline was overjoyed at what they'd come up with. "I hope we sell a ton on your fantastic desserts," joy bubbled in her laugh. "I'll make sure it's all transferred to the menu board before lunch."

"Thanks. I know Chloe will like what we worked out."

Caroline heard a tap at the front door. "I wonder who that could be? I hope it's not Tori."

"Yeah, me too." Ben followed her towards the front.

"I knew it, it is her." Caroline unlocked the door, "What's up? Why are you here?" She held the door for Tori to enter.

"Hey to you, too, Caroline." Tori turned and faced Ben. "I didn't expect to see you," and rolled her eyes.

Ben moved two steps back and he pursed his lips, "I was delivering desserts."

Caroline took charge. "What do you want?" And gave her a stern look. "Our last visit didn't end well."

"I'm glad you both are together. I don't want to cause more friction between the three of us." She stepped backward and stood by Ben. "It's amazing you two even know each other."

Ben's eyes sparkled. "It is isn't it?" He exhaled.

Before the two girls opened their mouths, Ben spoke, "Tori, now that you are here, I also need to get something off my chest."

Her head bent towards the floor, "Go ahead."

"I know you had no intentions of loving me, but can you explain your motives? I never got the looks you gave your fiancé, I knew when I saw the way you responded to him, he had your love."

"It's true, I love him. As for my motives?"

Caroline couldn't wait to hear her response and interrupted, "Yeah, I'd like to know as well."

Tori took a deep breath, "I thought I loved you once, Ben, but you're right, I never did. I live with my Uncle in London and several months ago, I started dating his head chef. Things didn't go well between us and we broke up. Well, he up and quit, leaving my uncle without a chef. As you can imagine, he's furious with me."

Ben rested his hands against his waist, "Wow."

"Yeah, he told me if I didn't get a replacement, he was going to kick me out and I can't afford to live in London on my own," she eyed the two of them. "That's when I thought of you. Will you forgive me?"

Ben pushed his hair back. "I'm glad you're telling the truth. I pray it will all work out for you," as he glanced at Caroline.

"Everyone desires forgiveness, Tori, I hope your uncle will forgive you."

Caroline turned towards Ben, "You are the nicest man I've ever met."

"What can I say?" and threw his hands up.

Tori touched his back, "I can't change your mind, can I?" She laughed.

Caroline knew she was serious, but hopefully Ben didn't.

"The answer is no, Tori. For one, I have a sick parent that I have to take care of, plus my brother just moved here and I will be looking after him and third, I love Camden and don't want to move," Ben smiled, "plus, I've got a gazillion desserts to make for Olli's every day."

Caroline and Tori laughed at the same time, "I thought I'd ask one last time," as she straightened her dress, "You never know. Listen, I'm on the way to the airport now. It's been nice seeing you both again.

Please pray my uncle won't kick me to the curb. Shoot, my stuff may be already on the sidewalk."

Caroline stepped up to her, "I will pray for you," and hugged her, "I'm sorry I got so mad." She paused as a smile surfaced on her face, "I'm glad we made up."

"Sorry for that, but you know how persistent I am." Tori grabbed ahold of Caroline one last time.

Together the three of them walked out of the restaurant and onto the sidewalk.

"I'll text you when I get back to London," Tori waved at a taxi to stop and got inside, waving as she rode away.

* * *

Boy was he glad the beautiful woman wouldn't be around to harass him any longer, "Bye, Tori," he waved.

Caroline and Ben stood on the sidewalk, glanced at each other, and shouted together, "GOOD RIDDANCE!" Laughter burst from them.

Ben stopped, "I wish I could stay, but I've got to get back to the bakery."

"I understand, will I see you later?"

Her features became more vibrant in the soft light when he followed her just inside the restaurant's front entrance. "Would you like to go out on an official date?" He was determined not to reveal his excitement when he saw her eyes brighten.

A slight gasp escaped her. "I'd like that."

"How about tomorrow night?" He tried to read her expression.

"That's wonderful, what do you want to do?"

"I'd like for you to go to church with me for our Wednesday Night Live. It's a potluck dinner with bible study afterwards. Tomorrow night we're having a guest speaker, Pastor Luke Anderson."

"Can you believe it? Pastor Luke is my pastor and I'd love to come." Caroline stepped back onto the sidewalk. "I waited on him when he came in to eat last Christmas and he invited me to church." She took a quick breath, "God knew I needed that, plus, so did Harry and Penny," She moved towards his Jeep, "It's been fantastic."

I know Pastor Luke and Corey through Chloe, my boss, Chloe and Corey used to be sister-in-law's.

"Really?" Caroline raised her brow. "Wow, small world."

"Yeah, Corey comes in the bakery sometimes. And... I'd love to visit your church with you." Ben pushed his sleeve away from his watch.

"How about next Wednesday?"

"As for tomorrow, can I bring Harry and Penny along?"

"I'd love for them to come," Ben turned to go. "I hate that I have to go, but..."

"I understand, I'll see you later," she brushed her hand against the sleeve of his hoodie.

He so wanted to hug her but refrained, "See you then. Call me if you need any more desserts."

"I will."

Ben jumped inside his Jeep and rummaged inside his pocket for his key. He drove a few blocks, stopped in the car park, and walked to the bakery. His immediate thoughts settled on Kandice. He'd hope she hadn't been too busy during his visit, "Kandice, I'm back," and ran into her at the shop's entry door to the kitchen. "Whoa!" Ben snickered.

She grabbed ahold of him not letting go. "Hey, I'm glad you're here."

She's not letting go. "Are you all right?"

Kandice pushed at him and cried, "I'm moving back to Colorado."

The shock hit him with full force, "What?"

"Yeah, I told Chloe."

"Is it because of me?" He had to know.

"No... yes... It seems like the last couple of days I've wanted us to be together, but I've seen how you've looked at Caroline and know I can never have that."

"Hey, wait a sec," as their eyes met, he felt a shock run through him, "Kandice, I don't know what to say." *She's so sweet, tell her.*

She folded her hands against her body. “Don’t be sad, I think my true love is waiting for me there.” Her voice broke off.

He was speechless. “When are you leaving?”

“Friday is my last day.”

His blue-spoked eyes widened with astonishment. “That soon?” He softened. “Kandice, when you find that special someone, he will be the most blessed man ever.” He lifted his eyes to see her better.

“Awe, thanks. But Ben, I think I have found him.”

He couldn’t believe what he was hearing “Wow, I’m so happy for you. Kandice... I’ll miss you. You’ve been my best-friend.”

“You’ve been mine, too.” She stood next to him. “My mom called and offered me a job making more than I make here.”

He was stunned by her news. “Gosh, this is hard to believe.”

“Yeah, it’s hard to believe, I know. I have always loved Denver and it will be so good to get back there. My mom’s bakery has grown over the last few years. Can you believe it? My mom asked me to manage the place and I’m so excited.”

Floored by her statements, he moved over to his work bench and sat on his stool. “I’m really happy for you. Kandice, I want you to know that your friendship means the world to me.” He stood and pulled her into an embrace and didn’t let go until he heard the bell above the door ring, “Someone’s here.”

“I’ll go,” Kandice ran towards the door, “Talk later.”

“I’ll be filling orders.” He wanted to call Chloe but would wait. Who would she get to replace Kandice? He glanced at the recipe beside him, then pulled a bowl from under his counter and upon filling it with three cups of flour, a stick of butter and four eggs, he started the mixer. After it mixed for several minutes, he poured in a cup of milk and a teaspoon of vanilla, and put in a cup of chocolate chips, nuts, and caramel chunks. “This looks so good.”

Kandice appeared, “There wasn’t anyone out there.”

Ben tilted his brow, looking at her with uncertainty, “I guess they changed their mind,” and finished his cookie mixture, putting in the remaining ingredients as he replayed Kandice's words that she would be leaving Camden Bakery.

"Ben!" Kandice yelled several minutes later, "Can you come up front and help me a second."

He dropped what he was doing and went to her aid. When he got there, ice cream had splattered all over her shirt and the two customers standing nearby were laughing. "I see our crazy machine messed up again, I'm sorry."

"Can you fix the darn thing, while I go clean up?" and stepped out of his way.

He began pulling it apart and fiddled with a few parts and then put it back together. Afterwards, he grabbed the half full large metal cup and whipped the shake as the customers watched. Their order was written on an order pad beside him. He added a little more ice cream, coffee, and milk and spun the mixture.

"Yay, you got it going again," Kandice cheered.

"Thank the good Lord," and placed the two shakes on the counter. "Here you are, please have a seat and I'll bring over your pastries."

"Thanks," the customers handled the two large glasses and headed over to a table.

Not wasting a moment, Ben hurried to the pastry display, grabbed a pair of gloves and saw that Kandice's smile had faded, "What?"

"I don't know why that old thing only messes up when I make a milkshake."

"It doesn't like you," Ben laughed and eyed the clean clothes she had on. "You spruced up fast."

"Yeah, I had clean clothes in the back."

He grabbed two apple fritters and three lemon squares and walked over to the customer's table. Was there a little tension in Kandice's voice? Should he ease up on her a little? When he returned, he stopped in front of her, "Listen, I'll finish up, you can start the two cake orders we need by 12:00 o'clock."

"Thanks," he saw tears at the corner of her eyes.

The nice couple left a few minutes later as Ben and Kandice stood by and watched, then headed to the back of the shop. "I still can't believe you're leaving."

"Yep. It happened so fast... I'm leaving and that's it," she scrunched her hair.

He would miss her crazy self. "I'll miss you," he smiled and as the rest of the afternoon slipped by, his thoughts were captured by a girl named Caroline.

16

At 4:00 p.m., Caroline pulled her cell phone from her hip pocket and dialed Camden Bakery, "Hello, may I speak with Ben please?"

"Sure, can you hold on a moment," replied a female voice.

Approximately one minute passed before he answered, "Hello, this is Ben, may I help you?"

Her stomached ached when she heard his voice. "This is Caroline, would it be possible to get another apple pie and a plain cheesecake before 6:00 p.m. today?"

"Sure, but you don't sound like yourself, is something wrong?" Ben questioned with a bizarre yelp at the end. "My bad I just choked."

She didn't want to respond, "Oh, before I forget, I can't have dinner with you tomorrow night."

He cleared his throat, "Are you mad?" He sighed with heavy breathing.

Her jaw clinched, "I don't..."

He interrupted, "Did I do something? What happened?"

She just wanted to hang up, "Uh, let's not talk about it now."

Ben took a quick snuffle, "I'm sorry, whatever it is."

"I'm going now, we'll talk later," she hung up and made a mad dash to the front of the restaurant where Tarsha was standing.

"Something's wrong, you're not acting right."

"Oh, it's nothing."

Tarsha got in her face "Spill it."

"Ben was with another woman."

"What?"

"I can't talk about it now."

* * *

What in the world? Heart palpitations fluttered as confusion mounted against his chest. *When he'd last seen her, everything was great.* He rattled his brain in thought as he rubbed his forehead at what he could have done. *The ring of the doorbell.* It must have been Caroline who left the bakery. It had to have been her and she saw him hugging Kandice. *It's all a misunderstanding.* And, why had she shown up at the bakery? She needed more desserts.

He gazed at the clock for the next 30 minutes wishing the time would zoom past five and was growing tired from the worry. Suddenly, he remembered the pie and cake Caroline needed and ran up front to check. One of each were in the display case. As the next ten minutes struggled to pass, he managed to pull a dozen mini tart pies from the oven and set them on the cooling rack, then dashed over to the counter beside the milkshake machine and grabbed an appropriate size box for each. He glanced at Kandice who was standing close by, waited a second, then blurted, "I hope you don't need that cheesecake and apple pie because I was going to deliver them to Olli's.

"No, I don't need them," Kandice squeezed her brown eyes tight, "You seem agitated."

"I am." His shoulders lifted, and he ran his hand through his hair as a flicker of apprehension roused his nerves. *I need to explain my actions.*

"You want to talk about it?" Kandice continued sorting recipes as she sat behind the counter.

"I wish, but I have a million things to do before we close," Ben responded.

He couldn't help his constant glancing at his watch. *Forget this* and rushed to collect the appropriate cleaning supplies from the storage closet then set them inside the deep wash sink beside the back door.

First, he emptied the trash cans and swept the back. "Kandice, do you want to help me finish my chores?"

"Not really, but I will," she snickered. "I'll clean everything out front and wash the dishes."

"I'll mop while you do that. I put the cleaning stuff in the mop sink."

"You seem such in a hurry, what's up with you? Relax, bud."

"I need to talk to Caroline." *Should I have told her that?*

Kandice stacked the recipe cards together, stuffed them inside the file and followed Ben to the other side of the shop. "I'll do your chores, if you want to go," she tugged at his arm, "You like her, don't you?"

What should he say, tell her the truth? *Okay, I will tell her what's up.* "Yes, I like her, and she's upset with me for some unknown reason." He paced the back of the shop, "I have an inkling why she's upset." He crossed over in front of Kandice and filled his cup full of water. "I was a little afraid to be honest, but you deserve the truth." He sat on a stool beside her and got right back up, "Are you upset with me that I like her?"

"You know a few days ago I would have said yes, I would have been... but," she shook her head, "Never mind."

"Tell me," he suggested.

"I'm all right with you dating Caroline, I really am." She giggled, "Let me tell you something. Do you remember I had a boyfriend named Chip, from Denver?"

The shock of her announcement brought relief. "Yeah, you use to talk about him a lot and, as I recall, you were engaged, weren't you?"

She brushed her hair back. "Yes, we were. When he went into the military, he broke it off and that devastated me to no end."

"How awful." He drew near to her, "Did he give you a reason for breaking up?"

"I think Chip was afraid he'd never come home." A tear brushed her cheek and she wiped it away.

"Why the tears?" He got the glass cleaner and started spraying the front door.

"I can't help but cry from what I heard last night. Chip told me he never stopped loving me."

"That's wonderful, Kandice, so tell me, is he still in the military?"

"No, he just got an honorable discharge a little over a month ago."

His smile broadened in approval, "Wow, that's awesome, I know that must make you happy."

"It does and listen to this, I can hardly believe it; we're going to dinner this Sunday night," an appealing grin appeared giving her features a glow.

Curiosity got the best of him as he saw the change in her eyes. "This Sunday?"

"Yeah, I'm driving home Friday after work." After getting the other cleaning supplies out of the sink, she went to spray the windows and started wiping. "Oh Ben, I've got to tell you," she turned her head to make sure he was paying close attention, "when I heard his voice on the phone, all the precious feelings I had for him flooded my heart."

She sought his opinion and from the look she gave him, his smile wasn't enough to satisfy the excitement in her voice. "It's hard to explain, I know, but anyway, I'm really excited to see and be with him." She exhaled, "And, I don't think I stopped loving him."

"That is wonderful," he agreed.

"I thought I did and, I tried to deny feelings for him a really long time, but now I don't have, too." Her huge smile brightened even more.

"I'm so glad you're happy. What's he doing now? I mean, is he working?"

"Yeah, he took over managing his father's hardware store, and guess what?" She glanced for more approval, "His store is right beside my mom's bakery." She laced her apron strings with her fingers and let out a bit of a sigh, "My busy body mother told Chip I was coming home, and he called me, but... I'm glad he did."

Ben was so relieved and wanted to grab her into a friendly hug, but refrained since the last time he did, it got him in trouble, at least he thought it got him in trouble with Caroline.

Kandice finished with the cleaner and then wiped down the tables. "I'll be finished in no time, go ahead and go."

"No, I'll finish mopping first." He busied himself, pushed and pulled the heavy-duty mop across every inch of the shop's floor, then returned the bucket to the supply closet, skedaddled and retrieved Caroline's desserts.

The front door opened and in walked his brother, "Hey," Ben approached him. "So, little brother, what brings you in to town?" He inquired as he finished boxing the desserts and tying the ribbons around each box.

Bradley rounded the corner, "I wanted to tell you how much I like it here."

Intense astonishment touched Ben's tanned face, "You met a girl, didn't you?"

"How could you tell?" Bradley smiled.

"You should see your face, what's her name?" Ben patted his brother's shoulder.

A smile tipped the corners of Bradley's mouth, "Kaitlyn."

"Is she in tenth grade, too?" Ben questioned.

"Yes, we have three classes together and guess what? She loves this bakery, it's her favorite place to eat." Bradley eased closer and threw back his head and let out a yelp, "I'm glad I met her and Ben, I think love is in the air." He stopped next to the display case when the pastries caught his eye, "Can I get her some donuts?" and touched the glass with his fingers.

"Don't touch the glass, we just cleaned it."

"Oh, my bad," and started wiping the area with his hand.

His brother's happiness was catching. "You're too funny, I'll clean it. Sure, you can pick out a few for her and I'll box them up." Bradley dashed behind the display and opened the case.

"Wait..." Ben hurried over, "You've got to pick them up with a piece of parchment paper, right there above your head."

"I see them," and grabbed one then collected a half dozen of assorted donuts while Ben held a box. The two stood silent for a moment as Ben folded the lid on top of the box, "I keep meaning to ask you how dad's truck's running; do you need gas money?"

"Actually, Mom gave me money this morning for gas and the truck is doing great." Bradley took the box from Ben.

"That's wonderful."

Bradley slowly followed after Ben, "You want to take mom, Kaitlyn and me to Olli's tonight? I'd love for you to meet her again, she's so pretty and guess what else?"

"Again, you sound like I know her or something."

"You do know her, and she knows your boss, Chloe."

"She does?" Ben thought of a girl named Kaitlyn from church, "I remember Kaitlyn now."

"Yeah, she's Miss Chloe's neighbor."

There wasn't much time to stand around, "Let me finish here and when I get home, we can decide about dinner." Now, all he had on his mind was seeing Caroline and figuring out why she was mad.

"Sure, sounds good." Bradley moseyed towards the door.

"Have you seen Mom today?"

"You wouldn't believe it if you saw it."

Ben felt his pulse start to rise as his mind jumped to her falling or worse. "What happened?"

"Nothing, she was moving around the kitchen cleaning up and stuff, it was unbelievable. I asked her if she should do that sort of stuff and she told me she was tired of sitting in her wheelchair."

"You're kidding, right?"

"I promise I'm not. She had a walker in front of her and acting like her leg wasn't bothering her at all."

"Really?"

"It shocked me."

Ben's heart sang with delight. "That's fantastic. You've brought nothing but good news in here. Thanks for coming in and now, I can't wait to see mom and get a firsthand look myself." He trailed his brother's footsteps, "Get out of here, I need to finish cleaning up."

"See ya, bro." Bradley skedaddled.

Quickly, he finished a few things then hurried to the edge of the kitchen, "Kandice, I'm leaving, I'll see you in the morning."

His best friend was leaving town, the girl of his dreams was furious with him, his mother was walking, and his brother happier than he could have ever imagined. *Thank God for girls! I think.*

Ben made a mad dash to his Jeep, slipped inside, buckled his seatbelt and spun the key. When he saw Caroline, would he be able to explain himself?

A few blocks down, he searched for a place to park. *Yes!* A space was available right in front of Olli's. He parallel parked, grabbed the two boxes and made his way inside. Searching, he scanned the front of the restaurant but didn't see her. The nice lady who'd waited on him several times before was standing at the hostess stand. He rushed to her, "Hey, is Caroline here?"

"You're Ben, aren't you?"

"Yes," he shifted his footing.

"She instructed me to get the desserts from you and let you know she won't be returning this evening."

A warning voice whispered in his head. *You must find her.* "Okay, thanks. I'll see her in the morning when I come to get the dessert inventory."

"Oh," the lady pulled on the sleeve of his jacket, "Your desserts have been a huge hit with the customers today. We need everything reordered for tomorrow."

"That's fantastic. I'll deliver them first thing in the morning."

"Thank you."

He stirred his uneasiness, *why not ask her where she went?* "You wouldn't by chance know where Miss Montgomery might have gone, would you?"

The lady shifted her eyes, "I suppose I'm not at liberty to say, but she went to her children's school for a play that Harry's in."

"Do they go to the elementary school on Elm Street?"

"Is that the one across from Bell's Drugs?" She queried.

"Yes, that's the one."

She got close to Ben, "I know this is none of my business, but I hope you get things worked out, Caroline was upset when she left a little while ago."

He leaned in, "It's all a big misunderstanding, I can assure you."

"You'd better hurry, the play starts at six."

Ben reached and hugged the gray headed woman, "I can't thank you enough."

"Awe, I want to see Caroline happy and I haven't seen that in a long, long time."

"You don't know how much I appreciate you for this information."

"Awe, get out of here."

"Thank you." Ben hurried back to his Jeep, cranked it and waited for the traffic to clear before he pulled away from the curb. After a few minutes and several left-hand turns, the school came into view. Tons of cars were everywhere. He turned into the school, followed several cars to the back, and eased his SUV to a halt in a field beside a bus loop. He locked the doors, then proceeded to follow a few folks inside the double doors at the building. It was a good thing that he wasn't the only late arrival for the play, because he probably wouldn't have been able to locate where the play was being performed.

A row of children lined the hallway with colorful costumes and to his left were others handing out programs. He took one from a cute boy dressed like a beaver, then followed the crowd into the cafetorium type multipurpose room where a stage was on one end and tables on the other and several hundred chairs were set up in the middle. He stood off to the side and searched for Caroline.

A tug against his pant leg startled him, "Hey, I know you," sounded a sweet voice.

Ben turned and saw Penny, "Hey, how are you?" He held out his hand to high-five hers.

She jumped and hit his hand and grabbed ahold of his waist. "Did you come to watch Harry's play?" She sprang up towards him.

With quickness, he caught her in his arms. "Yes, where's your mommy?"

"She's sitting right there." Penny pointed towards the stage.

Penny wiggled from his arms and grabbed his hand, "C'mon, I'll show you."

She pushed her way through the conglomeration of people and led the way. "Mommy, look who came to see Harry's play."

Caroline's eyes fluttered, "Oh my goodness, what are you doing here?"

He grew uncomfortable as dismay grew across her face, "I was hoping I could speak with you for a moment."

He wished she would smile or something. "I need to explain."

"Did Tarsha tell you we need the same desserts for tomorrow?" She looked away hastily, then shifted in her seat.

Not wanting to cause a scene, Ben leaned next to her ear, "Yes, she did. Can I please talk with you?"

Promptness took him by surprise as she stood and grabbed his hand. "Stay put Penny; I'll be right back." She led him into the hallway and stared. "You can't change what I saw."

His hands tightened against his folded arms, "Can I ask what you think you saw?"

"You and Kandice were arm in arm."

He shot her a twisted smile, "So, it was you that came to the bakery this afternoon?" He gazed into her eyes. "We heard the doorbell but when Kandice went up front, there wasn't anyone there and when I spoke to you later, I put two and two together. Why didn't you say something?"

"I was in pure shock and speechless. I came by to drop off your sunglasses you left at the restaurant." She reached into her purse and pulled them out, "Here you go," and shoved them at him.

His expression stilled and grew serious, "I'll get right to the point. What you saw between me and Kandice was me wishing her farewell."

Shock of this news hit her full force. "What is that supposed to mean?"

"Kandice is moving back to Denver. Caroline, we've been best friends for four plus years, and I was only hugging her to wish her the best."

Her green eyes twinkled and were full of life as her interested stare flattered him. "She's going to work in her mom's bakery."

"But I can't help wondering why you were holding her so tight. You looked like you enjoyed that embrace," She exhaled.

An amused gaze left his eyes, "We're just friends and like I told you, she's been my best bud since I moved here." He didn't want to complicate matters. "I love her like a sister."

"Oh?" She ran her hand down her scarf and tipped her watch. "We should go inside; the play is about to start."

Their eyes met and he spotted a gleam of curiosity in her eye. *She likes me.* His eyes brightened with pleasure.

He followed her to where Penny was sitting and grabbed a seat.

* * *

Why did Caroline care so much? She liked Ben plain and simple. She was already moving way to fast to have more than a friendship with this man. Before she would commit to a relationship with him, she would have to learn what makes him Ben and be able to trust him. She'd had too many troubled days with Eli to let down her guard. Remembering, the pain surrounded her, and she allowed a tear to fall. Both physical and mental stress was way too recent in her past and she would not go through that again, not now, not ever.

With the play starting soon, she turned and watched him. Penny was holding his hand; she's already fallen for him. *Was she falling too!* Was he right for her and her two children? Who was this man sitting beside her daughter? Could he be the daddy they were missing? As she continued to watch them, the curtain opened, and the crowd clapped. A beaver walked onto the stage, thanked everyone for coming and announced the play would start in less than two minutes.

Ben leaned in her direction a few minutes later after Harry spoke several adopted lion roaring lines, "Harry is doing so good," and smiled.

Caroline agreed, "I'm so proud of him."

Harry had the part of the lion and was doing everything he'd practiced just right. She bubbled over with relief that broke from her lips. Everyone, including her, stood and clapped for several minutes at the end.

"The play was great, Mommy," Penny reached for her and hugged her.

"Yes, it was. I'm so proud of Harry, let's go find him."

Caroline noticed Ben looking at her enigmatically, "Thanks for coming to Harry's program."

A demure smile appeared across his lips and she knew he was growing uncomfortable by the second, "Why don't we talk in the morning."

"I'll see you a little before eight."

* * *

A cold sweat poured from his body when he stepped outside. Why was he feeling the way he was? There wasn't an explanation. Sweat continued to form against his forehead even though a cold wind hit his face. He was glad to be out in the cold. Was it the warm school that got his temperature rising or Caroline? Either way, he cooled off by the time he reached his Jeep. He pondered his bad luck with women as he slipped inside his vehicle. He hadn't had success with any of them, ever, and he'd probably messed up any hopeful relationship he had started with Caroline, *Don' think like that.* Chloe, he was sure, would lend much-needed advice.

At the first stop light, he fingered Chloe's number on his phone and waited for her to answer. "Hey, how are you and the babies?"

"We're doing great, I guess you heard the news about Kandice."

"I can't believe it. What are we going to do?"

"I contacted a temporary agency today. They are sending a temp on Monday, plus I'm getting Mrs. Whitehurst to help you out front for a couple of weeks. By then I should be able to come back."

Her plan amazed him. "Are you sure you'll be ready to come back to work?"

"I'm working on a lot of things. My aunt Sharon is moving here to help me. She's going to rent a house near the bakery."

Always the planner that Chloe, "You've already got everything worked out. I was thinking I'd need to get things in gear, but I should have known you would've had it all worked out."

"How's your mother and brother doing?"

He almost couldn't wait to tell her the good news about his mother he'd heard from Bradley. "My mom is walking."

"Already?"

"Bradley came in the bakery this afternoon and told me. I can't wait to see her." Pensively, he looked out into the darkness. "One of the reasons I called is to get some advice."

"What's wrong?"

Questions hammered him, "I met someone."

"Ben, that's wonderful."

A little voice in his head screamed for him to ask for help. "I know you don't know much about my dating and messing up with girls my entire life, but, Chloe, I don't want to mess this one up."

"So, what's her name?"

His palms started to sweat thinking of her name. "Caroline."

"That's nice."

"I know. You got any advice on how to not mess things up?"

"Just be yourself and be confident. Ben, you're one of the most loving people I've ever met."

"Thanks."

"Is that why you've not dated since you've been in Camden?"

"Yeah, kind of, I don't really know, I always screw things up with girls. Since I was 12 it's always turned out bad. I really like Caroline, more than anyone in my past and guess what, she's already mad at me for hugging Kandice."

"What?"

He was almost home. When he got near his house, he waited for a car to pass before he turned into his driveway. *There goes Caroline.* He waved but knew she didn't see him.

"Caroline, the girl I like, moved into Mrs. Simpson's house across the street."

Chloe laughed, "So, she won't be too far away."

He took a deep breath. "If I don't do things just right... it won't matter where she lives."

"Don't worry, just take it slow and it should work out."

"I'll try, I promise." He hated how volatile he was and would try to overcome his dating woes.

17

The night sky radiated twinkling stars above as Ben parked in his driveway, eyeing the familiar landscape up and down the quaint street. As he sat there, he released his seatbelt, rolled down his window and breathed in the freezing crisp January air to clear his thoughts of the conversation between him and Caroline back at the elementary school. He spotted the beautiful woman, along with her two amazing kids as they exited their car and scurried inside their house. A smile tugged at his lips as he joggled his head picturing her beauty that had a lasting memory. Instead of letting it rest what transpired between him, Kandice and Caroline, he went around and around and over and over imagining what she possibly saw at the bakery. *The image to Caroline looked like he adored Kandice, or worse, that he loved her.* Boy how looks can be deceiving.

The front door opened, and Bradley stepped out.

"You're late," he tapped his watch.

Ben grimaced and jumped from his Jeep, "Yeah, I'm sorry, I had somewhere I had to go." *I forgot.* He stole a glance at his brother frowning, "Is it too late to go to Olli's?"

"Heck no, we're starving," Bradley rubbed his stomach.

Ben peered at his own watch. Five minutes past seven. He followed through the door to find his mom and Bradley's girlfriend sitting on the couch. And his brow lifted. *This girl is beautiful.* Her long flowing blond curls hung against her shoulders and from where he was standing, was a perfect match for his lanky brother who measured six foot four or five. "Hey, you must be Kaitlyn," Ben reached out his hand. When he got closer, "I've seen you at church."

Kaitlyn leaped to her feet. *Wow!* Kaitlyn stood several inches taller than him. She grabbed ahold of his hand, "I've seen you, too, and it's nice to formally meet you."

Her warm hand touched his freezing fingers and genuinely smiled at him.

"Same here," Ben uttered, "Sorry about my cold hand." He rubbed his fingers together after their handshake.

"Oh, it's okay," She tucked her head.

"Hey." Bradley interrupted and stepped in between them. "She's everything, plus some, huh, Ben?"

A chuckle escaped Ben, "She sure is." He turned to his mother and hugged her. "Mom, I hear you're walking," his mouth curved into an unconscious grin.

"I just couldn't stay in that wheelchair any longer." With a push off the couch, she stood. "Let me show you." Bit by bit, she took short steps until she reached the other side of the room. She spun around and waved her arms. "Can you believe it? And… my leg doesn't hurt all that bad."

Together, everyone stood and cheered. "Mom, you're amazing," Ben clapped his hands, then reached and pulled her into an embrace. "This is remarkable, Mom."

"Thank you." Tears formed against the corner of Emily's eyes, "You know, I don't think I've stopped to thank you for helping us, Ben." She brushed the tears that hit her cheeks and then touched his face, "I'm glad we're here. I didn't know if it would work out, but, you know, it's been easy, thanks to you."

"Awe, Mom, I'm glad you and Bradley are here." The tenderness in her expression amazed him. "This is your home now." *I can't believe that just came out of my mouth.* To his amazement, everything was settling into place. "Bradley told me you guys were starving. Are you ready to go to Olli's?" He shrugged his shoulders.

"Yes," Emily agreed. "I can't wait to try Olli's Lasagna that everyone at therapy keeps talking about."

"Let's go," Bradley pulled on the door handle. He picked up Kaitlyn's hand and pulled her to the door.

"I'm coming," Kaitlyn punched Bradley in the arm.

"Hey, you hit me."

Kaitlyn snickered. "It was a love pat."

Both Ben and Bradley helped Emily along the icy walk path, hanging on to her arms. "I need to sit in the front seat," she stated.

"By all means do sit in the front." Ben rounded the front of the SUV and poked his head inside, "I'll be right back, I'm going to get mom's walker, she may need it." He took off through the slushy snow packed yard and grabbed it.

"Everybody ready?" He buckled his seatbelt and proceeded to back out of the drive. Seconds later, he rounded the corner to the main road as Caroline crossed his mind for the umpteenth time. He downright liked her and wanted to tell her, but as he got closer to Olli's, the same old single man doubts crushed him. *She won't like me. She'll toss me to the wind even before we have time for a real date.* The silence in the Jeep was mind boggling as he drove through the busy streets along the edge of Camden's downtown district. "It's so quiet in here."

"I guess we're too hungry to talk," Emily chuckled as she readjusted her seating.

"Camden's a really cool place. I like it here," Bradley broke the ice.

"I really appreciate you sharing that, Bradley," Ben looked in the rearview mirror at Kaitlyn, "Did you grow up in Camden?"

"Yep, lived here my whole life." She took a quick breath, "My dad's a fisherman and my mom's a nurse at Camden Hospital.

Ben loved her bright facial expression. "I know your boss, Miss Chloe."

"Yeah, that's what Bradley was telling me."

She shifted her body towards the center console to get a little closer to Ben and Emily, "I'm so excited about her twins. Do you know if she's named them yet?"

Ben gripped the stirring wheel as he slowed the vehicle around the steep curve. "Yeah, she named them Morgan and Mack."

"I love those names," Kaitlyn's greenish blue eyes were beaming.

Ben looked over at his mom. He was *astounded* by the progress she was making. "Did you check with your doctor about you walking so soon?"

"No," She turned and gazed out the window.

He couldn't stop his pondering, "Do you think you should?"

Her disgusted face jeered at him, "I'll tell them at therapy tomorrow," Emily folded her arms, "I'm doing good."

Ben shook his head, "I didn't mean for you to get mad; I was just a bit concerned."

"Don't baby me, you know I don't like that sort of thing." Emily let go of her arms and shifted her shoulders, "I'm also going to find out if I can go back to work. It's getting so boring just sitting around the house all day."

Despite his alarms, it was a thrill to see her accomplishments. "Gosh, Mom, do you think you're going about it too fast. It's only been, what, almost two weeks since the incident?"

"Yes, I know, but, regardless, I'm going to ask. I also need to help bring income into the house."

Ben halted the car at the first stop light in town. "I appreciate you wanting to get a job, but please don't push yourself. Listen to what your doctors tell you."

She huffed, "I will."

They arrived at Olli's a few minutes later and had to park in the back-parking lot. He knew Caroline wouldn't be there, but as soon as they entered, he scanned the eatery for her gorgeous face. Nowhere could he see her, so he turned his attention to his family who'd walked ahead and were standing at the hostess stand.

"Good evening folks. A table for four?" Tarsha solicited, who he'd spoken with a little earlier that day and waved in his direction, "It's so nice to see you again. I didn't think I'd see you tonight, though."

"My family was starving, so here we are." He laughed as he threw his hands in an upward motion, "No one can stay away from Olli's too long."

She checked the seating chart on the hostess stand. "Would you like to sit by the bay this evening? I have an available table."

"That would be great, thank you," Ben nodded in a thankful gesture and allowed her to pass in front of him. Tarsha led them to the rear of the restaurant. The picturesque view of boats along the docks in the moonlit evening, was beautiful. Ben got so close to Tarsha, they rubbed shoulders and in a small voice, he asked, "Is the boss lady here tonight?"

Tarsha cupped her hand around her mouth. "No, she's at home this evening. Did you get your problem worked out?"

"Not exactly."

"Keep at it, she's worth it, I promise." She winked at him.

He thanked God he'd received encouragement from someone close to Caroline. After being seated, they ordered their entrees, then discussed different topics. He imagined their stomachs were growling like his as the smell of grilled meat filtered into their noses. In less than five minutes salads and bread sticks, along with their beverages were put in front of them. Ben looked at this mom, then around the table, "Would you like for me to ask the blessing?"

Emily gave him a thumbs up signal, "Thank you."

Ben bowed his head and blessed the food. He felt eyes glued to him and looked up to see Kaitlyn staring at him. "Are you okay?" He asked.

"Yes. Thanks for that sweet prayer. I appreciate you wanting to pray before our meal. You don't see that much anymore."

Ben smiled. "I'm thankful."

As soon as he was about to speak, their entrees appeared. "That was quick."

Kaitlyn laughed, "It's because you prayed."

They all broke into laughter and it felt good.

"You're right," Ben cackled along with the rest.

As usual their dinner was fantastic, yet his mind wouldn't clear of Caroline.

* * *

Little feet echoed throughout the house, "Did you get ready for bed?" Caroline asked Penny and Harry.

A sudden stop of feet, "Yes, Mommy."

"Where are you two?" She stepped out of her bedroom and found them crouched in the hall. Without hesitation, Penny slipped something behind her back. "What are you two up, too?"

Harry sat still looking at a picture and with a sudden move, he proceeded to hide the picture behind his back. "We want to get this picture."

Caroline squinted. "What kind of picture is it?"

Harry, instead of hiding it, lifted it up into the air and put it in her hand, "It's a puppy doggy."

Caroline studied the photo of a Labrador puppy, "Awe, he's so cute."

"That's the dog we want."

Caroline touched her finger to the picture. "Yeah, that's right, we agreed to get a dog, didn't we?"

Penny pulled out another picture from behind her back, "Look at this one."

Caroline took the slick paper from her, "It's the same dog."

"Where did you get these?" Her curiosity started to rise.

"We got them from the library."

Caroline bent to the floor and sat beside them, "Listen, I need to ask you a question."

Four eyes intently stared at her. "Did you tear these pictures out of a magazine?"

In a low voice, Harry answered, "Yes, Ma'am."

Caroline's lips straightened in a flat line, "Do you know that you can get in trouble for this?"

"But, Mommy," Penny screeched. "The teacher gave us the magazine. We didn't tear them out until we got to the day care this afternoon.

She took a deep breath. "Gosh, I'm so glad."

"Can we have one, please, Mommy?" Harry blurted.

"I'll start looking tomorrow"

"Where do you get a puppy?" Penny questioned.

"Different places. I'll look online first and if I can't find one there, then I'll pick up a newspaper."

"Can we help you look on your laptop?" Harry asked.

She looked at Harry, then at Penny, "Right now?"

"Please, please," Penny got off the floor and started dancing in a circle. "We're going to get a puppy," she shouted.

Caroline looked at the clock in the kitchen, "I guess we can look for a few minutes." Penny and Harry followed her to her room and jumped on her bed. Caroline unplugged the power cord from her laptop and climbed into bed. "Let's see what we can find."

Together, the three of them searched the internet for puppies for sale in the Camden area. "Here's one," Caroline enlarged the picture to get a better view.

"Awe, he's so cute," Harry announced.

The blond Labrador stared back at them. She picked up her phone and dialed the number listed under the ad. "Hello, do you still have the puppy for sale?"

"Yes, we do," the man responded.

A quick breath, "When can I come and look at him?"

"Any time after three most afternoons."

"How's tomorrow sound?" Caroline asked, "I'd like to bring my children along if that's okay?"

"That will be fine."

"Okay, we'll see you tomorrow. Can you give me your address?"

The man repeated his address for Caroline to write it down and she affirmed that she would give him a call when they were on their way.

After she disconnected the call, she looked at the two of them, "Okay, if we get a puppy tomorrow, you have to help take care of him and now it's time for you to get ready for bed. Run and brush your teeth and wash your faces."

"Yes, Mommy," Harry answered for them both.

A dog? She loved puppies and was excited about them getting one. She went to check on Harry and Penny and found them in the bathroom. Toothpaste was all over the counter. "What happened?" She picked up a washcloth and started cleaning the smears.

"Harry squeezed the toothpaste too much."

"Oh, my goodness, you two get in bed and I'll clean this mess up." Caroline wet the cloth and proceeded to wipe the counter. *At least it smells good in here.*

A minute or so later, she went to Harry's room and tucked him into bed and then found Penny inside her closet. "What are you doing?"

"I need to find the perfect outfit for doggy shopping tomorrow."

Caroline smiled, "Your grey t-shirt with the dog on it will be good."

"Yes, I like that, can you help me find it?"

"Sure, honey," They started searching for the shirt and several minutes later, Caroline put her hand on it, "Here it is," and put the shirt beside Penny's bed. "You can wear these blue jeans."

"I can't wait to get the puppy."

"Me, too."

After night kisses and their prayers, Caroline went to the den to relax and turned on the TV to watch the news. She pulled a blanket over her legs and pondered what had transpired between her and Ben at the school. She wondered if she could trust him after seeing what she'd seen between him and Kandice. Was the explanation he gave her good enough? His handsome face entered her thoughts as she gazed at the TV, and the longer she sat there, the more she tried to convince herself to like him. *But... his smile* as she closed her eyes. What was she doing and shook her head, stop this? He may be like Eli. She'd have to find out.

Her cell phone rang. "Hello."

"Hey, it's Ben."

Caroline scrunched her hair. "I was just thinking about you." She fell against the couch.

"I've been thinking about you, too. Would you like me to bring you a cup of coffee? I just got in from having dinner at Olli's with my family and was thinking about making a pot."

"Gosh, Ben, the kids are in bed and I'm tired, so I don't think, not tonight."

What could he say to change her mind? "I could bring the coffee to you and we could sit on your porch, how does that sound?"

"Cold."

A rumble of laughter escaped him, "I tried."

"Why don't we talk in the morning when you bring the desserts."

Not wanting to push the issue or sound disappointed, he uttered, "Okay, I'll see you around eight."

He tapped his phone with his finger. *She was thinking of me.* He felt a huge smile instinctively surface as a great mound of confidence rose within him. Come up with a plan of action and don't mess this up. He slipped from his room to check on his mother before going to bed. "Mom, you accomplished a lot today and I'm super proud of you."

"Thank you. I can't wait to go to therapy tomorrow and tell them what I did."

"I hope you hear good news." He stepped to the sink, got a glass off the shelf and filled it with water. "Is Bradley taking you?"

"Yes."

"That's good. I think I'm going to bed, I'm exhausted. Let me know how your therapy goes."

As he drifted off to sleep, his mind filled with thoughts of Caroline. He yawned a couple of times, turned over and fell asleep."

18

The image of Ben swirled across her thoughts as she tugged the comforter closer to her chest. *It's useless.* A look around her small master bedroom, she twisted and gazed at the clock on her nightstand. 9:24 p.m. *I can't sleep.* She grabbed her phone and puffed out her cheeks. *Should she call him?* As thoughts of him continuously churned through her mind, a sudden change to him hugging Kandice flew to the forefront of her thoughts for the umpteenth time that day. *Stop thinking about that.* Was he telling the truth and didn't have any feelings for Kandice? Would she be able to believe him, ever? What difference did it make? She had zero time for a relationship with him or anyone. As she contemplated whether to call him, his handsome face became vivid in her mind again. Everything about him she liked. The temptation was too much for her to take and pushed the talk button. "Ben, hey, it's Caroline."

"Well, hello there, I wasn't expecting you to call."

"Do you still want to come over?" Caroline squeezed her eyes shut waiting for his reply.

"I'd love to. It will take about ten minutes to make us a cappuccino."

"Okay, sounds good." She tossed the nagging notions of him hugging Kandice aside. *Trust him*! Not wasting time, she hopped out of bed, dashed to her closet, threw off her nightgown and slung it onto her old blue leather chair she'd had ever since she was a little girl. With her undergarments under her arm, she grabbed a sweatshirt and a pair of jeans, hurried and snapped her bra into place, then tugged at her tight jeans. Lastly, she pulled on the loose-fitting sweatshirt with South Carolina Gamecocks inscribed on it.

A few minutes later, while standing at her kitchen sink, a text message buzzed on her phone, 'On the way.' *He will be here in less than a minute.* She ran her hands through her hair, dashed to the hall closet and gathered two woolen blankets. Before he could ring the door-bell and wake Harry and Penny, she slipped outside and perched on the white bench she'd just purchased the evening before and as she waited, a strong wind blew right through her and sent chills up her arms. *It's freezing.*

The streetlights shone the silhouette of a man crossing the street with two gigantic mugs of hot steaming coffee. He nodded, "Good evening."

A growing, now annoying, itch on her middle of her back overwhelmingly bothered her. She squirmed to try and locate the spot. "This is bit weird, but would you mind scratching my back?"

The shadowy beard across his face was so handsome and his half smile made her heart skip a beat. "Where?" He put the mugs on the small table beside the bench and proceeded to scratch her back up and down, and sideways.

"You found it, thank you. Wow, you got over here quick."

"My espresso machine is fast." He pulled on her sleeve. "That's a nice sweatshirt, are you a Gamecock fan?"

"No, not really." She ran her palm down the front of her shirt. "I got it from their football coach when their team came into Olli's one night. They were in town playing Maine Maritime Academy."

"Wow! Was it the old ball coach who gave it to you?" Ben started to beam.

She laughed, "I'm not really sure, it was ages ago." With an abrupt turn, Caroline grabbed the blankets, "Please have a seat."

Their fingers touched when he gave her the mug. "This looks amazing." Whipped cream was stacked two inches above the steaming liquid.

"I hope you enjoy it."

Caroline picked up one of the blankets and put it in the chair beside the bench, then sniffed the sweet brew. "The scent is heavenly."

The frigid air blew his hair and he tugged at his coat. "It's super cold tonight."

As they sat in silence, Caroline's mind exploded with questions. Now that she wanted to date Ben, her curiosity to know more about him rocketed. She breathed in and let out an anxious gasp. "Would you be willing to answer a few questions?"

He busted out laughing. "Am I on trial?"

"No, silly. I just want to know you better."

Clamping his mouth tight, the only thing he could do was stare.

Seconds passed. "I just..."

"Go ahead, I'm an open book."

"Would you mind if I spoke with Kandice about your relationship with her?" She gazed at his face to examine his expression.

"You can talk with her."

His reaction was what she wished he'd say. "There's something else. You may prefer not to answer, but here goes... do you ever become aggressive?"

He glared, "What?"

"I mean... do you ever get so mad that you let rage take over your emotions?"

"Whoa, whoa, whoa!" Ben's mouth dropped open. "Are you asking if I'd hit you like your late husband did? Caroline, the answer is, no. I'd never hurt you."

Her head bobbled. *He's staring.* "I'm having trouble trusting anyone since Eli beat me." Reaching out, she stroked his arm and grinned, "You're shivering."

He bent his neck in a downward motion. "I'm cold." Without a second thought, he laid his mug on the small table and readjusted the cover he'd wrapped around himself. "There, that's better."

"Sit with me," Caroline patted the bench.

Obliging, he wiggled into the small space, covers and all. "How's your cappuccino?"

She sipped, "It's great," and a frown etched her forehead. "How did you know this is my favorite drink?"

"I took a chance."

"I love it."

Ben coughed several times as he slid to the edge of the stool.

An edginess inched up her spine. "Are you the type that likes to rush into things, like dating?"

"No, not really." He stopped midstream and fixed his eyes on her, then drew a deep breath, "I haven't done well with that, gee, Caroline, I haven't dated anyone in over nine years."

"That's bizarre, why?" She shivered and pulled the blanket over her shoulders.

"I suppose it's because every girl in my past did me wrong." He shook his noggin.

She shifted, "Tell me what happened?"

"Well for one, Tori cheated on me with my best friend and like every other girl I dated."

"As handsome as you are, I can't believe that anyone would do that to you."

"Uh, thanks." He leaned in, "You, Caroline Montgomery, are beautiful."

"I didn't say that to get a compliment." A smile crossed her lips. "But...I appreciate you telling me."

"I want to tell you every time I see you."

"That's sweet." Caroline's expression changed, "The right person hasn't come along yet."

"I guess you're right." He diverted his eyes and looked at her concrete floor. It's been unbelievable lately." He gripped her hand tight. "And amid all the fiasco... I met you." A twinkle of moonlight caught his eyes as he glanced at her.

The touch of his hand was suddenly almost unbearable in its tenderness. Something she'd not experienced before. "May I?" She leaned close to him.

"Yes, Ma'am," he reached and held her snugly against his chest.

Caroline touched his cheek with her lips. *He smells wonderful.* "You are so sweet."

"You're amazing." Ben pulled her into an embrace.

"I need to be going. If you wish to talk to Kandice, please come to the bakery tomorrow."

"What time does she come in?"

"I believe she's scheduled to be there at six."

"In the a.m.?"

"Yep."

* * *

Thank God she called me. Ben drifted toward the bottom step of her porch.

Caroline unwrapped her blanket. "What time do you go in every morning?"

"Anywhere from 2:30 a.m. to 3:00 a.m. On the norm, Chloe, my boss and I switch off opening, but since she's out with the babies, it's all on me."

"You love the bakery, don't you?" Caroline followed him to the edge of her yard.

"I get awful tired sometimes, but I love working for Chloe." He stopped at the road. "Catch you tomorrow." He dared not take the chance and give her a goodnight kiss and backed away, not taking his eyes off her, "Bye."

Something, he couldn't explain, glued them to the grass without moving.

Caroline smiled, "Go."

"See you later." He shifted his shoulders, "tomorrow." He took one step backward, moved slowly across her yard and it felt like he was floating. When he finally shifted his feet into the direction of his house a huge grin surfaced upon his face as a happy, giddy feeling invaded his chest. *Thank you, Jesus, for Caroline. Help us rescue each other.* With quick feet, he took off and raced the rest of the way to his porch and spun to take one last glimpse. She was standing at her cracked door and blew him a kiss. He reached into the air and caught it pulling it to his lips. He loved her and wanted more than anything to trust her, but would she be like all the rest? He lowered his head and prayed.

* * *

At 2 a.m. the sound of his alarm clock blared and with a stretch of his arms, he slung the covers away from himself then sat on the side of the bed. Immediately Caroline entered his thoughts. Had it been a dream that they met on her porch, it sure felt like it as the same giddy titillation soared through him when he entered the bathroom. It was for real.

After a long hot shower, he dressed and moseyed to brew a pot of coffee and found his mom was sitting at the table. "Hey, why are you up?"

"I couldn't sleep so I decided to start a pot of coffee for you, my dear." She stood and limped over to the cabinet and grabbed several cups. "Almost done."

"Thanks." He yanked a chair, sat and watched her move around with hardly any difficulty. "You're getting around fantastic, Mom."

"I am and I'm so glad, here you go," and placed a mug in front of him. "You can doctor it up yourself."

"Thanks. It feels like I'm back home."

"That's just it..." Emily raised her brow. "We don't have our home anymore."

"This is your home now, how many times do I have to tell you?"

"A billion because this is your house, but hey, I'll carry on the best way possible. You know it's not like me to depend on anyone."

Her expression was unreadable, except for the single tear that hit her cheek. "Mom, it will all work out, please give it time."

"I'll try." Her body shifted as she cradled the table for support.

"I've got to go. Love you, Mom." He leaned over and kissed her forehead. "Have a great day and please don't stress over it."

Reaching his Wrangler, he pulled on the door handle, jumped in and cranked it, backed out and at the far end of his street he exited onto the main thoroughfare. He drove the few miles to the bakery and as soon as his feet touched the pavement of the car park, an old guy with dirty, smelly clothes approached him. Startled, he lurched backward, "Can I help you, Mister?"

"Do you have an extra dollar you can spare?"

"Uh, no sir, but I'd be glad to get you something hot to drink and give you a Danish once I go inside the Camden Bakery, I work there." Ben pointed towards the shop. The man looked down on his luck, "Are you on your way somewhere?"

"Yeah, I'm going to my sister's."

Halfway to the door, Ben slowed his step, "You want to come inside and warm up a few minutes?"

"No, thanks though. My sister's house is a few blocks from here."

"Well then, I wish you luck." Ben unlocked the door, slipped inside, twisted the deadbolt and flipped on the light switches. He gazed through the side window and noticed the dude was moving slowly along the sidewalk, "Poor guy." He looked towards the ceiling, "Help him, Lord."

Hastening with quickness, Ben stopped at the sink, washed his hands and then tied his favorite apron around himself. He found his baker's cap and slid it on his head. Afterwards, he gathered the usual recipes for the morning pastries, dashed by the ovens and flipped them on, then pressed the fryer switch to 375 degrees. As he stood at his workstation, he felt colder than normal as a shiver went down his spine. "Huh..." *the ovens would warm it up in here and it should be toasty in no time,* he hoped.

Getting the donut batch ready would be a breeze, then he'd have to figure out the measurements for five dozen blueberry scones. *They were a customer favorite.* After adding all the items in a gigantic bowl, he spun the dough. Within a few minutes, he placed the scones in the oven, and shortly after getting a cup of coffee, he started the bagels that was next on his daily list. Upon retrieving all the ingredients, he washed out the same bowl, measured, mixed and stirred the bagel dough, then kneaded it and arranged four dozen on six trays and plopped them into the oven. Upon finishing that task, he readied his favorite thing they offered, brownies. *This is a thick batter.* The two brownie recipes he used were a little different and one called for nuts. He measured out the pecans and folded them in. The chocolaty smell was so rich, he couldn't refuse a little taste. With a clean spoon, he dipped it into the mix and savored the rich fudgy taste. *Yum!* He grabbed four baking pans, sprayed them with oil spray, then emptied the bowls and into the oven they went.

As the morning ticked by Ben moved around mimicking a mad man as he prepared all kinds of desserts. When a sweet treat was complete, he set them on the cooling rack and proceeded until all were done. He loved being busy. A knock at the rear door sounded. *Could it be Kandice?* He walked over to the large metal entryway, "Who is it?" No answer. Another thump, "Who's there? Kandice is that you?" Ben shouted at the metal door.

"Open up," he heard a low voice yell back at him.

No way would he do that. He shot to his workstation, grabbed his phone and dialed 911. "Hello. This is Ben Matney from Camden Bakery. Someone is at our rear entrance telling me to open the door. Can you please send a deputy?" He rattled off the bakery's address, ended the call and flew to the exit.

"The police have dispatched an officer, please go away."

Another thump, "Open this door."

Not wasting another second, Ben flew and stood behind the front counter to wait for the officer's arrival. *I can't deal with this.*

Several minutes later blue lights flashed throughout the shop. *Thank God.* A police deputy knocked on one of the windowpanes. Ben hurried over and with a quick twist of the lock, he allowed the officer to come inside. "I appreciate you coming so quickly. Someone's at the rear entrance and keeps asking me to open the door."

"I'll check it out, stay here."

"Here's the key." Ben handed the large bunch of keys over to him.

The heavy-set officer ambled through the shop and he jangled the keys along the way. Ben stayed put until he couldn't stand it any longer because he wanted to check out what was going on and slipped to the back. "I hope it's okay for me to be back here."

With the door ajar, the officer stepped outside, "Sir, what are you doing?"

Ben froze, squinting to see who was out there.

"You will freeze to death if you don't get out of this horrible weather," the officer spoke in a commanding voice.

"I believe that young man in there will give me a drink and something to eat."

"Wait a minute." Ben scrambled to the entryway and peered at the skinny man who'd refused his offer earlier. "It's you. I thought you were going to your sister's."

"I did, but she told me to return when it was daylight."

Ben swung his head. "Officer, I did offer him something to drink earlier. I also told him he could warm up inside." He pointed to the old fellow. "Why did you come back here?"

"For that drink." The man stumbled. "When I didn't see you from the front, I walked to this door."

The deputy grabbed ahold of the old fellow, "Are you all right?"

"I'll be fine." The old man straightened himself.

The officer turned to Ben. "I'll take him to the police department."

"Many thanks, Officer. Would you two like a few fresh donuts?" Ben pointed to the officer, "You, sir, can I get you a donut?"

The young deputy nodded. "I'd appreciate a few, thank you."

"Can I have that coffee you attempted to give me earlier?" The dirty dressed man looked at Ben. "It would be really nice to have something hot to drink."

Ben dashed over to the cooling racks, pulled a half dozen donuts and boxed them up for the two, then poured several cups of coffee, "Here you are. The cream and sugar are on that bar over there." He handed the tired man his box first and then the officer and gave them their steaming cups of joe.

"I drink my coffee black," the old guy smiled at Ben.

"What's your name?" the deputy asked the man, "and whose residence were you going to?"

"My name is Henry Weathers and my sister is Mary Milson who lives on Anchor Drive."

A queer look crossed the officer's face. "Mary Milson is my mother, so that would make you my uncle."

The man's head shifted. "Maddy?" He blinked, then rubbed his eyes a few times, squinted and gazed at the young officer a second time.

The deputy drew closer to Henry. "No one's called me by that name in years. Uncle Henry?"

"Yes, that's me." A broad smile crossed the elderly man's face.

The officer placed his hand on the man's shoulder, "I remember you. How many years has it been since we've seen you, ten or more?"

"Yeah, I think longer than that." A sadness took over the man's countenance.

"Come with me, instead of going to the police department we'll go to my mom's."

* * *

Funny how things turn out. At 5:30 a.m., his phone buzzed. *Who could that be?* Crossing the room, he wiped his hands on a rag and picked up his phone. *A text from Kandice.* 'Ben, I'm sick. So sorry, I won't be in this morning. I'll call you later.'

Ben released a pent-up breath realizing he'd have to work the shop by himself all day. No need to get in touch with Chloe, he'd handle it.

A little after 6 a.m., while stuffing the display case with every kind of pastry one could imagine, a tap at the entrance echoed throughout the quiet building. He lifted his head to discover Caroline standing at the entrance. *I can't believe it.* He ran to her, unbolted the door and swung it open. "Hey."

"How are you?"

Ben put his arm around her shoulder and leaned against her, "I'm good, thanks.

"I came to visit Kandice." She stepped in from the freezing frigid wind that blew her long curls every which away.

"Uh, Kandice isn't here, she's sick."

"No kidding." Caroline smoothed her hair as she unzipped her heavy jacket. "You're going to be shorthanded, aren't you?"

A quick thought... she could help him. That would be marvelous, but she's got her own business to tend to. "I'll manage, I've done it before. The only thing, sometimes customers get impatient, if you know what I mean." He swirled around and rapped his forehead.

The heavy lashes that shadowed her cheeks flew up. "Believe it or not, it's my day off and I'd be glad to help out today."

His insides somersaulted with delight, "You'd do that?"

"Sure, until my kids get out of school, why not?"

"That would be fabulous, c'mon, I'll show you around." Rushing behind the computer, he punched keys and brought the system to life, explained the different processes for sales, then moved over to the quirky espresso machine. "This old thing needs to be replaced, but it's all we have for now." He pushed knobs and pulled handles showing her how it worked. "If it messes up, holler and I'll fix it for you. Why don't we make an espresso so I can show you how it works?"

An oven timer buzzed. "The brownies! C'mon, we can make the espresso in a minute."

"This is going to be fun." Caroline smiled as she followed him, "Can I have a sample of the brownies?"

"Yeah." He gave her a glance. "You need an apron." He stopped in the middle of the large kitchen, "Are you certain about this?"

"Yes," She took a quick breath. "What can I do first?" Her voice broke. "Am I working the front when we open?"

They both froze in a stunned tableau, but Ben broke their stare and spoke, "If you wouldn't mind."

"Not at all, that's what I was thinking," Her eyes met his.

"That way I can keep up with the incoming orders," he winked.

With two clean bowls, Ben slid one across the counter towards her. "Here's the recipes of the last few things I still need to get done." He pointed at the papers sitting in between them.

At a glance, Caroline flipped through the formulas for petit fours, orange rolls, cinnamon rolls, coco puffs with Chantilly frosting, and apple pies.

"I'll take a shot at this one," she pulled the pie recipe. "The others look too hard."

He drew near her and felt a shock run through his bones. *I love her being here.* "We can start with the pies and work together on the other three, how does that sound?"

"Perfect. Show me where I can get the ingredients."

"Follow me." He led her around the kitchen and together they collected the ingredients for the pies.

As he stirred his mixture, he took a second and gazed at her. His heart turned over in response to her smile. It amazed him at how well Caroline was adapting to the kitchen, "You're getting the hang of things pretty darn quick."

"This kitchen reminds me of Olli's." She lifted her spatula, "What's wrong with Kandice?"

"She sent me a text telling me she was sick."

"Um, I was hoping to talk to her."

"Maybe she'll be in this afternoon."

They finished the pies and started working on the orange rolls. 7 a.m. approached without either one of them realizing it when Ben heard a knock at the door. "Oh gosh, look at the time, we've got to open up." When he bolted to the front, customers jammed the opened door. "Welcome everyone, sorry for the wait." He looked at Caroline, "Here we go, you ready?"

"I sure am."

Ben stepped behind the counter, "Can I get your order?" He wrote down what they wanted and filled their drink orders while Caroline boxed up pastries. "Will you take the next person's order while I fry two egg sandwiches with bacon for this order.

"Okay." She stepped up with a pad in hand, "Hey, can I get your order."

The customer ordered and the next and the next while Ben filled them.

* * *

Caroline looked out among the packed tables and realized an hour had ticked by and moved over next to Ben, "I could get use to this, I'm having a wonderful time." She ran her hand against the sleeve of his shirt, "We make a great team."

The longer she worked with him the more she became comfortable around him. *He's unlike anyone I've ever been around, nothing like Eli.* She couldn't help but compare the two. Eli never had the gentleness of Ben. She stood back as he was talking with several customers and watched him. He was so genuine, a perfect gentleman and wonderful to be with.

"Miss Montgomery, will you make another egg sandwich with bacon?"

That broke her train of thought, "Yes, of course." She got right to it and the sizzle of the bacon and the melting of the butter on the griddle gave her sweet memories of her childhood when she watched her mother make her breakfast at their old family restaurant when she was a girl. The sweetness of her mother flooded her heart. She would stop by with Harry and Penny after school in the p.m.

Ben checked the container of eggs in the cooler. "We need more eggs; I'll be right back."

"I'll start on these café mochas," she glanced at the written order beside Ben.

Her jade-spoked eyes fluttered when he returned, "I'm glad I got to work with you today."

"I can't thank you enough. It's been crazy this morning," he smiled. "Maybe we can do this again sometime. You know," he took a quick breath, "I prefer to work the front, but I don't have that option right now since Chloe's not here." The customers lagged and the front of the shop got quiet. He picked up a rag and wiped the display case when it was clear of customers. He put the rag in the sink beside the drink machine, "Since it's not busy, I'll be in the back whipping up some petit fours until you need me."

Ten minutes passed and all was quiet. It was crazy for her to remain on the stool beside the display case, so she tiptoed to the entryway to the kitchen. "What cha doing?"

"About to start a wedding cake."

Her voice rose, "Can I help? It's slow out front."

"I'd love that because wedding cakes are not my cup of tea," he whimpered. "Chloe usually makes them."

"Really?"

"I'll wait on the customers when they come in."

She stood by and observed him studying a recipe, "Is that the recipe?"

"Yeah, here." He handed it over. "I'll get you the ingredients." He lifted his brow, "Thanks for this. See that large bowl under the counter there? That's the one you need for this huge cake," then hurried about and gathered the items she would need.

Left alone, Caroline read over the recipe, picked up the measuring cup to her left and measured out six cups of flour. Ben put all the things she needed for the cake in front of her and scooted to the front. She busied herself whipping up the cake and minutes later she heard someone enter the front door. "Hey, how are you doing?" Caroline heard, dropped what she was doing and tiptoed to see who he was talking to. *Kandice.*

"I'm feeling much better." Kandice eased up to Ben. "Were you busy?"

"Hey, Kandice," Caroline interjected in between their sentences.

Kandice jumped, "Where did you come from?"

"I came in earlier to see Ben and he told me you were sick, so I pitched in and helped."

"That's fantastic, you didn't have to be at your own place?" She grinned in Caroline's direction.

"No, I'm off today."

Kandice laughed, "I bet he got you to start that wedding cake we need to finish today."

Caroline snickered, "He did."

A deep cackle escaped Kandice, "I remembered we had to get it ready today, so I took some aspirin and came in." She moved towards her. "Ben despises making a wedding cake. I'll help you."

"That would be wonderful." Caroline put her hands against her hips.

"It can get pretty hectic making the cake that the customers requested, did he show you a picture of the one we have to get done?" Kandice took off her wrap and hung it on the coatrack.

"No, he didn't. When I got to the decorating part, I was going to ask him what to do."

"I'll show you." They walked to the back and left Ben alone. "How much did you get done?"

"I just started measuring out the flour when I heard you come in." She let Kandice pass in front of her.

It was wonderful that Kandice took charge. She stood by and noticed how efficient Kandice was around the grand kitchen, "You are a pro at this."

Kandice threw her hand in the air, "Well... I've had a lot of practice. Will you measure out eight cups of sugar while I start the egg mixture." She glanced at the order slip in front of her. "Oh, let me get that picture for you to see." She looked under her counter and pulled out a book. It's on page seven, I think."

Caroline turned to the page. In front of her was a six-tier cake with flowered decorations. "It's beautiful."

"This cake has four flavors." Kandice ran her finger along the order form, a second time, "The top layer is supposed to be chocolate."

Busy as bees, Caroline and Kandice worked on the cake. "I came by this morning to see you."

"Oh?"

"Yeah, I wanted to ask you some questions about Ben."

A broad smile crossed Kandice's face, "Ben's a great guy."

Caroline beamed when her thoughts flooded of him. "You probably already know this, but I have feelings for him." She lifted her arms into the air. "Is it okay if I tell you something first?"

"Sure." Kandice stopped whipping her mixture and leaned in pulling the bowl with her.

"My ex-husband was a wife beater..."

Kandice gasped, "Ooh, I'm so sorry."

"It started on our honeymoon. I did nothing about it until he almost killed me."

The look on Kandice's face made her stomach churn, "I'm so sorry."

"Don't apologize. But here's my question for you... do you think Ben would have those tendencies?"

"Seriously, look at me," she put her spoon on the counter, "Ben is a gentle man and he's so loving. Caroline, if you become a couple, he will treat you with utmost respect. He... I must say, is a little skittish with relationships, though."

A slight grin spread across her face, "Yeah, he shared that with me last night." Caroline picked up the vanilla and a measuring spoon, "Do you want me to add this?"

"Yes, that's great."

"I hear you're moving to Colorado."

"That's right. My mother owns a bakery there and needs my help. Her health isn't the best these days."

"Oh?"

"Yeah, she has pretty bad arthritis and can't move around like she used to do. Friday will be my last day."

"I bet you're excited?" Caroline began to recognize Kandice's unselfishness.

"I'm super excited," and turned towards her. "To be honest, I'm thrilled about seeing my boyfriend again. He says he can't wait for me come home." Kandice's face lit up. "We dated years ago before he went into the military."

"Wow, I know you must miss him."

"I really do. I didn't realize it until I talked with him this week."

Another thought washed over her, "What about Ben?"

"What about Ben?" Kandice looked Caroline square in the face.

"Can I be candid?"

"I wouldn't want it any other way."

"Do you love Ben?"

"To tell you the truth, I thought I did. He's so amazing, but no, I'm not in love with him that way. He made me realize that. Ben's my best friend or like he would say, I'm like his sister."

Thank God.

The two finished the cake layers and put them on the cooling rack. "Now to the hard part. We need to lay the frosting on the layers and put the cake together, then decorate it."

"You'll have to show me since I've never done this before." Caroline stepped to her side and watched.

"Why don't you practice making rose petals with the green icing while I start the frosting."

"What if I mess up?"

"We'll scoop it up and put it back into the container."

"Oh, I get it."

"It's easy, I'll show you." Kandice took some parchment paper and squeezed green icing into a rose pedal, "Okay, your turn," and handed it over to her.

She was doing great at making the roses, and little by little, the cake became a magnificent piece of art. "Thanks for listening to me about Ben, I feel so much better now and I hope I can get past my inward fears."

"God can take away your fears."

The undeniable facts were true. "You are so spot on. I do need to give him my fears and trust Ben." She would fight this battle and give it all to God.

Ben entered. "It's quiet in here. What are you guys doing?"

Kandice reached and hit Ben's arm. "Having a girl talk and it is none of your business."

Caroline snickered. "Yeah, it's girl talk."

"Kandice, we need to have Mrs. Black's order ready by one. Gosh, look at that cake, Chloe would be so proud."

Caroline beamed, "Kandice did most of it."

"I can't take all the credit because you helped a lot." Kandice looked at Ben. "Was Mrs. Black's order for a strawberry shortcake, two dozen brownies, two apple pies and three dozen lemon squares?" She gazed at him, "I'll go see."

"You don't need to check, you remembered correctly because I just looked and you're right."

Caroline cleared her throat. "Kandice, I can help and Ben, you can work the front, if that's okay?"

"I see you girls don't need me," and he walked to the front.

With ever slow feet, she walked up behind him and tapped his back. The thrill of knowing Kandice approved of Ben made her insides calm. *Lord, is Ben the man for me? Take my fears away and help me trust this man I'm falling in love with.*

Throughout the rest of the day the three worked together and finished all the cakes, scones, pies, and such.

19

Ben dialed Caroline's number, "Hey there."

"Hi, it's like I haven't spoken with you in, like, forever."

"I feel the same," he laughed "and it's only been ten minutes since I saw you. I was wondering if you still want to go to the Wednesday Night Live at church this evening?"

"Oh, that's right, Pastor Luke's going to be there!"

"You remembered?"

"I did, and, yes, I'd love, too."

"Can I pick you and the kids up in let's say 15 minutes?"

"That would be great, we'll be ready."

He could no longer deny feelings for her and would tell her the next time they were alone. After a quick shower, he dressed, dried his hair, brushed his teeth and was out the door. His mother and brother had already left for church in his father's truck and he rushed to crank up his Jeep, then backed out of the driveway and immediately inched up Caroline's drive. He flung his hair, smoothed his tongue over his teeth, then found his breath spray in his center console, squirting it into his mouth. Without second guessing what to say, he exited his Wrangler and scooted onto her porch. *He wanted to kiss her and hold her and tell her he loved her.*

A tap on the door, he stood and waited.

The door opened and a huge smile was on Caroline's face, "Ben, you're right on time."

"You guys ready?"

Harry and Penny darted to him and hugged his legs. "Ben," they both shouted at the same time.

"Hey, you two."

"We go to church with you?" Harry patted Ben's back.

"Yeah, do you like hamburgers?"

"I love them." Harry rubbed his tummy, "I hun-gee."

"Me too," Penny rammed up against Harry's body. "I get inside first." She took off and ran to Ben's Jeep.

"Wait, let Ben help you." Quickly, Caroline ran to the vehicle. "Thanks for picking us up. Gosh. I need to get their car seats out of my car."

"Yeah, right, we need them."

They transferred the seats to Ben's Wrangler and buckled up. "I can't wait to hear your Pastor tonight."

"You will really like him."

As they drove away from their neighborhood, his admission of his feelings was beyond logic, it was a must. Love bubbled from him and he wanted to shout it to the world. A quick scan of her beauty made him twinge, "You look lovely this evening."

"Thank you," she smoothed her sweater wrap with her hand.

The red blouse against her blond hair made his blood soar. "Nice blouse."

"Thanks," she pulled her shawl tighter to herself, "I should have worn a coat."

"I think your wrap is great, but it is cold out tonight."

"I got it a few weeks ago and this is the first time I've worn it."

Ben's thoughts were driving him bonkers, "I need to tell you something."

"Yeah?" She readjusted her seating and faced him.

He took a quick breath, "I love you, Caroline."

"Ben," her lips spread into a grin and she opened her mouth.

"Don't say anything." He touched her hand. "It's been burning inside me to tell you... I've loved you since the day you walked inside the bakery."

A quick turn into the church yard, Harry and Penny started to shout, "We're here, I hun-gee, Mommy," Penny unbuckled her car seat.

"I can't get mine undone," Harry squirmed, "Help me, Mommy."

"Can we take a walk after we get them settled?" She stared.

"I'd like that." Upon getting the children out of the Jeep, his hand lightly touched the small of her back as the four of them hurried to the door of the gym.

* * *

He loves me. Her insides melted at the thought. Could she be as open and tell him the same? *Yes.*

Once they were inside the large building, she noticed a line had formed at the opened window at the kitchen. "Harry, get a plate, you too, Penny."

Penny reached above her head for a plate and got one for Harry. "Ben, here's a plate for you," Penny reached and handed him one, too.

Ben obliged and took it from her small hands then stood behind them not taking his eyes off Caroline.

"You're staring, Mr. Matney. Hey, there's Pastor Luke," and waved in his direction. "We'll speak to him once we get Harry and Penny settled."

The line moved fast, and each got a burger, chips, a cookie and a drink. The condiment table was to the left and Caroline waited behind several folks to put a small amount of ketchup, mustard, mayonnaise, and cheese on Harry and Penny's burgers then loaded hers up. If it wasn't dripping with mayonnaise and mustard, a burger wasn't worth eating in her opinion. She looked at Ben, "you like a messy burger, too?"

"That's the only way to eat it." He grinned and lifted his brow, "I see you like it the way I do."

"A man after my own heart." Caroline put her plate on the table and helped get Harry and Penny into the chairs they selected, "I'm going to speak to Pastor Luke. Harry, Penny, sit here and eat, please."

"Yes, Mommy," Harry agreed as he picked up his burger and took a huge bite.

Penny nodded acknowledging her mother's request.

"C'mon, Ben, I'll introduce you to Pastor Luke." Ben followed at her heels. "Pastor Luke," Caroline's voice rose over the mingling crowd of people.

"Well hello, Caroline, what finds you here?" He leaned and gave her a hug.

"I was invited by my friend, Ben," she glanced his way.

Ben held out his hand and shook the pastor's hand, "It's nice to see you again. I've heard great things about you from Caroline," and gave him a pat on his shoulder.

"Thank you."

Corey turned to Ben, It's been way to long since I brought the girls by the bakery for some donuts."

"Yeah, I've missed seeing you and the girls."

"We go and visit Chloe and the babies every chance we get, so coming by the bakery hasn't been a priority."

Corey grabbed the sleeve of Ben's jacket, "Chloe's in the nursery."

"Really?" It was like a family reunion around there. "I can't wait to see her." He put his arm high in the air, "I'm the guilty one for not stopping by and seeing Morgan and Mack."

Everyone laughed.

"I think Chloe understands, Ben."

"Corey," Caroline rushed over and hugged her. "Let me look at that dress you've got on; I just love it."

Corey twirled around, "It's the first dress Luke bought me before we got married last Christmas."

Caroline pulled on Ben's arm, "Look who just came in?"

* * *

There in the line was his mother, Bradley and Kaitlyn inching up to the counter to get their burgers. Ben excused himself and skipped across the floor to his mother, "Hey, Mom," and put his arm around her shoulder, then pulled his brother into a hug and shook Kaitlyn's hand, "How are you doing?"

"I'm great."

Kaitlyn fluffed her hair, "I'm starved, how about you?"

"I already fixed my plate. I'm with Caroline and her two children. Mom, will you sit with us?" Despite his eagerness to get back to Caroline, he waited and made sure his mother was set with her food and drink. He cupped his arm around hers and guided her to where Caroline was, "Here we are."

"Mom, this is Harry, and this is Penny."

With gleaming faces, ketchup smears and all, Harry and Penny looked her way. Penny put down her burger, got down from her chair and wiped Harry's face with her napkin then rubbed her own face.

"It's so nice to finally met you." Penny dropped the ketchup stained napkin and ran to Ben's mother, grabbing ahold of her, "Hey, I love your shirt."

Emily pulled at her shirt. "You do?"

"Yeah, it's pretty." Penny smiled then immediately took off towards her mother. "Mommy, Ben's mommy's here."

Caroline ambled over to Ben, his mother, Bradley and Kaitlyn. "Hey everyone, I'm Caroline."

Everyone shook hands and sat down to eat their burgers and small talk began between them. Out of the corner of Ben's eye, he saw Chloe come into the gym. "Excuse me for a moment." He rose and went to greet her. "Hey there and grabbed her to himself, "How are you doing?"

Chloe hugged him. "The question is, how in the world are you?" She pushed at him. "Let me see your face." She studied him, squinted and released him.

"I'm fine." He leaned to her ear, "I'm in love."

"What? With that sweet girl you mentioned earlier?"

With gentleness, he gripped her arms. "Yes, her name again, is Caroline Montgomery and she's here with me. Over there with my mom."

"Ben, I haven't met your mother, yet."

He hit his noggin, "That's right, c'mon, I'll introduce you." Ben slipped up behind his mother and turned to make sure Chloe was with him, "Mom, I'd like to introduce you to my boss, Chloe Terrison."

Emily reached out her hand, "It's so nice to meet you, dear. I've heard wonderful things about you."

"How are you doing? I heard all about your terrible incident." Chloe sat beside her in a vacant chair.

"I'm doing much better than expected. The doctor told me today that I can start looking for a part-time job."

"How's it been getting settled in at Ben's?"

Chloe's husband, Mitchell stepped up to the table. "Hey Mitchell. Congratulations," Ben stood greeting him.

Mitchell grabbed ahold of Ben, "I can't thank you enough for what you did for Chloe, Morgan and Mack." A tear hit his cheek.

"Gosh, Mitchell, I would do it again tomorrow if I had, too. It was the most thrilling thing I've ever experienced." He turned to Caroline. "Everyone, please meet Caroline, my friend." *He wanted to say his girl.*

Caroline stood, "Ben, what are you talking about?"

"I guess I didn't tell you. I delivered Chloe's babies at the bakery."

"Wow. That's amazing."

As the night worn on, everyone finished their meal, Ben led Harry and Penny to the children's department for their program and came back and found Caroline in the large bible study class, along with his mother, Chloe, Mitchell and another hundred folks. Pastor Luke introduced himself and had everyone read over his scripture for the evening. Funny how it was on building relationships.

Upon reading the bible verses, Pastor Luke stopped to greet everyone. "Thank you for having me tonight. Our study this evening is on relationships and trust. We need to trust and love."

He continued for 20 minutes and led everyone in prayer. As the night ended, Caroline followed the other parents to where Harry and Penny were.

Ben walked his mother to Bradley's truck and helped her inside, "Bye, Mom, I'll see at home," then ran to the other side of the truck. "Bradley, take good care of these beautiful women, bye Kaitlyn."

Bradley laughed. "I will."

He hurried inside and found Pastor Luke gathering his personal items, "I really appreciated your message tonight, if for no one else, it was for me."

"Thank you, it was good seeing you. Come visit sometime."

As they were leaving the gymnasium, Caroline pulled on his arm. "Can we sit on the porch when we get back?"

"I'd like that."

The ride back to Water Edge Way was silent. Ben looked in the rearview mirror finding that Harry and Penny had fallen asleep. His mind reeled of things he wanted to say to Caroline.

She spun in her seat, "Oh look, the twins are asleep, I thought it got awfully quiet in here."

"I'll help you get them inside when we get back." He turned into Caroline's driveway within the next few minutes. Once they got the twins inside and into bed, Ben sat on Caroline's living room couch and looked around the small room, decorated beautifully in greys with accents. *It's nice.*

"Thanks for tonight. I so enjoyed being with you."

"It was a good night. You wanted to talk to me?"

She sat next to him, "I have so many things I want to tell you."

"I want to tell you things, too." He gazed into her eyes.

"You first," Caroline put her hand over his.

"Remember what I told you on the way to church?"

"Yes, that you loved me."

"Caroline, I do. I love you and I want you to be mine."

"I received a confirmation tonight from Pastor Luke's message."

Her intense stare made a chill spike through him.

"I love you, Ben Matney. I realized that when we worked together at the bakery today. It was so special being with you. You are loving, you have a servant's heart and tonight, I know I can trust you, that you will not be like Eli, like I previously thought. You are gentle with my children and I want you to know that I trust and love you.

"I love you, Caroline." He reached and grabbed her into his arms. He felt her lips touch his like a whisper and gradually he deepened their kiss.

After a few seconds she pushed away and touched his face with her hand. "You are so loving."

They sat and chatted about their wants and dreams. Ben brushed his lips against her forehead. "Will you be my wife someday?"

He drew her hand into his, "Oh, Ben, yes, I will. I love you. I hope someday will be sooner than later," she smiled and kissed his cheek.

"We will start planning our future tomorrow, but for now, let's enjoy this moment so we can remember it forever."

The End

About Jeannie Sharpe

Jeannie Sharpe has a deep love for writing Christian Romance novels, but she has also published two children's books: *Once There Was an Orange Truck* and *Orange Truck Helps Katie the Kangaroo Find Her Friends*. Over the past several years, she has sold eight-thousand copies of these two titles. Jeannie's other two romance novels are *The Baker's Husband* and *Her Daughter's Preacher*.

A career in writing is a dream coming true, but Jeannie especially loves to sing with her talented husband, Vance, in many venues around the United States and Canada. Be on the lookout for new books by this passionate author.

Connect with Jeannie Sharpe

Facebook: https://www.facebook.com/jeannie.sharpe
Twitter: https://twitter.com/Jws415Sharpe
Instagram: https://www.instagram.com/jeanniesharpe/

Fresh Ink Group
Independent Multi-media Publisher

Fresh Ink Group / Push Pull Press

ଷ

Hardcovers
Softcovers
All Ebook Platforms
Audiobooks
Worldwide Distribution

ଷ

Indie Author Services
Book Development, Editing, Proofing
Graphic/Cover Design
Video/Trailer Production
Website Creation
Social Media Management
Writing Contests
Writers' Blogs
Podcasts

ଷ

Authors
Editors
Artists
Experts
Professionals

ଷ

The Choice: unexpected heroes is the sequel to *The Contract: between heaven and earth*. In the first book, a catastrophic political event threatens Earth. The heavenly leadership decides to execute extraordinary measures to ensure the survival and long-term viability of the planet. Two volunteer souls return to Earth and take human form as Brad Channing and Sarah O'Brien. They are ultimately successful in preventing the catastrophe, but lose their lives in the process.

The Choice picks up where the first book ends, at an Air Force Base in northern California. The base commander invites Brad's former Navy SEAL instructor to help him determine who is behind the murder of Brad and Sarah. It is evident that their deaths are part of a bigger plan, and the commander has an urgent need to thwart that plan.

A mystery unfolds which implicates key Washington D.C. officials. A confidential team studies the evidence and pursues leads. Eventually, they uncover a traitorous conspiracy that has as its goal: world domination. The pressing question is who can be trusted and who cannot.

Read it now!

www.ingramcontent.com/pod-product-compliance
Lightning Source LLC
Chambersburg PA
CBHW060557310726
48982CB00008B/1150/J

* 9 7 8 1 9 4 7 8 6 7 7 4 1 *